BLACKLANDS

www.**rbooks**.co.uk

Belinda Bauer lives in Wales. *Blacklands* is her first novel.

BLACKLANDS

BELINDA BAUER

BANTAM PRESS

LONDON • TORONTO • SYDNEY • AUCKLAND • JOHANNESBURG

TRANSWORLD PUBLISHERS
61–63 Uxbridge Road, London W5 5SA
A Random House Group Company
www.rbooks.co.uk

First published in Great Britain
in 2010 by Bantam Press
an imprint of Transworld Publishers

A CIP catalogue record for this book
is available from the British Library.

ISBNs 9780593062944 (cased)
9780593062951 (tpb)

Addresses for Random House Group Ltd companies outside the UK
can be found at: www.randomhouse.co.uk
The Random House Group Ltd Reg. No. 954009

The Random House Group Limited supports The Forest Stewardship
Council (FSC), the leading international forest-certification organization. All our
titles that are printed on Greenpeace-approved FSC-certified paper carry the FSC logo.
Our paper procurement policy can be found at www.rbooks.co.uk/environment

Typeset in 11.5/15pt Caslon 540 by
Falcon Oast Graphic Art Ltd

Printed in the Great Britain by
CPI Mackays, Chatham ME5 8TD

2 4 6 8 10 9 7 5 3 1

Mixed Sources
Product group from well-managed
forests and other controlled sources
www.fsc.org Cert no. TT-COC-2139
© 1996 Forest Stewardship Council
FSC

To my mother, who gave us everything and
never thought it was enough

1

Exmoor dripped with dirty bracken, rough, colourless grass, prickly gorse and last year's heather, so black it looked as if wet fire had swept across the landscape, taking the trees with it and leaving the moor cold and exposed to face the winter unprotected. Drizzle dissolved the close horizons and blurred heaven and earth into a grey cocoon around the only visible landmark – a twelve-year-old boy in slick black waterproof trousers but no hat, alone with a spade.

It had rained for three days, but the roots of grass and heather and gorse twisting through the soil still resisted the spade's intrusion. Steven's expression did not change; he dug the blade in again, feeling a satisfying little impact all the way up to his armpits. This time he made a mark – a thin human mark in the great swathe of nature around him.

Before Steven could make the next mark, the first narrow stripe had filled with water and disappeared.

*

Three boys slouched through the Shipcott rain, their hands deep in their pockets, their hoodies over their faces, their shoulders hunched as if they couldn't wait to get out of the rain. But they had nowhere to hurry to, so they meandered and bumped along and laughed and swore too loudly at nothing at all, just to let the world know they were there and still had expectations.

The street was narrow and winding and, in summer, passing tourists smiled at the seaside-painted terraces with their doors opening right on to the pavement and their quaint shutters. But the rain made the yellow and pink and sky-blue houses a faded reminder of sunshine, and a refuge only for those too young, too old or too poor to leave.

Steven's nan looked out of the window with a steady gaze.

She had started life as Gloria Manners. Then she became Ron Peters's wife. After that, she was Lettie's mum, then Lettie and Billy's mum. Then for a long time she was Poor Mrs Peters. Now she was Steven's nan. But underneath she would always be Poor Mrs Peters; nothing could change that, not even her grandsons.

Above the half-nets, the front window was spotted with rain. The people over the road already had their lights on. The roofs were as different as the walls. Some still wore their old pottery tiles, rough with moss. Others, flat grey slate that reflected the watery sky. Above the roofs, the top of the moor was just visible through the mist – a gentle, rounded thing from this distance. From the warmth of a front room with central heating and the kettle starting to whistle in the kitchen, it even looked innocent.

The shortest of the boys struck the window with the flat of his palm and Steven's nan recoiled in fright.

The boys laughed and ran although no one was chasing

them and they knew no one was likely to. 'Nosey old bag!' one of them shouted back, although it was hard to see which, with their hoods so low on their faces.

Lettie hurried in, breathless and alarmed. 'What was that?'

But Steven's nan was back in the window. She didn't look round at her daughter. 'Is tea ready?' she said.

Steven walked off the moor with his anorak slung over one shoulder and his T-shirt soaked and steaming with recent effort. The track carved through the heather by generations of walkers was thick with mud. He stopped – his rusty spade slung over his other shoulder like a rifle – and looked down at the village. The street lamps were already on and Steven felt like an angel or an alien, observing the darkening dwellings from on high, detached from the tiny lives being lived below. He ducked instinctively as he saw the three hoodies run down the wet road.

He hid the spade behind a rock near the slippery stile. It was rusty but, still, someone might take it, and he couldn't carry it home with him; that might lead to questions he could not – or dared not – answer.

He walked down the narrow passage beside the house. He was cooling now, and shivered as he took off his trainers to run them under the garden tap. They'd been white once, with blue flashes. His mum would go mad if she saw them like this. He rubbed them with his thumbs and squeezed the mud out of them until they were only dirty, then shook them hard. Muddy water sprayed up the side of the house, but rain washed it quickly away. His grey school socks were heavy and sodden; he peeled them off, his feet a shocking cold white.

'You're soaking.' His mother peered from the back door, her face pinched and her dark blue eyes as dull as a northern sea. Rain spattered the straw hair that was dragged back into a small, functional ponytail. She jerked her head back inside to keep it dry.

'I got caught in it.'

'Where were you?'

'With Lewis.'

This was not strictly a lie. He had been with Lewis immediately after school.

'What were you doing?'

'Nothing. Just. You know.'

From the kitchen he heard his nan say, 'He should come straight home from school!'

Steven's mother glared at his wetness. 'Those trainers were only new at Christmas.'

'Sorry, Mum.' He looked crestfallen; it often worked.

She sighed. 'Tea's ready.'

Steven ate as fast as he dared and as much as he could. Lettie stood at the sink and smoked and dropped her ash down the plughole. At the old house – before they came to live with Nan – his mum used to sit at the table with him and Davey. She used to eat. She used to talk to him. Now her mouth was always shut tight, even when it held a cigarette.

Davey sucked the ketchup off his chips then carefully pushed each one to the side of his plate.

Nan cut little pieces off her breaded fish, inspecting each with a suspicious look before eating it.

'Something wrong with it, Mum?' Lettie flicked her ash with undue vigour. Steven looked at her nervously.

'Bones.'

'It's a fillet. Says so on the box. Plaice fillet.'

'They always miss some. You can't be too careful.'

There was a long silence in which Steven listened to the sound of his own food inside his head.

'Eat your chips, Davey.'

Davey screwed up his face. 'They're all wet.'

'Should've thought of that before you sucked them, shouldn't you? Shouldn't you?'

At the repeated question, Steven stopped chewing, but Nan's fork scraped the plate.

Lettie moved swiftly to Davey's side and picked up a soggy chip. 'Eat it!'

Davey shook his head and his lower lip started to wobble.

With quiet spite, Nan murmured: 'Leaving food. Kids nowadays don't know they're born.'

Lettie bent down and slapped Davey sharply on the bare thigh below his shorts. Steven watched the white handprint on his brother's skin quickly turn red. He loved Davey, but seeing someone other than himself get into trouble always gave Steven a small thrill, and now – watching her hustling his brother out of the kitchen and up the stairs, bawling his head off – he felt as if he had somehow been accorded an honour: the honour of being spared the pent-up irritation of his mother. God knows, she'd taken her feelings for Nan out on him often enough. But this was further proof of what Steven had been hoping for some time – that Davey was finally old enough, at five, to suffer his share of the discipline pool. It wasn't a deep pool, or a dangerous one, but what the hell; his mother had a short fuse and a punishment shared was a punishment halved in Steven's eyes. Maybe even a punishment escaped altogether.

His nan had not stopped eating throughout, although each mouthful was apparently a minefield.

Even though Davey's sobs were now muffled, Steven

sought eye contact with Nan and finally she glanced at him, giving him a chance to roll his eyes, as if the burden of the naughty child was shared and the sharing made them closer.

'You're no better,' she said, and went back to her fish.

Steven reddened. He knew he was better! If only he could prove it to Nan, everything would be different – he just knew it.

Of course, it was all Billy's fault – as usual.

Steven held his breath. He could hear his mother washing up – the underwater clunking of china – and his nan drying – the higher musical scraping of plates leaving the rack. Then he slowly opened the door of Billy's room. It smelled old and sweet, like an orange left under the bed. Steven felt the door click gently behind him.

The curtains were drawn – always drawn. They matched the bedspread in pale and dark blue squares that clashed with the swirly brown carpet. A half-built Lego space station was on the floor and since Steven's last visit a small spider had spun a web on what looked like a crude docking station. Now it sat there, waiting to capture satellite flies from the outer space of the dingy bedroom.

There was a drooping scarf pinned to the wall over the bed – sky-blue and white, Manchester City – and Steven felt the familiar pang of pity and anger at Billy: still a loser even in death.

Steven crept in here sometimes, as if Billy might reach across the years and whisper secrets and solutions into the ear of this nephew who had already lived to see one more birth-day than he himself had managed.

Steven had long ago given up the hope of finding real-life clues. At first he liked to imagine that Uncle Billy might have left some evidence of a precognition of his own death. A *Famous Five* book dog-eared at a key page; the initials 'AA' scratched into the wooden top of the bedside table; Lego scattered to show the points of the compass and X marks the spot. Something which – after the event – an observant boy might discover and decipher.

But there was nothing. Just this smell of history and bitter sadness, and a school photo of a thin, fair child with pink cheeks and crooked teeth and dark blue eyes almost squeezed shut by the size of his smile. It had been a long time before Steven had realized that this photo must have been placed here later – that no boy worth his salt has a photo of himself on his bedside table unless it shows him holding a fish or a trophy.

Nineteen years ago this eleven-year-old boy – probably much like himself – had tired of his fantasy space game and gone outside to play on a warm summer evening, apparently – infuriatingly – unaware that he would never return to put his toys away or to wave his Man City scarf at the TV on a Sunday afternoon, or even to make his bed, which his mother – Steven's nan – had done much later.

Some time after 7.15pm, when Mr Jacoby from the newsagent sold him a bag of Maltesers, Uncle Billy had moved out of the realm of childhood make-believe and into the realm of living nightmare. In the 200 yards between the newsagent's and this very house – a 200 yards Steven walked every morning and every night to and from school – Uncle Billy had simply disappeared.

Steven's nan had waited until 8.30 before sending Lettie out to look for her brother, and until 9.30, when darkness was falling, to go outside herself. In the light summer evenings children played long past their winter bedtimes. But it was not until Ted Randall next door said perhaps they should call the police that Steven's nan changed for ever from Billy's Mum into Poor Mrs Peters.

Poor Mrs Peters – whose husband had been stupidly killed wobbling off his bicycle into the path of the Barnstaple bus six years before – had waited for Billy to come home.

At first she waited at the door. She stood there all day, every day for a month, barely noticing fourteen-year-old Lettie brushing past her to go to school, and returning promptly at 3.50 to save her mother worrying even more – if such a thing were possible.

When the weather broke, Poor Mrs Peters waited in the window from where she could see up and down the road. She grew the look of a dog in a thunderstorm – alert, wide-eyed and nervous. Any movement in the street made her heart leap so hard in her chest that she flinched. Then would come the slump, as Mr Jacoby or Sally Blunkett or the Tithecott twins grew so distinct that no desperate stretch of her imagination could keep them looking like a ruddy-cheeked eleven-year-old boy with a blond crew-cut, new Nike trainers and a half-eaten bag of Maltesers in his hand.

Lettie learned to cook and to clean and to stay in her room so she didn't have to watch her mother flinching at the road. She had always suspected that Billy was the favourite and now, in his absence, her mother no longer had the strength to hide this fact.

So Lettie worked on a shell of anger and rebellion to protect the soft centre of herself, which was fourteen and scared and missed her brother and her mother in equal measure, as if both had been snatched from her on that warm July evening.

*

How could Uncle Billy not know? Once more Steven felt that flicker of anger as he looked about the clueless, lifeless room. How could anyone not know that something like that was about to happen to them?

2

A year after Billy disappeared a delivery driver from Exeter was arrested for something else, somewhere else.

At first, police merely questioned Arnold Avery after a boy called Mason Dingle accused him of flashing at him.

It was not the first time Arnold Avery had exposed himself to a child – although, of course, this was not what he told police initially – but, in luring fifteen-year-old Mason Dingle to his van for directions, Avery had unwittingly met his nemesis.

Mason Dingle was himself not unknown to the police. His small size and choirboy features were merely a lucky lie, which hid the true face of the terror of Plymouth's Lapwing estate. Graffiti, demanding money with menaces, breaking and entering were all in Mason Dingle's blood, and the police knew it was only a matter of time before young master Dingle followed his brothers in the family tradition – a life of some sort of ongoing detention.

But before he got there (which he absolutely did) Mason Dingle helped to catch the man the tabloids later dubbed the Van Strangler.

Naturally, the police did not even know that such a child killer was on the loose. Children disappeared all the time, and a few turned up dead. But this happened all over the country and police forces in the 1980s did not have the resources to compare notes in any but the most high-profile murder cases. For all the government's Orwellian bleating about improvements and manpower and databases, the police detection rates remained at roughly the level that they would have achieved by periodically sticking a pin in a list of the usual suspects.

And anyway – until Mason Dingle took a hand in proceedings – none of Arnold Avery's victims had been found and Avery himself had never been arrested or even speed-ticketed, so all the databases in the world would not have thrown his name across the desks of investigating officers.

So when he saw Mason Dingle all alone, scratching something no doubt filthy into the seat of a red plastic swing in the battered Lapwing playground, Avery pulled over in his white van, got himself ready, and whistled to get the boy's attention – confident in the inabilities of the Devon & Cornwall, or any other police force.

Mason looked up and Avery's heart lifted to see his sweet face. He waved the boy over and Mason sauntered towards the van.

'Gimme directions?'

Mason Dingle lifted his eyebrows in assent. Everything about him, Avery saw now, was like a small man. Here was a boy with older brothers, if he'd ever seen one. The way he slouched, his manly under-eagerness to help, the cigarette tucked behind his tender little ear beside the shaven temples. But oh, his face! The face of an angel!

Mason bent down to the window of the van, looking off into the distance as if he barely had time in his busy schedule for this.

'Right, mate?'

'Yeah,' said Avery, 'can you show me on this map where the business park is?'

'Just down there and take a left, mate.'

'Can you show me on this map?'

Mason sighed, then poked his head inside the van to look down at the map spread across Avery's lap.

'Can you point at it for me?'

For a second Mason Dingle couldn't take in what he was seeing, then he jerked slightly, bumping his head on the door frame. Avery had seen this reaction before. Now one of two things would happen: either the boy would start to redden and stammer and back rapidly away, or he would start to redden and stammer and feel compelled – *because Avery was an adult who had asked him a question* – to point at the area on the map, so that his hand was mere inches from it. When that happened, things could go anywhere – and sometimes had. Avery preferred the second reaction because it prolonged the encounter, but the first was good too – to see the fear and confusion – and the guilt – on their faces because, at the end of the day, they all wanted it. He himself was just more honest about it.

But Mason Dingle took a third path; as he pulled backwards through the van window, he twisted the keys from the ignition. 'You dirty old bastard!' he said, grinning, and held the keys up.

Avery was instantly furious. 'Give those back, you little

shit!' He got out of the van, zipping himself up with some difficulty.

Mason danced away from him, laughing. 'Fuck you!' he yelled – and ran.

Arnold Avery re-evaluated Mason Dingle. Appearances had been deceptive. He had the face of an angel but obviously he was a tough kid. Therefore Avery expected the boy to re-appear shortly with his keys and either a demand for money, or at least one older male relative or the police.

The thought didn't scare Avery. Mason Dingle's street-smarts had worked for him so far, but Avery guessed that they could also be used against him. Nobody believed nice children about things like this – let alone troublesome brats. Especially when the man being accused of such filth and per-version just sat around and waited for the police to arrive instead of behaving as if he had something to hide. So Avery lit a cigarette and waited in the playground – where he could not be surprised – for Mason Dingle to return.

At first the police were disinclined to take Mason Dingle seriously. But he knew his rights and he was insistent, so two policemen finally put him in a squad car – with much warning about wasting police time – and drove him back to the play-ground, where they found the white van. They were checking that the keys Mason had produced did indeed fit the van when Arnold Avery approached angrily, and told them that the boy had stolen his keys and tried to hold them to ransom.

'He said if I didn't pay him he'd tell the police I tried to fiddle with him!'

The police focus switched back to Mason and, while the boy told the truth in remarkable detail, Avery could see that the police believed his own version of events only too eagerly.

And so everything was going Avery's way until, with a sinking feeling, he saw a small boy approaching with a man who looked like a father on the warpath.

While he maintained his composure with the two police officers, inside Avery was cursing his own stupidity. All he'd had to do was wait! Everything would have been OK if he'd only waited! But it was a playground, and playgrounds attracted children and even though the stocky eight-year-old now bawling his way towards him wasn't really his type, the first boy had taken so long to come back! What was he supposed to do?

So, in the final analysis, it was all Mason Dingle's fault. Although when Arnold Avery ventured this opinion to a homicide officer – after half a dozen small bodies had been discovered in shallow graves on a rainswept Exmoor – the officer broke his nose with a single backhander, and his own solicitor merely shrugged.

It all fell apart.

Slowly but inexorably, connections were made, dots were joined, and Arnold Avery was charged with six counts of murder and three more of child abduction. The murder charges were limited to the number of bodies they could find on the moor, and the abduction charges limited by the items found in Avery's home and car which could be positively linked to missing children – although Avery never admitted taking any of them. A one-armed Barbie doll belonged to ten-year-old Mariel Oxenburg of Winchester; a maroon blazer with a unicorn crest on the pocket had once warmed Paul Barrett of Westward Ho!, and a pair of nearly new Nike trainers found under the front passenger seat of the white van were proudly marked in felt tip under the tongues: Billy Peters.

3

Dear Sir,

My grandmother choked and died on a bone in your plaice. On the box it said it was a fillit.

What are you going to do about it, please?

Yours sincerely,

Steven Lamb, Shipcott.

Mrs O'Leary said that 'sincerely' was the wrong word. In business, one wrote 'yours faithfully'. Steven changed it but thought she must be wrong. He would rather be faithful to people he knew and loved than to the manager of the local supermarket whose fish had fallen so far below the advertised standards as to kill his grandmother.

When he wrote his personal letter, 'sincerely' sounded so stiff and formal. But, he thought pragmatically, it was Mrs O'Leary doing the marking, so he'd better stick to her version.

Mrs O'Leary pointed out his spelling error too, but didn't fuss too much. She said his letter was very good; very authentic – and read it to the class.

Steven wished she hadn't. He felt the eyes of other boys branding him like laser tattoos. We'll get you later for this, you arse-creeper, is what they burned on the back of his neck. To be singled out so in class was to be doomed in the playground and he sighed at the thought of the next few days of dodging and hiding and sticking close to the teacher – 'What's wrong with you, Lamb? Go and play!'

Luckily it didn't happen often that he was so marked. Steven was only an average student, a quiet boy who rarely gave cause for concern, or even attention. When Mrs O'Leary wrote the end of term reports, it took a second or two to recall the skinny dark-haired boy who matched the name on her register. Along with Chantelle Cox, Taylor Laughlan and Vivienne Khan, Steven Lamb was a child only truly visible by his absence, when a cross next to his name gave him fleeting statistical interest.

Steven spent lunchtime near the gym doors with Lewis, as usual. Lewis had cheese and pickle sandwiches and a Mars bar and Steven had fish paste and a two-fingered Kit Kat.

Lewis refused to swap anything, and Steven couldn't blame him.

The three hooded boys played footie on the tarmac netball court, and only occasionally had the time to leer threateningly at Steven or to call him a wanker as the ball came down the left. One of them did pretend to throw it in his face, making Steven blink comically, and the boy cackled joylessly at him, but it was all bearable.

'You want me to beat him up for you?' Lewis enquired through chocolate lips.

'Nah, it's all right.' Steven shrugged. 'Thanks though.'

'Any time. You just let me know.'

Lewis was a little shorter than Steven, but outweighed him by 20lb of pure ego. Steven had never actually seen Lewis fight but it was generally accepted by both of them that Lewis was a match for anybody right up to – but not including – Year 8. Michael Cox, brother of semi-visible Chantelle, was in Year 8 and he was over six foot tall and was black, to boot. Everyone knew the black kids were tougher and that Michael Cox was the toughest of them all.

Other than Michael Cox, Steven reckoned Lewis was a match for anybody. But even Lewis couldn't fight all three hoodies, and that was surely what he'd get if he decided to fight one. They both knew it, so they changed the subject by unspoken agreement.

'The old man's taking me to the match tomorrow. Want to come?'

The match, Steven knew, involved the local team, the Blacklanders. In the absence of a nearby top-class league soccer team, Lewis and his father had plunged headlong into pragmatic support for the Blacklanders – a motley collection of local half-talent – and Lewis followed their fortunes with the same fervour that his classmates did Liverpool or Manchester United.

Going to the football was the only thing Lewis and his dad ever did together.

His dad was a short, ginger, bespectacled man who rarely spoke. He wore slacks beyond his years and did something in an office in Minehead but Lewis had never cared enough to find out exactly what. 'Something in the law,' he'd shrugged when Steven asked. At home Lewis's dad did the *Telegraph* crossword and researched his family tree online. Once a week in the winter, he and Lewis's mother went to the village hall to play badminton – a risible game made even worse by the occasional glimpse Steven had had of them in their kit, his pale curly leg hairs and her maxi thighs in a miniskirt.

In all the years Steven and Lewis had been friends, Lewis's dad had only ever said three different things directly to him: 'Hello, Steven,' on many occasions, 'You boys having fun?' whenever he accidentally stumbled on them engaged in spying, and once – embarrassingly – 'Who traipsed dog shit through the bloody kitchen?'

In common with his much larger, more vibrant mother, Lewis generally ignored his dad. In Steven's company he greeted everything his dad said with an eye-rolling tut or truculent silence.

Once Steven had gone to Minehead with Lewis's family to see a sandcastle competition. By the time they got there a summer downpour had reduced the magnificent creations to vague, melting mounds, so that the fairytale castle looked like the *Titanic*, and the life-size orca looked like a rugby ball. Lewis's dad had nevertheless wandered from lump to lump in his Berghaus waterproofs, photographing each from several angles and trying to enthuse Lewis by repeating variations on the theme of 'You can see how it *would* have looked!' All the while Lewis and his mother shivered under a flapping umbrella, rolling their eyes and whining loudly about getting inside for a cream tea.

While he hadn't quite had the guts to abandon Lewis and show support for the sandcastles, Steven had stood a little way away from his friend, his mother and the umbrella. He preferred to get wet than to be associated with their scornful dismissal of such sad enthusiasm.

He thought it was a waste of a father.

Lewis brought him back to the here and now by adding temptingly: 'Batten's off the injury list.'

Steven shook his head. 'Can't.'

'But it's Saturday.'

Steven shrugged. Lewis shook his head pityingly. 'Your loss, mate.'

Steven doubted that; he'd seen the Blacklanders play.

Saturday was dry and, if not warm, at least not particularly cold for January. Steven dug two complete holes by lunchtime and ate a strawberry jam sandwich. He always made his own Saturday sandwiches, so never had to suffer the indignity of fish paste. He'd taken the crusts – nobody cared about crusts. One of them had a speck of mould on it and he picked it off with a grimy finger. It made him think of Uncle Jude.

Of all the uncles Steven had had, Uncle Jude was his favourite. Uncle Jude was tall – really tall, and had thick, louring eyebrows and a deep, Hammer Horror voice.

Uncle Jude was a gardener and he had a four-year-old truck and employed three men, but his fingernails were always dirty, which Nan hated. Steven's mum always said it was good clean dirt – not what she called gutter grime. Of course, that was before they broke up. After that, his mum's only answer to Nan's criticism of Uncle Jude was a slight tightening around the lips and a shorter fuse with Steven and Davey.

It was Uncle Jude who had given Steven his spade. Steven had told him he wanted to dig a vegetable patch in the back yard. Of course he never had but Uncle Jude was cool about it. He'd come into the kitchen and peer through the rain at the bramble-choked jungle and say: 'How are the tomatoes, Steve?' Or 'I see the beans are really taking off.' And he and Steven would exchange wry smiles that made Steven's heart expand a little in his chest.

Sometimes, after tea, Uncle Jude played Frankenstein, which meant he would chase Steven and Davey around the house, lurching slowly from room to room with his arms out-spread to catch the boys, booming menacingly, '*Ho ho ho!* Run and hide but Frankenstein will find you!'

Steven was nearly ten at the time and old enough to know better, but Uncle Jude's huge size, and three-year-old Davey's hysterical shrieks, would inject genuine fear into him. He'd pretend to be playing for Davey's sake, but – hidden behind the sofa or wrapped in the front-room curtain with his hair twisted up into the thick green cloth, waiting for Uncle Jude to find them – he knew that his shallow, flutter-ing breath and hammering heart could not lie.

Unable to bear the tension, Davey invariably cracked, and would bounce up from their hiding place and rush implor-ingly at Uncle Jude's legs, crying: 'I'm Frankenstein's friend!' Steven would grab the opportunity to stand up too, rolling his eyes at Davey for spoiling the game; secretly relieved it was over.

The watery winter sun warmed his back a little as he thought of Uncle Jude. He was two uncles back. After him had been Uncle Neil, who had only lasted about two weeks before disappearing with his mother's purse and half a chicken dinner, and most recently there was Uncle Brett, who sat and watched TV with religious fervour until his nan and his mum had a blazing row over his head during *Countdown*. When Uncle Brett told them to shut up for the conundrum, they both turned on him. After that he didn't come back.

His mother was between uncles now. Steven didn't always like his uncles but he was always sorry when they left. His was a small, lonely family and any swelling of the ranks was to be welcomed, even if it always turned out to be temporary.

His spade bit into the ground and hit something hard. Steven bent and picked the soil aside with his hands. Usually what he hit was a rock or a root, but this sounded different.

Steven's stomach flipped as he saw the pale bone smoothness exposed in the rich dark earth. He knelt and scratched at the thick, root-enmeshed dirt of the moor. He had no other tools, just the brute spade, and he felt the soil pressing up painfully under his nails.

He could get his finger under it now, and tried to lever it out. It budged only millimetres, but enough to expose a tooth.

A tooth.

With his breath stuck somewhere hard in his chest, Steven leaned down and touched the tooth.

It wobbled slightly within the jawbone.

He sat back on his heels. The sky and the heather swirled around him. He looked to one side and retched into the gorse. Strings of mucus ran from his mouth and nose to the ground and, for a vivid second, he felt his own fluids tying him to the moor, tugging him downwards face-first into the soil, pulling him under so that his nose and mouth became clogged with dirt and roots and mulch and small biting insects.

He jerked his head up and scrambled backwards to his feet.

Steven wiped his nose and mouth on his bare arm, and spat several times to clear his throat. The acid taste of sick lingered in the back of his mouth.

From a dozen feet away, he peered gingerly into the shallow hole. He had to take two steps forward before he could see the jawbone, then he stood still.

He had done it.

He had done what the police with their heat-seeking rays and their sniffer dogs and their fingertip searches could not do with all their manpower and technology.

He had found Billy Peters.

And he had touched his tooth.

His stomach heaved again at the thought, but he swallowed it.

Suddenly Steven felt weak. He sat down heavily on a cushion of heather and cotton grass.

His sense of relief was palpable.

He *was* better!

And now his nan would see that and everything would change. She would stop standing at the window waiting for an impossible boy to come home; she would start to notice him and Davey, and not just in a mean, spiteful way, but in ways that a grandmother should notice them – with love, and secrets, and 50p for sweets.

And if Nan loved him and Davey, maybe she and Mum would be nicer to each other; and if Nan and Mum were nicer to each other, they would all be happier, and be a normal family, and . . . well . . . just everything would be . . . better.

And this was what it all came down to – this smooth, cream-coloured curve of bone and the boy-tooth within it. Steven thought about Uncle Billy's toothbrush sweeping over that yellowing molar and had to quickly push the image away.

He shuffled back to the exposed jawbone slowly, but determined, and with excitement starting to bubble inside him.

New possibilities burst open in Steven's mind like fireworks illuminating a door to a future that he'd barely dared hope existed. He would be a hero! He would be in the newspapers. Mrs Cancheski would make an announcement in assembly and everybody would be astonished at this ordinary boy who had done an extraordinary thing. Maybe there'd be a reward, or a medal. Mum and Nan would be so proud and grateful. They would offer him the world but he would only ask for a skateboard so that he could go to the ramp with the bigger boys and learn to be a teenager with baggy jeans and keychains and battle scars. Even better, a plaster cast – but it wouldn't stop him skating. Of course, he would fall off at first, but soon he'd be flying and he'd be the best in the village. He'd teach Davey how to skate and he'd be patient with him and grip his hand to help him up when he fell. And girls would giggle at each other and follow him with their eyes as he walked home with his custom deck under his arm, drinking a Coke. Maybe with a baseball cap. And with white earphone cables running across his bare chest as the evening sun sank in the blue-green sky. Everybody would want to be his friend, but he'd stay loyal to Lewis; Lewis was a true friend, even if he wouldn't swap a Mars bar for a two-fingered Kit Kat.

The open door scared him. If he thought too much about those things, the potential for disappointment was vast. Better to expect nothing and get a bit, his mum always said. So he allowed the fireworks to pop and fizzle out, smoking like sparklers in a bucket of water. He could almost smell that smell of wet flames on a dry November night. He was conscious of breathing again for the first time in minutes.

And he was back on Exmoor.

A chilling wind had sprung up and rainclouds were gathering over his shoulder, so Steven knew he had to work fast if the glory was to start.

He found his hands were shaking, the way Uncle Roger's used to before a drink.

Trying to clear his head of the school picture of Billy with his wide grin showing lots of his small white teeth, Steven worked around the jawbone until finally he was able to pull it from the soil.

He stared at it stupidly for long minutes.

It was wrong.

It was all wrong.

Steven touched the point of his own jaw to feel how it moved and connected. Here was the bit that went up the side of the face to the ear. That looked all right, but this was where it wasn't right. The jaw was too long. And the teeth were wrong too. They were not neat boy-teeth – they were long and flat and yellow. Steven ran his finger across the teeth in his own lower jaw. The molars gave way at the broad front to sharp incisors. But the jawbone in his hand held big fat molars and only a couple of long incisors at the narrow front. Everything was wrong.

Steven felt sick again, although this time he did not vomit. He felt sick and tired and as if this life of waiting and disappointment would never be over. That he was a fool to think it ever could be.

This jawbone belonged to a sheep.

Of course it belonged to a sheep. There were sheep and cattle and ponies all over the moor and they died out here just as they lived – all the time. Their bones must outnumber those of murdered children a thousand – a million – to one.

How could he be so stupid? Steven glanced around to make sure nobody was witnessing this humiliation. He felt the pain of failure and, more deeply, the pain of the loss of the future that he'd glimpsed so briefly, yet so gloriously.

He dragged himself upright and let the jawbone fall from his slack fingers back into the miserable patch of earth it had taken him two hours to scuff out of the moor. He picked up the spade and rained blows on the jawbone until exhaustion made him stop. It was in four pieces, and most of the teeth had been knocked out. He kicked soil over it.

Tears burning his eyes, Steven shouldered his spade and walked home.

4

Mr Lovejoy droned on and on and on about the Romans, but Steven's mind was elsewhere. Strangely, he was thinking not about football or dinner but about Mrs O'Leary's English class.

The writing of letters. An ancient art.

Steven did not have a computer at home – or a mobile phone, much to his embarrassment – but Lewis had both, so Steven knew how to email and how to text, although he was so slow at texting that Lewis would often growl in frustration and snatch his phone back to complete the message for him. It kind of destroyed the whole point of letting Steven practise, but when Steven saw how quickly Lewis's fingers flickered over the keys he understood how irritating it must be for him to watch his own feeble efforts.

But letters were different. He was good at letters, Mrs O'Leary had said so. His letters were authentic.

Mrs O'Leary might have already forgotten that Steven wrote a good letter and resumed her near-ignorance of his existence, but Steven had not forgotten her praise. He rarely experienced it, and now he sat in Mr Lovejoy's history class and rolled that nugget of praise around in his head, examining it from every side, watching the light reflect off it and – like any prospector – wondering what it might be worth.

Almost by accident, he had stumbled on this talent for letters. It was not a talent he would ever have chosen – skateboarding or playing bass guitar would have been better – but he was not a boy to discard a thing without first determining its potential value.

When he was ten, he remembered suddenly, he'd found a child's buggy twisted out of shape and dumped in a layby. Everything about it was ruined, as if a car had rolled over it. Everything except the three wheels. They were good wheels, with proper rubber tyres and metal spokes. It was one of those posh all-terrain buggies, as if the parents who'd bought it were planning an ascent of Everest with their infant in tow.

Steven had taken the wheels home and kept them. And kept them. Until, almost a year later, Nan's shopping trolley had broken on the way home from Mr Jacoby's. Her trolley was an embarrassing tartan box on two stupid metal wheels with hard rubber rims, but she had had it a long time and when a wheel broke she was upset. She would have to buy a new one now and they were ridiculously expensive, just like everything else nowadays.

Steven worked on the trolley in the back garden. Mr Randall lent him a few old tools and even showed him how to use washers to keep the bigger, wider all-terrain wheels from brushing the sides of the shopping bag itself.

When Steven presented the rejuvenated trolley to his nan,

she pursed her lips suspiciously and jerked it roughly back and forth across the floor as if she could make the wheels fall off this instant if she only tried hard enough. But Steven had been careful – so careful – to tighten and retighten every nut, and the trolley remained whole.

'Looks silly,' said Nan.

'They're all-terrain wheels,' Steven ventured. 'They'll bounce over stones and kerbs and stuff much better.'

'Hmph. That's all I need – some kind of cross-country shopping trolley.'

Petulantly she bounced it up and down a few more times and Steven held his breath but the wheels stayed put.

'We'll see,' was all she said.

But she did see. And so did Steven. He saw how much easier it was for Nan to pull the trolley along behind her. It never got jammed on stones and fairly leaped up and down kerbs. Other old women stopped and admired it and, on one unforgettable occasion, he saw Nan actually touch one of the tyres with her walking stick with an unmistakable sense of pride.

She never said thank you, but Steven didn't care.

He didn't know why he'd thought of the shopping trolley while he was trying to think about his letters, but suddenly another thought led on from it, which made him sit up a little.

He had shown Uncle Jude the trolley and Uncle Jude had examined it carefully, turning it this way and that – taking it seriously. Finally he'd said: 'Good job, Steven,' and Steven thought he'd burst with joy inside, although outside he just nodded and said nothing.

Then Uncle Jude had stood up and said, 'That's the secret of life you know.' Steven had nodded solemnly, as if he already knew what Uncle Jude was going to say, but he was all ears to hear the secret of life.

'Decide what you want and then work out how to get it.'

At the time Steven had been a little disappointed that the secret of life according to Uncle Jude was not something more spectacular, or at least mysterious. But now he sat in the hot classroom, not hearing about the mosaics in Kent, and thought it through properly for the first time.

He already knew what he wanted.

Now he just needed to work out how this new weapon in his limited armoury might be used to get it for him.

5

Lewis was a garrulous boy with a wide circle of friends but he considered Steven to be the best of them. The two boys had been born just three doors and five months apart.

Lewis was as robust as Steven was bony; as freckled and ginger as Steven was pale and dark-haired; as bumptious as Steven was shy. And yet somehow the two had always rubbed along in the same way that can make lifelong friends of strangers thrown together by chance. As the elder, Lewis had always taken the lead but he would have anyway, they both knew.

Until three years ago, Lewis had also decided everything. Where to play, what to play, who to play with, when to go home, what to eat for tea, what was cool to have for packed lunch and what was not, whom they liked and whom they hated.

After some trial and error they had got into a routine of

perfection which saw them do pretty much the same thing every day. They played snipers in Steven's garden; football in Lewis's; Lego or computer games in Lewis's house. Anthony Ring, Lalo Bryant and Chris Potter were acceptable play-mates and Chantelle Cox was on the fringes if they were desperate and she agreed to be the sniper target or the goalie; they went home when Lewis got bored; they ate beans or fish fingers and oven chips. Sandwiches containing peanut butter, cheese and pickle or red jam were acceptable, as was any kind of chocolate, although a two-fingered Kit Kat was deemed to be the lowest rung of the chocolate ladder. Sandwiches con-taining egg, salad, or any other colour of jam were frowned upon, and fruit was grounds for derision and only good for throwing. They liked Mr Lovejoy and Miss McCartney at school and Mr Jacoby in the shop; they hated the hoodies. Once Lewis suggested they hate Steven's nan too as she was such a grumpy old cow, but Steven did not immediately fall into line, so Lewis made it into a joke and they never mentioned it again.

Then Steven found out – and things changed for ever.

When they were nine they were caught in Billy's room.

They knew they weren't supposed to be in there and weren't allowed to touch anything, but Lewis's Lego ran out before they'd finished the terrorist headquarters and he was desperate for bricks.

'I know where we can get some,' said Steven.

Lewis was sceptical. He was the solver of problems in this partnership and he thought it unlikely that Steven would be able to conjure Lego from nowhere when he didn't even own a set himself. Still, it wouldn't hurt to see what he had in mind.

Steven steered Lewis quietly past the living room, where the TV was blaring cartoons for Davey and where Steven's nan stared out of the window, and led him up the stairs.

They went past the small, messy room with the big messy bed that Steven shared with Davey, and Steven cracked open the door at the end of the hallway.

Lewis knew this was Uncle Billy's room and he knew Uncle Billy had died young. Furthermore, he knew that no one was allowed in Uncle Billy's room. That was all either of them knew right then, although things were about to change.

With more furtive glances downstairs, they entered Uncle Billy's room, made sub-aqua by the blue curtains drawn across the window.

Lewis squeaked when he saw the space station.

'We can't take it all,' warned Steven. 'Nan comes in here all the time. She'd notice.'

'Still, we can take bits off the back and sides,' and Lewis started to do just that.

'Not so much!'

Lewis's pockets were bulging with half the docking station.

'He's not going to play with them, is he? He's dead!'

'Sssh.'

'What?'

Steven never got a chance to answer. There was a creak on the floorboards right outside the door and they looked at each other in alarm. Too late to hide . . .

Then the door opened and Nan was looking down at them.

Lewis still felt uncomfortable when he remembered that afternoon. He tried not to think of it but sometimes it popped into his head unbidden. When it did, it knocked all the stuffing out of him – and there was plenty to knock.

Nan had not shouted and she hadn't hit them. Lewis

couldn't remember quite why it was so frightening; he only remembered rebuilding the docking station with hands that shook so hard he could barely hold the bricks, while Steven stood and sobbed loudly beside him, his socks wet with piss.

Lewis squirmed as he recalled that sudden dizzy fall from anti-terror sniper agents to little boys bawling and peeing like babies as the old woman loomed over them.

He had not seen Steven for two days afterwards, but when he did Steven had a story to tell which was the best story he'd ever heard in his whole life and which – to a very great extent – made up for the humiliation and fear they'd suffered in Billy's bedroom.

Steven's uncle Billy – the very boy whose hands had constructed the space station – had been murdered!

Lewis had felt the hairs stand up on his arms when Steven said it. Even better, he'd been murdered by a serial killer and – best of all – his body was most likely still buried somewhere on Exmoor! On the very moor which he, Lewis, could see from his bedroom window!

At the time Steven was still cowed by the tellings-off and the tears in his household, and the sadness which came with the sudden shocking understanding of his own family's suffering. But safely ensconced three doors down, Lewis was merely drunk with the gruesome thrill of it all.

It was – naturally – Lewis's idea to find Billy's body, and he and Steven spent the summer of their tenth year tramping across the moor looking for lumps under the heather or signs of disturbed ground. Snipers and Lego lost their charms in the face of the real possibility of the corpse of a long-dead child. They called the new game Bodyhunt.

But when the evenings grew short and the rain grew cold, Lewis inexplicably tired of Bodyhunt and rediscovered his passion for small coloured bricks and beans and chips.

Surprisingly, Steven did not. Even more surprisingly, that winter he acquired a rusty spade and an Ordnance Survey map of the moor and started a more systematic search.

Sometimes Lewis would accompany him but more often he did not. He covered his guilt at this abandonment by loyally maintaining the secrecy of Steven's operation, and by demanding frequent and fulsome reports of where Steven had been and what he had found. Then he would pore over the map and decide where Steven should dig next. This gave the impression that Lewis was not only involved but in charge, which both of them felt comfortable with and neither believed.

At first, when Lewis became bored by the search, and was trying to get Steven to be bored by it too, he had asked his friend why he wanted to continue.

'I just want to find him, that's all.'

If he had been put on a rack and stretched, Steven could not have been any less vague about why he continued to dig when Lewis had decreed that they should desist. He only knew that digging had become an itch he needed to scratch.

Lewis could only sigh. His best efforts were met with friendly but determined shrugs and finally he decided to let Steven be. They were still best friends at school but Lalo Bryant became his main after-school friend, even though Lalo had a lot of his own ideas about snipers and Lego, which made their relationship more difficult for Lewis.

And so Lewis and Steven developed a new, less perfect routine: one in which they hung out at school, compared – and sometimes swapped – sandwiches, and avoided the hoodies. Then Lewis went home to play with his Lego, and Steven went out on to the moor to search for the corpse of a long-dead child.

6

Steven lay in the heather, hidden from every eye but those of passing birds. His spade lay beside him, but without fresh soil on it. The unusual gift of February sun warmed his eyelids and made the breath that flowed evenly from his nostrils feel uncommonly cool.

Under his lids, his eyes flickered minutely as he dreamed a dream . . .

In his dream, he was hot and it was stuffy and he could hardly move. His arms were pinned to his sides and soft darkness pressed on his face; a slight pulling sensation on the top of his head . . .

From somewhere he felt Davey's tiny hand touch his, groping for comfort; he squeezed it, but could not otherwise move. He could feel the fear coming through Davey's hand, the small, hot fingers sliding through his, the boy's body pressed against his legs . . .

Steven knew they must be wound in the heavy green curtain in the front room, the musty cloth wrapped around his head and spiralling upwards to the pelmet, taking a twist of his hair with it. Then Davey's breathing jerked and his own breathing stopped and suddenly all he could hear was the sound of his own heart thudding in his ears, and Steven knew Uncle Jude had entered the room. Steven didn't move – he couldn't move – but he could feel Davey tense against him, and their intertwined hands gripped so hard it hurt.

Uncle Jude wasn't *Ho-ho-ho*-ing. He wasn't giving them any warning. But Steven and Davey could hear the floorboards creak under his enormous feet, closer and closer, and Steven was suddenly seized by a terrible knowledge that what was coming to get them was not Uncle Jude at all, and that an old green curtain was their only protection from the evil thing that now moved towards them . . . Then Davey was crying: 'I'm Frankenstein's friend!' and breaking cover and giving them away but Steven felt no relief – only terror that this time the game was not about to end. This time it was only just beginning.

He jerked awake with a whimper.

He knew what he had to do.

7

DEAR MR AVERY

Arnold Avery stopped reading and sat back on his bunk and gazed at the ceiling while the words floated around in his head like a magic spell.

Dear.

Mr.

Avery.

How long had it been since he'd had a letter thus addressed? Nineteen years? Twenty? Before he'd been inside, certainly.

Since he'd been driven through the gates of Heavitree prison in Gloucestershire and marched to his cell through a gauntlet of spit and hatred, he'd had letters which started in a variety of ways: 'Mr Avery' from his hopeless cut-rate solicitor, 'Dear Son' from his hopeless cut-rate mother, 'You fucking piece of shit' – or variations on the theme – from many hopeless cut-rate strangers.

The thought gave him a pang. 'Dear Mr Avery' made him think of gas bills and insurance salesmen and Lucy Amwell, who'd gone off half-cocked trying to organize a school reunion, like they'd all grown up in California instead of a smoggy dump in Wolverhampton. But still, they were people who'd wanted to be nice to him and interact with him without judging and whining and grimacing with that cold look of disgust they couldn't hide.

Dear Mr Avery. That was who he really was! Why couldn't other people see it? He read it again.

> DEAR MR AVERY
>
> I AM LOOKING FOR WP. CAN YOU HELP ME?
>
> SINCERELY,
>
> SL, 111 BARNSTAPLE ROAD, SHIPCOTT,
> SOMERSET.

If Arnold Avery had had a cellmate, he would have been struck by the total stillness that descended suddenly on this slightly built killer of small and helpless things. It was a stillness more marked even than sleep – as if Avery had slipped rapidly into a coma and the world was turning without him. His pale green eyes half closed and his breathing became almost imperceptible. That cellmate would also have seen Avery's sun-starved skin break out in gooseflesh.

But if the hypothetical cellmate had been privy to the workings of Avery's brain he might have been shocked by the sudden surge in activity.

The carefully hand-printed words on the page had exploded in Avery's brain like a bomb. He knew who WP was, of course, just as he knew MO, and LD, and all the others. They were triggers in the loaded gun of his mind, which he could use to fire off streams of exciting memories whenever he wanted. His brain was a filing cabinet of useful information. Now, as his body shut down to allow his mind to work more efficiently, he allowed himself to slide open the drawer marked WP and to peer inside – something he had not done for some years.

WP was not his favourite. Generally he used MO or TD; they had been the best. But WP was not to be sniffed at and, inside that mental drawer, Avery hoarded a wealth of information gleaned from his experience, from newspaper and TV reports of the child's disappearance and, later, from his own trial, which had been moved to the picturesque Crown Court in Cardiff – supposedly to give him a fighting chance, which was laughable, when you thought about it.

William Peters, aged eleven. Fair hair in a fringe over dark blue eyes, pink cheeks on pale skin and – for a short while – a grin that almost swallowed his ears it was so wide.

Avery had stopped at the crappy little village shop. He'd bought a ham sandwich because burying Luke Dewberry had been hungry work. Out of habit, he'd glanced at the local paper, the *Exmoor Bugle*.

Local papers were a rich source of information for a man like him. They were filled with photos of children. Children dressed as pirates for charity; children who had won silver medals at national clarinet competitions; children who had been picked for the Under-13s even though they were only eleven; whole teams of children in soccer or cricket or running kit, each with his or her name conveniently printed in the caption below. Sometimes he would call them, pretending to be another reporter wanting the story for another newspaper. It was so easy. Big-headed parents were only too happy to milk their child's paltry success and would hand over the phone. Only rarely did they snatch the phone from their child's ear in time – alerted by the confused shock on a young face.

Sometimes he just used a child's name and details to strike up conversation with random kids in parks and playgrounds. 'How old are you? You must know my nephew, Grant? The one who just got the lifesaving award, you know? Yeah, that's right. I'm his uncle Mac.' And he'd be off.

Anyway.

He'd just got back in his van with the sandwich when he saw William Peters – Billy, his mother called him later in the papers – go into the shop. Avery only caught a fleeting glimpse of Billy but it was worth waiting until he came out, he thought. He ate the ham sandwich while he did just that. He hadn't bought the *Exmoor Bugle* on the basis that it was too close to home. He didn't live on Exmoor but this was where he'd just buried a body, so he'd made a mental note to avoid local children. But there was something about Billy . . .

The boy took a while and when he came out, Avery knew.

Now, all these years on, Avery still managed to recapture some of the thrill of that moment when he identified a target. The way he hardened, and spit filled his mouth, so that he had to swallow to keep from drooling like an idiot.

Billy was kind of on the thin side, but he had a little-boy jauntiness that was very appealing. He walked away from

Avery's van, blissfully unaware that he'd just chosen the last meal of his young life – a bag of Maltesers. It made Avery smile to watch the child swagger down the street, crunching on his sweets, kicking a plastic milk bottle along the gutter. He liked a confident child; a confident child was far more likely to be eager to help – to lean through the window just that little bit further . . .

He put the van into gear and rolled down the street, pulling his map towards him . . .

Avery shivered.

'Goose walk over your grave?'

Officer Ryan Finlay leered through the hatch at Avery, his drinker's nose poking into Avery's space; his watery blue eyes darting about. The killer in the cell felt himself knot inside with hatred.

'Officer Finlay. How are you?'

'Right enough, Arnold.'

Avery hated him some more.

Arnold.

As if they were old friends. As if one night soon Ryan Finlay might crook an arm at him at lockup and say, 'Come on, lad, let's you and me put a couple away down the Keys.' As if Avery might even enjoy the craic, sipping a black and tan, surrounded by a forest of thick-necked, thick-headed screws talking about how hard it was to lock and unlock doors and shepherd docile thieves between floors.

'Anything interesting?' Finlay nodded at the letter in Avery's hands. In that instant, Avery knew that Finlay had already read it, that Finlay had been disappointed at being unable to stick his thick black pen through anything in it, and that this question now was a clumsy attempt to probe for the information he knew must somehow be contained therein.

'Just a letter, Officer Finlay.'

'While since you had one, isn't it?'

'Yes, it is.'

'Well, that's nice.'

'Isn't it?'

Finlay took a moment to think of his next lumbering line of attack.

'News from home?'

'Yes.'

Again Finlay was momentarily lost. He took his time picking something troublesome out of his left nostril. Avery controlled himself admirably.

'What's happening there then?'

While Finlay had picked his nose, Avery had anticipated this very question and prepared for it in full.

'Nothing special. My cousin. He's a computer nut. I had an old word processor – an Amstrad. He says it's a collectable or some such. Always trying to get it off me.'

'Geek, is he?'

'A geek. That's right.'

Finlay looked around, acting casual. 'You going to let him have it?'

Avery shrugged. Then he smiled, putting everything into it. 'We'll see.'

Finlay was a prison officer with twenty-four years on the job, but in the face of that smile, his suspicion melted away and he couldn't help feeling that he and Avery suddenly shared some secret that was really quite wonderful.

Finlay had interrupted his train of thought, but that was good, really. That train was too good to stop in daylight. It was a night-time train, though not a sleeper. He smiled inwardly at that. He'd go back over WP tonight; right now he was interested in the possibilities that this odd little letter represented. Possibilities were the first casualty of prison life. They were curtailed as soon as the cell door clanged. And for most prisoners they would never be properly recovered. Even men who served only months or a few years suddenly discovered that the possibilities in their lives had been confiscated like shoelaces. Before they had hoped for office jobs, now they could expect only labouring or the dole. Cons lived by a whole different concept of possibility. For lifers, possibilities came to mean even smaller things: the possibility of chips instead of mash, chops instead of mince.

Avery didn't know who SL was, but for clarity he decided to think of SL as male.

SL had been very careful about this letter. He'd been smart enough to realize or to learn that letters did not pass to and from paedophiles and serial killers without the busy pen of the censor crawling all over them. So he'd kept it short and cryptic. He'd also been smart enough to know that bare initials would mean something to Avery.

But of course, the return address was the giveaway. When he'd first been incarcerated, Avery had had dozens of letters from in and around Shipcott. Most had been insulting or pleading, and those were easily forgotten, but he'd had one from Billy Peters's sister, if memory served (as it would have to – he'd not been allowed to keep his huge volumes of correspondence). It was the usual thing – wanting to know what had happened to Billy; where he was buried. She had begged Avery to put her mother out of her misery. He'd written back pointing out the charming coincidence – that Billy had begged him to do the same for him.

Avery seriously doubted that Billy Peters's sister had ever

got that letter. This conviction was strengthened by the fact that a day after he put it in the prison mail, he found himself led to the B-wing showers. The screws had told him that the Segregation showers were being replumbed. The issue of plumbing with its accompanying vocabulary of pipes, bores and plungers seemed to amuse both the screws quite a lot on the way to B-wing and once they'd left him in the showers – naked but for his shitty flannel-sized prison-issue towel – he'd understood why.

He'd been in the hospital for two weeks – the first of them face-down.

Ironically, just two years ago the showers in the Vulnerable Prisoners Unit here at Longmoor really had been renovated; Avery had declined to bathe for the twelve days the job took to complete.

And, for Avery, that was a serious decision.

Arnold Avery hated to be dirty. Hated it like the plague. Sometimes just being touched by another prisoner or screw could send him hurrying to the shower room to scrub his clothes and his skin.

After each murder – and each burial – he'd had to scrub and scrub.

Cleanliness was next to godliness.

Strangulation was as clean as he could make it, but still – some of them vomited, some of them pissed in terror, some of them did worse than that. And when they did, disgust doused his passion and made him hate them all the more for ruining the experience for him. On more than one occasion he'd had to hose them down before he could bear to finish them off.

And once they were dead, they repulsed him. Even the helpless tears that got him so hot while they were alive became slimy trails of disgust on their cooling faces.

Anyway.

He couldn't be certain, but he thought it quite possible that the letter from WP's sister had come from the same address: 111 Barnstaple Road.

So, SL was who? A crusading neighbour? WP's mother? A cousin? A grandchild? Another, much later, son or daughter conceived in an effort to create a new family to fill the black hole which the last one had become? Avery mused momentarily, but they all seemed equally possible so he didn't waste too much time.

Dear Mr Avery was good. WP was good. The appeal for help was nice and to the point.

But what really impressed Arnold Avery was the word 'Sincerely'.

The first letter Steven Lamb wrote to Arnold Avery had been returned to him so blotted by thick black felt tip that it was unreadable. The censor had finally given up three-quarters of the way through and had not even passed it on to the prisoner. He had merely scrawled 'Unacceptable' across the last quarter of the letter and sent it back to Shipcott.

Steven was humiliated. He felt like a little kid who had been caught sneaking into an 18 film in a false moustache.

It was days before he forgave himself and regained the confidence to make another attempt. He was only twelve, he reasoned; he couldn't be expected to get stuff like writing to serial killers right first time.

Over the next week he composed the letter again and again in his mind, each time paring and shaving and whittling until he decided to start from the other end of the scale of information required. That resulted in the first 90 per cent of the letter.

What took him another two weeks to wrestle with was whether to use Yours sincerely or Yours faithfully.

Although this was a personal letter where the name of the intended recipient was known to him, Yours sincerely stuck in Steven's craw. He just couldn't do it.

And yet Mrs O'Leary would have quibbled over Yours faithfully.

It kept Steven awake at night and left him staring vacantly into space in history and geography classes. His pre-occupation reached its climax when he sat next to Lewis the whole of one break-time without saying a word. After three attempts to engage Steven in conversation, Lewis called him a 'tosser' and stalked off.

Steven knew he had to commit to one or the other.

It was only when he actually put pen to paper – using his neatest block capitals – that he suddenly had the brainwave of writing 'Sincerely' instead of 'Yours sincerely'. It solved every problem he'd had. He was sincere in his request, but he sure as hell wasn't Yours.

Steven posted the short letter with high hopes.

Ten days later, he received a reply.

> Dear SL
> I don't know what you're talking about.
> Have a nice day.
> Sincerely
> AA

8

'Scum-sucking egg and tomato.' Lewis glared at his sandwich, then squinted up at Steven. 'What you got?'

Steven leaned on his spade and wiped sweat off his face with his bare arm. He hesitated as if he might lie, but finally it was too much trouble.

'Peanut butter.'

'Peanut butter!' Lewis got up. 'You want to swap?'

'Not really.'

Lewis knew he wouldn't want to swap. Tomato made Steven sick. He knew that, and he knew Steven knew that he knew that, but the thought of peanut butter instead of egg and tomato made him selfish.

'Ah, bollocks; you can take it out. Half and half. Can't say fairer than that.'

He was already rummaging in Steven's Spar bag. Mr Jacoby's shop used to be Mr Jacoby's shop. Now it was a Spar and Mr Jacoby had to wear a green Aertex shirt with an arrow-head logo on his ample bosom.

Steven looked helplessly at Lewis's back.

'Don't take the good half.'

He sighed inwardly. Having Lewis with him was a mixed blessing.

When he was on his own, Steven dug and dug and dug and ate his sandwiches and drank his water and dug some more. On a good Saturday he could dig five holes. Each was the length, depth and breadth of an eleven-year-old boy, although Steven was not stupid enough to think that this gave him any advantage. He understood that he'd have stood a similar chance of success if he had dug a series of two-foot-wide, four-foot-deep holes shaped like elephants. But he was looking for a body of a particular size and shape, and the holes he dug were a constant reminder of that. It was an exhausting and usually solitary pursuit, but a strangely satisfying one.

But when Lewis made his occasional forays on to the moor everything changed. Certainly, it was more companionable and there was less chance of the hoodies chasing him home, but there were drawbacks.

For a start, Lewis always arrived with the words 'Want some help?' but no help was ever forthcoming. Lewis never brought his own spade or offered to relieve Steven of his.

What's more, Lewis's very presence – far from helping Steven – actually hindered him. Lewis talked and asked questions, which Steven felt compelled to answer. Lewis pointed things out too – things which Steven, with his head bent over the heather, would never have seen, much less cared about – and wanted to discuss them.

'Shit! Look at that!'

'What?'

'That. There!'

And Steven would have to look up and lean on his spade.

'What is it?'

'I don't know. I think it was an eagle.'

'Buzzard, most like. There are tons of them around here.'

'What do you think I am? Some kind of moron? I know a buzzard and this wasn't a buzzard.'

Steven would shrug and turn back to his hole. Lewis would sit and look around, or pick up the Ordnance Survey map with its blue biro crosses, denoting where Steven had dug, scattered like a constellation.

'This is a bad place to dig.'

'It's as good as anywhere.'

'No, it's not.' Long silence. 'You know why?'

'Why?'

'You don't think like a murderer.'

'Yeah?' Steven would wrestle with a knot of vegetation, grunting and twisting.

'Yeah. What you got to do, see, is think: if I murdered someone, where would I bury them?'

'But he buried them all between here and Dunkery Beacon.'

Lewis would be silent, but only for a moment.

'Maybe that's where everybody's gone wrong. See, if I killed six people and buried them here, maybe I'd start somewhere else after that. Over there. Or up at Blacklands. Reduce the chances of anyone finding them, see?'

Long silence.

'Steven? See?'

'Yeah. I see.'

'Next time I come up to help, I'm digging at Blacklands.'

The other thing that Lewis did was eat his sandwiches. Steven had tried lying about what was in them, but Lewis always checked and then ate them anyway. And then Steven would have to eat Lewis's sandwiches immediately, whether he was hungry yet or not, otherwise Lewis would eat them too and he'd be left with nothing.

And Lewis got bored. Rare was the day when he did not start demanding that they go home by four o'clock, when there was still a good three hours' digging to be done.

Steven couldn't remember ever digging more than three holes while Lewis was with him. Even so, when Lewis said he was coming to help, Steven always encouraged him. Having his friend there made Steven feel less weird – as if digging up half of Exmoor for a corpse was quite normal, as long as one had a companion.

Now he threw down the spade and pulled the Spar bag open.

'You took the good half!'

'I didn't!'

'You did! You took the half with the top crust!'

A look of astonished innocence passed over Lewis's broad, freckled face. 'You call that the good half? Sorry, mate.'

Steven sighed. What was the point? He and Lewis had discussed the good half of a sandwich on at least six occasions. Lewis knew the good half as well as he did, but in the face of such blatant denial, what could he do? Was the good half of a peanut butter sandwich worth losing a friend for?

Of course, Steven knew the answer was 'no' – but he felt dimly that at some point in the future, the moment might come when all the bad-half sandwiches he'd had to swallow would explode out of him and wash Lewis away on an un-stoppable tide of resentment.

He ate his own sandwich quickly, then picked the tomato out of the half of egg sandwich Lewis had left him – the bad half again, he noticed wearily – and ate that too.

Steven had not told Lewis about the letter. He was em-barrassed by it, as if he'd written a letter to Steven Gerrard asking for an autograph.

Of course, if he had Steven Gerrard's autograph, every boy in the school would have wanted to look and touch (except for Uncle Billy, the loser Man City fan, thought Steven fleet-ingly). But until such an autograph was granted, the request and its author would have had scorn – and possibly physical violence – poured on to him on a daily basis.

No, only if and when it ultimately yielded up the body of William Peters did anyone have to know about the letter.

Then Steven would admit what he had done, in the certain knowledge that Nan and Mum would agree – and be thankful for the fact – that the end had justified the means.

Steven's initial thrill at receiving Arnold Avery's letter was supplanted by disappointment when he read it. At first.

After a few days, however, the two neatly written sentences contained therein had begun to take on a deeper meaning in his mind. The very fact that – apart from Avery's prison and cell numbers along the top of the page – there were only two sentences required that they be pored over and analysed in a way that a six-page rant never would have been.

I don't know what you're talking about.

After a couple of days, Steven decided that this was just not true. Could not be true!

Contrary to Lewis's assertion, Steven had done his very best to think like a murderer when writing the letter, and he had more knowledge of how murderers thought than most twelve-year-olds.

After the bedroom incident when he had pissed his pants (which, mercifully, neither he nor Lewis ever referred to), Mum had told him about what happened to Uncle Billy.

At first Steven had been numbed with horror but, with Lewis's excited encouragement, he slowly learned to be fascinated. His mother had told him Avery's name, but would say little else about him. Instead, over the next year or so, Steven had read about serial killers. He'd thought it best to do this in secret, hiding library books in his kit bag and reading under the sheets by torchlight.

With many nervous moments spent hearing footsteps creak towards him outside the protective duvet cocoon, he learned more about murder than any boy his age should ever know.

He learned of organized killers and disorganized killers; of thrill-seekers and trophy-takers; of those who stalked their prey and those who just pounced as the mood seized them. He read of crushed puppies and skinned cats; of bullies and bullied; of peeping toms and firestarters; of frenzied hacking and clinical dissection.

Steven's manic reading had two major effects. For a start, in a single year his school-tested reading age leaped from seven years to twelve. Secondly, he learned that despite the seemingly crazy nature of their work, serial killers like Arnold Avery were in fact unusually methodical. This told him that if he was true to type, Avery was likely to remember those he had killed quite vividly.

For a start, each of his victims had been chosen deliberately and, if Avery hadn't known their names when he killed them, he sure took the trouble to find out afterwards.

In the fifteen minutes of free internet time he could devote to his search on any one day at the school library, Steven had found only a couple of online archived reports of Avery's trial, but from them he discovered that Avery had picked Yasmin Gregory's name from the *Bracknell & District News*. Yasmin had presented a bouquet of ugly orange lilies to Princess Anne. There was a photo of her curtseying. The cutting had later been found in the house Avery shared with his widowed mother, along with newspaper reports of her family's appeal for her safe return. The cuttings were discovered by police in a shoebox along with Yasmin's yellow knickers with 'Tuesday' in glitter-writing across the front. The knickers had been laundered; the report said Avery was 'disgusted by bodily fluids'.

The report also said Yasmin had been kept alive for at least two days. Steven searched again and found a photo of Yasmin in a cornflower-blue dress – a gap-toothed blonde child with a lazy eye. The photo had been cropped to show Yasmin alone, but Steven could tell she'd been hugging a dog when it was taken.

Steven shivered, although the tiny school library was oppressively hot.

Yasmin Gregory, who'd hugged a big yellow dog. Yasmin Gregory, who'd probably thought that being teased at school about her eye was as bad as it got. Yasmin Gregory who'd left home in her Tuesday knickers but who hadn't been killed until Thursday . . . Steven quickly switched off the computer.

How long had Avery kept Uncle Billy alive?

The librarian tutted behind him. 'You're supposed to log off, you know. If you can't play with it properly, you won't be allowed on it again.'

'Sorry,' said Steven.

He walked home slowly, his mind whirring.

Slicing through every social norm, evading capture with supernatural ease, and preying on the small, the vulnerable and the trusting, Avery had swept down like the angel of death and pulled a pin out of his family. Then he hadn't even stuck around to watch it explode.

Steven's mind could only snatch fleetingly at Avery's crimes. He could think the words, but shortly after thinking them, the concept of what Avery had done kept slipping away from him, too evil and illogical to stick in his head for long. Avery played by different rules – rules that few human beings were even aware of. Rules that seemed to have emanated from another world entirely.

Once – unexpectedly – Steven caught sight of the world Arnold Avery inhabited, and it scared him cold.

One day in geography Mrs James showed them a photo of the Milky Way. When she pointed out their solar system within it, Steven felt a jolt run through him. How small! How tiny! How completely and utterly insignificant it was! And somewhere inside that speck of light was a dot of a planet and they were merely microbes on its surface.

No wonder Arnold Avery did what he did! Why shouldn't he? What did it matter in the whole scheme of things? Wasn't it he, Steven Lamb, who was the fool for caring what had happened to a single one of those microbes on a dot inside a speck of light? What was everyone getting so hot under the microbial collar about? It was Avery who saw the bigger picture; Avery who knew that the true value of human life was precisely nothing. That taking it was the same as not taking it; that conscience was just a self-imposed bar to pleasure; that suffering was so transitory that a million children might be tortured and killed in the merest blink of a cosmic eye.

The feeling passed and Steven's cheeks and ears prickled with the horror of it. It was as if something quite alien had momentarily invaded his mind and tried to tug him clear of reality and set him adrift on a sea of black nothingness. He looked up to see Mrs James and the rest of the class staring at him with a mixture of interest and contempt. He never knew what he'd missed, or what he'd done to draw their stares, and he never cared; he was just relieved to be back.

Later, it was remembering this incident that made Steven realize why he was keeping his letter secret. This was much much worse than writing to a footballer or a pop star. What he was doing was writing to the bogeyman; to Santa Claus; to ET the Extraterrestrial – to someone who did not even exist on this plane of reality.

Steven was writing to the Devil and asking for mercy.

So, with his reading and his research and his epiphany in geography, by the time he wrote his letter Steven felt he knew plenty about Arnold Avery.

That was why he was convinced that Avery knew only too well what he was talking about. And if he'd lied about that, then wasn't 'Have a nice day' equally suspect? Once he'd thought it, Steven was convinced he was right about that too, and started to work out what Avery might really have meant.

Surely those four words had no place in any flat-out rejection of his request? Steven had not studied semantics or even heard the word, but Arnold Avery's letter was a good introduction to the subject and Mrs O'Leary would have been impressed by his deductions.

Steven lived in Somerset, but he was no bumpkin. He had an Eminem CD and had seen any number of loud and bullet-riddled Hollywood gangsta movies. Drawing on the experiences of those strange people in a strange land, he figured that a flat-out rejection would have looked something like this: 'Don't write to me again, shitbag.' Or 'Fuck you and your mother.' Steven didn't know what irony was either, but he could feel *something* coming off the page at him. He knew the four words did not mean what they claimed to. By day three, 'Have a nice day' had become a code in Steven's mind for 'You're a brave kid.' By day five it seemed to be saying: 'I admire your attempt to get this information.'

By day seven he was pretty convinced it meant: 'Better luck next time . . .'

9

Spring had taken the day off and Barnstaple in the rain was something even the most enlightened town planner had no solution to.

A blustery wind threw rain into faces, and raised a million ripples on the wide, mud-brown surface of the Taw.

Even the high street chain stores looked besieged by the weather, huddled in the shelter of the battered Victorian buildings above them. Marks & Spencer was temporary home to this year's strappy fashions and, in its doorway, an angry one-legged drunk shouting, 'Fuck the *Big Issue*.'

Hanging baskets dripped miserably on to wet shoppers – the petals of the primulas and winter pansies plastered against their own leaves, or drooping, heads heavy with water.

Steven knew how they felt. Rain stuck his hair to his forehead and trickled under his collar. Nan didn't agree with baseball caps and Steven declined to wear the laughable yellow sou'wester type of hat that Davey was too young to refuse. Now and then he tried to edge under Lettie's umbrella without making it obvious.

Nan wore a see-through plastic headscarf that tied under her chin. It was the kind of thing that most people would have worn a couple of times then thrown away or lost; Nan had had hers for as long as Steven had been alive – at least. He knew that when they got home she would lay it over a radiator to dry, then fold it like a fan into a ruler-sized strip. Then she'd roll it up and put an elastic band around it to keep it neat in her bag.

When Steven's last trainers had been put out with the bins after two years of constant hard labour, she had been sour for a week because he hadn't removed the 'perfectly good' laces.

Now Lettie rummaged through her purse and brought out a list which she frowned at as people jostled past them.

'Right,' she said. 'I've got to go to Butchers' Row, the market and Banbury's.'

Tiverton was easier and closer, but Barnstaple had Banbury's.

'What do you need in Banburys?' said Nan suspiciously.

'Just some undies.' Steven heard the brittle tone in her voice – stretching it to keep it light.

'What's wrong with your old ones?'

'I don't really want to discuss it here, Mum!' She smiled with her mouth but not with her eyes. The lighter her voice got, the thinner it got; more likely to crack.

Nan shrugged to show it was no concern of hers if Lettie wanted to waste money on underwear.

Lettie put her shopping list away and turned to Steven. 'You take Davey to spend his birthday money and we'll all meet at twelve thirty.'

Davey brightened. 'In the cake place?'

'Yes, in the cake place.'

Behind Lettie, Nan decided to air her views after all and said quite loudly: 'It's not as if anyone's going to see your knickers.'

Lettie didn't turn away from the boys, but Steven saw her lips tighten across her teeth. Davey's excitement became anxiety in an instant as he looked from his mother to his grandmother, not understanding the words, only their effect.

Lettie gripped Steven's anorak by the collar and yanked the zip up as far as it would go, knocking his chin.

'I swear, Steven, you deserve to catch a cold!'

He said nothing.

'Now take Davey to spend his money. And don't let him waste it, understand?'

Steven knew he'd get stuck with Davey. Bloody Nan! If only she'd kept her mouth shut Mum would have been happy to let her have custody of Davey, and he could have gone to the library. Now he had Davey in tow.

Davey had birthday money. Three pounds. Steven fidgeted impatiently while Davey picked every rubber dinosaur out of a box and looked at it and then didn't even buy one. He moved on to the next box, which was full of small clear balls with even cheaper toys inside them. After long and careful deliberation he chose one filled with pink plastic jacks; it cost 75p.

Steven took Davey's hand and hurried him towards the library but Davey made himself heavy and awkward as they passed a sweet shop and once again Steven had to wait while Davey peered at every bar, every packet, and into every jar until finally he emerged with a quarter of jelly worms and a

Curly Wurly. He tried to stop again at the shop on the corner selling radio-controlled cars, but Steven yanked him onwards.

Without the sun to struggle through its high, dirty windows the library was gloomy and cold.

The librarian – a young man with an earring, a zig-zag shaved into the side of his head, and a name tag reading 'Oliver' – led Steven to what he grandly called 'the archives' with a suspicious air. The archives were an alcove behind the reference section – and out of sight of his desk.

'What year?'

'June '90.'

'1890 or 1990?'

Steven pulled a puzzled face. It had never occurred to him that they would have newspapers going back to 1890.

'1990.'

Oliver sighed and peered up at the giant books on the top shelves. Then he turned on a pulsing fluorescent and looked again.

Then he looked intently at Steven and Davey as if trying to find something wrong with them – something that would give him an excuse not to help them.

'He can't eat those in here.'

'I know,' said Steven. 'He won't.'

Oliver snorted and held out his hand for the sweets. Davey instinctively withdrew them.

'I'm not having Curly Wurly all over my archives.'

Davey looked at Steven for guidance.

'Give them to him, Davey. He'll keep them safe for you.'

Reluctantly Davey handed them over.

Oliver kicked a stool noisily across the floor and climbed on to it, dragging down a huge bound volume which he then dropped on to the desk with a petulant bang.

'No eating, no cutting out, no folding or licking the pages.'

Steven blinked; why would he lick the pages?

'Got it?'

'Got it.'

Steven sat on the only chair and Davey sat on the floor and started to open his jacks. Oliver hovered in the doorway but Steven ignored him until he left, then opened the giant book.

The *Western Morning News* used to be much much bigger. It was weird to see the same banner title on this huge news-paper. Steven felt like an elf reading a human book as he paged carefully through the tome. He giggled at the thought and Davey looked up at him.

'What's funny?'

'Nothing.'

The internet had been OK but patchy. Avery's case pre-dated the internet, and Steven had the frustrating feeling that there was lots it wasn't telling him. At least the internet didn't smell like old socks, though.

Davey was struggling to open the plastic sphere, his tongue stuck out in concentration.

'You want me to do that?'

'I can do it.'

The paper was yellowing and painfully thin. In places the ragged edges were torn. Steven stood up so he could handle the tome more efficiently.

'ABUSED, TORTURED, KILLED'. The headline ended Steven's search.

There was a picture of Arnold Avery – the first Steven had seen. He instinctively drew closer to the page so as not to miss a single detail. The photo would have looked equally at home on the sports pages – a young man who'd scored twice against Exmoor Colts or taken three wickets for the Blacklanders.

Steven was thrown. He had expected . . . well, what *had* he expected? His mental image of Avery up until now had been vague – maybe not even human. Avery had been a dark shape in an Exmoor fog, a collage of movement and muffled sound lingering on the edges of a nightmare.

But here was the real Avery, staring into a policeman's camera with a shameless directness, his dark fringe flopped fashionably over one eye, his slightly snubbed nose giving him an amiable look, his wide mouth almost shut and almost smiling. Steven noted that Avery's lips were very red. It was a black-and-white photo, but he could tell that much. As he studied it more closely, he could also see that the reason Avery's mouth was only almost shut was that he had protruding teeth. A pixel of white suggested it.

Steven tried to get disturbed by the picture but Avery looked more like a victim than the perpetrator of the crimes of which he'd been convicted.

There were pictures of Avery's victims, although at this point in the proceedings the *News* called them 'alleged' victims.

Little Toby Dunstan was described in the caption as 'youngest victim'. A laughing six-year-old with sticky-out ears and freckles even on his eyelids. Steven grinned: Toby looked like fun. Then he remembered – Toby was dead.

There was a graphic on the front page too. It was a map of Exmoor. Steven unfolded a scrap of paper from his pocket and copied the shape – a rough, crinkled rugby ball. The graves of the six children who had been found were marked with Xs and arrows which pointed to six photos – one of each confirmed victim. The same picture of Toby Dunstan, a different one of Yasmin Gregory, then Milly Lewis-Crupp, Luke Dewberry, Louise Leverett and John Elliot.

Steven marked each child's initials inside the rugby ball with a red pen. All of them were roughly clustered in the centre of the moor. Shipcott was not marked but Steven could see the gravesites were between there and Dunkery Beacon. Three of them were on the west side of the Beacon itself.

He had never seen the exact location of the graves marked before and was relieved that he'd been digging in the right general area all this time. Of course, what was a half-inch square on this map was several miles of open moorland in reality. But Steven felt new impetus seep through him just by dint of being reminded of his quest.

He carefully folded up the scrap of paper, and started to read.

The tenth of June had been the first day of the trial at Cardiff. What this meant, Steven quickly realized, was that the prosecution told the court the highlights. It was like *Match of the Day* or those slick American TV dramas that always started with 'Previously on *ER* . . .'

Previously on Arnold Avery – Serial Killer . . .

The prosecution barrister, whose name had been (and likely still was) Mr Pritchard-Quinn QC, made it all sound as if Avery was undoubtedly, indisputably, irrevocably guilty. There was no room in his mouth for 'perhaps' or 'maybe' because it was so full of words like 'callous', 'cold-blooded' and 'brutal'.

Mr Pritchard-Quinn told the court how Avery had approached children and asked them for directions. Then he would offer them a ride home. If they took it, they were dead. If they didn't, they were quite often dead anyway, once he had tugged them head-first through the driver's window.

Steven marvelled at the sheer cheek of it. The simplicity! No stalking, no hiding, no grabbing and running, just a child leaning over too far – a little off-balance – and a shockingly strong and fast hand. Steven thought of Uncle Billy's feet kicking through the open window and felt his stomach slowly roll over.

'Make it work.'

Steven looked up. Davey had brought the pink jacks to the table. Now he held two of them out to Steven, pressing them together.

'What?'

'Make it work!'

'What do you mean?'

Davey got his grizzly face on. 'It won't stick! Make it stick!' At the same time he tried to force the two jacks together as if willpower alone could meld matter.

'They don't go together. That's not what they're for.'

Davey looked at the jacks with mounting discontent.

'Look, I'll show you.'

Steven picked the jacks off the floor and found the small red rubber ball where it had rolled against the wall. He bounced the ball and picked up a jack, then bounced it again and picked up two.

'See? That's how it works.'

The disgust on Davey's face was plain.

'You want to try?'

Davey shook his head, slowly working out that he'd spent a large portion of his birthday money on something he had no interest in.

'I don't want them,' he said crossly. 'I want my Curly Wurly.'

'You can have it when we go,' said Steven.

He knew the moment the words were out of his mouth that they were an invitation to Davey, and Davey seized it and RSVPd in an instant . . .

'I want to go.'

'In a minute.'

'I want to go now!'

'In a minute, Davey.'

Davey threw himself on to the dusty tiled floor and started to grizzle loudly, flailing his arms and legs about and scattering his jacks across the room.

'Shut up!' Steven shushed but it was too late.

Oliver appeared in the doorway, and they were out.

The rain had stopped and the sun was trying its best but the cars still hissed past and sprayed unwary pedestrians.

Steven knew he was walking too fast for Davey but he didn't care; he yanked and tugged at his little brother to keep him going, ignoring the boy's whines as he half jogged to keep up. It had been a wasted day; they only came to Barnstaple three times a year – Christmas, school clothes shopping in August and for birthdays. Steven's was in December, so his birthday trip was combined with the Christmas trip, but this was Davey's birthday trip – 1 March – so it would be months before Mum brought them back in to moan about the size of Steven's feet and the rips in his school shirts.

And what did he have to show for it? Nothing. A crude map and an enemy in the form of Oliver, who would probably never let him back into the archive, or perhaps even the library. Stupid Davey with his stupid jacks.

As they hurried, the faces of the throng of shoppers started to emerge at Steven as if he were noticing for the first time that a crowd was made up of individuals.

Individual whats? Individual farmers? Chemists? Perverts? Killers?

Steven felt a sudden eerie fascination with the shoppers of Barnstaple. Arnold Avery would have shopped. He would have appeared normal to his neighbours, wouldn't he? The books Steven had read under his sheets were filled with quotes from friends – even family members – who were baffled when their 'normal' neighbour, son, brother, cousin was exposed as a homicidal maniac. The thought of Arnold Avery or someone like him walking free on this street made Steven feel nervous. He looked around him warily and his grip tightened on Davey's hand.

A grey-haired man stared about as his wife cooed over something in Monsoon's window, his eyes hooded and predatory.

A girl in a dirty skirt played an old guitar badly and sang 'A Whiter Shade Of Pale' in a dull monotone while her lurcher shivered on a wet blanket, too dispirited to make a break for it.

A young man walked towards them. Scruffy yellow hair like Kurt Cobain, a brown goatee, bike jacket. Alone. Was alone bad? Steven caught his eye and wished he hadn't. The young man appeared uninterested, but maybe that was a ruse. Maybe he would walk past Steven and Davey to lull them into unwariness and then turn and slip his fingers around Davey's right arm, starting a tug-of-war which a screaming, pleading Steven could never hope to win, as shoppers stepped politely around them, not wanting to get involved . . .

'Ow, Stevie! You're hurting!'

'Sorry,' he said.

They were almost at Banbury's.

'Where you going, Lamb?'

The hoodies.

Steven's heart bumped hard, then sank; he was a good runner and fear made him a very good one. On a Saturday in Barnstaple he would have lost the hoodies easily. Without Davey, that is. His anger at his brother flared again.

'Nowhere.' Steven didn't look into their faces.

'We're going to meet Mummy,' said Davey. 'We're going to have cakes.'

The hoodies laughed, and one made his voice squeaky and gay. 'Going to meet Mummy. Going to have cakes.'

Davey laughed too and Steven suddenly felt his anger swing from his brother and redirect itself at the leering hoodies. He couldn't fight them, and if he stayed where he was he was going to get pounded. His only advantage was surprise – right now, while Davey was laughing . . .

Emboldened by the crowds of shoppers, Steven lunged past the hoodies, almost pulling Davey off his feet. The three boys were momentarily stunned by his sheer nerve. Then they came after him.

Davey was initially surprised by the speed of the move but one look at Steven's face told him this was serious and he did his best to keep up. Elbows and hips banged his head as Steven towed him heedlessly through the crowds. The pair of them bounced off shoppers like two small, scared pinballs.

If he'd been alone, Steven would have run as far and as fast as he could, but with Davey in tow he knew he had to make every step count, so he headed straight for Banbury's glass doors a mere twenty yards away.

The hoodies realized his destination and tried to cut Steven off. They weren't as fast, but they were more brutal and less inclined to go around people. Davey screamed as the crowds parted to show the hoodies just feet away from him.

A woman with a buggy wandered unsuspectingly into their path.

'Fuck!'

One of the hoodies crashed over the buggy and the other two were distracted long enough for Steven and Davey to burst through the glass doors of Banbury's.

A fat, middle-aged security guard immediately turned towards them, and Steven forced himself to stop running. Davey peered behind them, scared although he didn't know why.

Outside, the hoodies were hurling insults at the angry mother, and barrelling towards the doors.

'Stevie . . . ?'

'Ssssh!' Steven jerked his hand to make him pay attention and led him at a sedate pace towards the racks of bags, beads and belts. The security guard frowned – stymied in his readiness for action now that the two boys had slowed right down and started to look like customers.

The glass doors banged open and the hoodies ran straight into the guard.

Steven looked back as he and Davey stepped on to the escalator. The hoodies were angrily yelling about their rights while the security guard hustled them out of the doors.

'We'll get you, Lamb!'

Polite shoppers looked around, confused. Steven reddened and looked straight ahead; Davey gripped his hand as if he'd never let go.

10

DEAR MR AVERY,

THANK YOU FOR YOUR LETTER.

WISH YOU WERE HERE.

SINCERELY,

SL, 111 BARNSTAPLE ROAD, SHIPCOTT.

Avery was surprised. The letter said nothing! It did not beg, it did not plead, did not offer to help him at his parole hearings – the first of which had already taken place without him, and had led to his transfer from Heavitree to the lower-category Longmoor.

He read the letter again and a slow anger started to smoulder inside him. His own letter had been offhand and cryptic; he knew, because he'd taken some days to work out the precise tone he wanted to convey – ignorant, to get past the censors, and yet with enough of a tease in it to tempt a smart and determined reader into an answer. Avery's in-tray had been empty for eighteen long years and he barely dared admit even to himself the thrill it gave him to receive a letter. Even more, to receive a letter dealing with his favourite subject. And – the ultimate – to receive a letter from someone connected in some way with the family of one of the children.

SL's first letter had opened for Arnold Avery a Pandora's box of memory and excitement. He had started with WP and examined that memory from every aspect; it had taken him days – and those were days when he was no longer held at Her Majesty's pleasure, but in the grip of his own; days when Officer Finlay's blue-veined nose lost the power to provoke him; days when being handed a small paper tub of snot instead of mustard with his hamburger was water off a duck's back. They were days when he was free.

Then he had gone back to the beginning and savoured each of the children anew, and prolonged the ecstasy to almost a month's duration.

And now this letter.

SL had promised to be a serious correspondent but he was

a tease. Like a woman! Like a child! In fact, he wouldn't be surprised if SL was a woman after all! How dare SL start a correspondence and then send him this nothing of a letter? SL could go fuck herself!

Angrily he folded the single A5 sheet to tear it to pieces – then noticed something on the back of the paper.

Avery frowned and held it up to the light but that made it disappear. He tilted the page until he could see what it was. His heart lurched in his chest.

Arnold Avery hammered on his cell door and shouted for a pencil.

The A5 paper SL had used was good quality. It was better than good quality – it was thick, almost card-like. Avery had taken art at school and thought it was watercolour paper, with its slightly textured finish.

Avery took a long careful time to rub over the back of the letter with the blunt pencil he'd had to sign for through the hatch.

Drawing on a piece of paper laid over this one, SL (whom he now thought of as a man once more, for the cleverness of this communication) had impressed a single wavering, yet somehow deliberate line which travelled crookedly round from the top of the paper in a large loop. Inside the line were the initials LD and a short way below LD were the initials SL.

The only other symbol impressed on the page was a question mark.

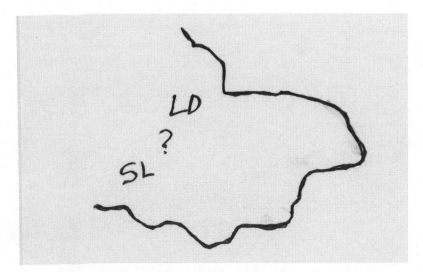

Avery almost laughed. The message was childlike in its simplicity. With a line and four letters which would mean nothing to anyone but him, SL was showing him the outline of Exmoor; he was showing Avery he knew where Luke Dewberry's body had been found and where he was in relation to that, and he was asking again – where is Billy Peters?

Arnold Avery smiled happily. He had his correspondence.

11

When he was younger, good things seemed to happen too fast for Arnold Avery. Things died too easily and too soon. Birds – which he lured to a seed-table and caught in a net – were despicable in their surrender. A friend's white mouse sat meek and trusting as he stamped on its head. The struggles of Lenny, his grandmother's fat tabby, were explosive at first but faded quickly as he held it underwater in her bright white bathtub.

None of them challenged him. None of them pleaded, begged, lied or threatened him. Sure, Lenny had scratched him but that was avoidable; the next cat he drowned – black-and-white Bibs – tore madly at the motorcycle gauntlets he'd stolen from a car boot sale.

From an early age he read reports of children snatched from cars or playgrounds and found strangled just hours later, and was confused by the waste. If someone went to all the risk of stealing the ultimate prize – a child – why murder it so shortly after abduction? It made no sense to Avery.

At the age of thirteen he locked a smaller boy in an old coal bunker and kept him there for almost a whole day – afraid to damage him but enjoying the control he had over him. Eight-year-old Timothy Reed had laughed at first, then asked, then demanded, then hammered on the doors, then threatened to tell, then threatened to kill, then had become very, very quiet. After that the pleading had started – the cajoling, the promises, the desperate entreaties, the tears. Avery had been thrilled as much by his own daring as by Timothy's pathetic cries. He had let him out before it got dark and told him it was a test which he had passed. He and Timothy were now secret friends. The younger boy shook in terror as he agreed that Arnold was his secret friend and never to tell.

And he meant to keep that secret.

After a few weeks of wariness, Timothy Reed started to respond to Arnold's friendly hellos. He could not help accept-ing the stolen Scuba Action Man or the pilfered sweets. Two months after the bunker incident, Timothy Reed watched as Arnold tortured a weedy nine-year-old bully to tears and a grovelling apology. The bully sent out word in the playground and Timothy was pathetically grateful to have an older, bigger boy as an ally and protector.

And once Timothy Reed looked on him as a hero, Arnold sensed the time was right to call in the kind of favour only a very close – very secret – friend might grant.

Arnold Avery abused Timothy Reed until the child's reversals of behaviour and plummeting schoolwork prompted serious enquiries from his parents and – quickly thereafter – the police.

So Arnold learned his first lesson – that the advantage of animals was that they could not tell.

At the age of fourteen Arnold Avery was sent to a young offenders' institution, where every night of his three-month sentence – and some days – were spent learning that real sexual power lay not in asking and getting, but in simply taking. The fact that he was initially on the painful end of that equation only heightened the value of this, his second lesson.

He went home, but he never went back.

It took him another seven years before he killed Paul Barrett (who bore a surprising resemblance to Timothy Reed) but it was worth waiting for. Avery kept Paul alive for sixteen hours, then buried him near Dunkery Beacon. Nobody suspected Avery. Nobody questioned him, nobody gave him a second glance as he drove his van round and round the West Country, reading local papers, calling local homes, chatting to local children.

And nobody found Paul Barrett's body; when they searched it was near the boy's home in Westward Ho!

So Dunkery Beacon was a safe place to bury a body, thought Avery.

And he made good use of it.

12

The heather on the hill had been drenched into submission by the rain, and now dripped eerily on to the wet turf as Steven dug.

He dug two holes then ate a cheese sandwich and dug one more.

Since what he'd come to think of as the Sheepsjaw Incident, the digging had lost some of its appeal. That intense high and the crashing low had thrown the hopelessness of his mission into sharp relief. Now every jar of his elbows, every ache in his back, every splinter in his palm somehow seemed more wearing.

At the root of his new bad mood was an itchy discontent that made him distant with Lewis and snappy with Davey. Even out here on the moor, where sheer hard work usually drove everything from his mind but a kind of dim exhaustion, he was dissatisfied and grouchy – though there was no one to be grouchy with bar himself, his spade and the endless moor beneath his feet.

He had not heard from Avery. It had been almost two weeks since he sent the letter with the symbols on the back. Was it possible that he had been too careful? So careful that Avery himself had failed to spot the secret message? Had the killer of Uncle Billy merely read the meaningless words on the front of the paper and tossed it into a bin? Or, if Avery had seen it, had he understood it? In Steven's murderous mind, he had thought he'd given enough to tempt Avery into answering, but maybe Avery couldn't crack the code. Or maybe he just didn't want to. Maybe he didn't want to play mouse to Steven's teasing cat. As the days dragged by without an answer from Longmoor, Steven could not suppress a sick feeling of failure. He wished he could tell Lewis of his fears, but he knew this was something he had to keep to himself. Nobody else would understand what he'd done. In fact, Steven could see himself getting into some awkward conversations if he revealed anything about the correspondence.

He had already taken pains to make sure he was always there when the post came. Their post came early – around 7am – and Steven had started setting his alarm for quarter to so as to ensure he was at the top of the stairs when Frank Tithecott walked up the path. The last thing he needed was his mum or nan picking up a letter addressed to him. Steven had never had anything personal come through the letter box – not even a Christmas card – and he imagined questions would be asked. But the anticipatory moments spent with cold toes at the top of the stairs were more than outweighed by mounting disappointment.

He started on another hole but had only made one stab

at the fibrous ground before he flung the spade down, and himself disconsolately after it.

Almost instantly the wet started to seep through his cheap waterproof trousers. The chill earth gripped him below and the wet heather curled over him in a dripping shroud. The sweat he'd worked up dried all too fast and he started to shiver.

A sea mist crept silently over the land in a damp blanket smelling of rotten kelp.

Steven felt himself shrinking under its blind vastness. The image of the galaxy came back to him. He was an atom on a microbe on a speck on a mote on a pinprick in the middle of nowhere. Moments before he'd been upright and strong and emanating heat. Now, just seconds later, he was a corpse-in-waiting adrift in space. Avery was right. It all meant nothing.

Steven's eyes became superheated and – with no further warning – he started to cry. At first it was just his eyes but his body soon followed and he started to sob and bawl like an abandoned baby stretched out in the heather, his chest heaving and hitching, his stomach muscles tensing with effort, his white-cold hands curled into loose, upturned fists of hopelessness.

For a few minutes he lay there weeping, not understanding what this feeling was or where it had come from; his only coherent emotion was a vague, detached concern about whether he had gone mad.

His crying slowed and stopped and his hot eyes were cooled by the mizzle swirling soundlessly from the nothing-white sky. He blinked and found the effort almost beyond him. Tiredness seeped from his heart and through every part of him like lead, pressing him down on to the moor, and then there was nothing left for his body to do but lie there and await instructions.

Inside his complete physical stillness, Steven's mind came back to him from a long way off, a bit at a time. At first he felt very sorry for himself; he wished his mother would come and find him and wrap him in a fluffy white towel and carry him home and feed him stew and chocolate pudding. A little after-sob escaped him at the knowledge that this wasn't going to happen – not just now, but ever again. And another, colder stab in his heart told him that this memory-wish had probably *never* happened. He had no real recollection of fluffy towels, or of stew, or of his mother enveloping him in safe, warm arms when he was wet and cold. He had plenty of memories of her roughly stripping wet socks off his feet, of shouting about the filth in the laundry basket, of drying his hair too roughly with one of their mismatched, thinning towels that were hung up at night but were always still damp in the morning. That made him think of the stained bathroom carpet, which played host to big reddish fungal growths behind the toilet in winter, as if the outside was slowly seeping inside their house, filling it with cold and creeping things. Davey cried when he first saw the fungus, and wet the bed rather than go near it. But now, like all of them, he ignored it. Sometimes they even joked about the mushrooms and the mildew, but more often, when Steven came back from Lewis's spotless house, the smell of the damp hit him as he opened the front door. He could not smell it on his own clothes but – from the fresh flowery aqua-blue washing powder scents of his classmates – he had an uncomfortable feeling that he carried that stench of poverty around on him like a yellow star.

He never felt clean. Not when he came off the moors covered in mud, not when he climbed out of the tepid baths

he shared with Davey, not when he first arose from the bed
they shared and pulled on yesterday's school shirt.

What had happened to him? Steven felt his mind whirl
with confusion. How had it happened? Where had he gone?
Somewhere, somehow, the little boy who used to be him had
disappeared and been replaced by the new him. The new
Steven did not watch *Match of the Day* or queue in the Blue
Dolphin for 50p's worth of batter bits. He did not want Steven
Gerrard in his Soccer Stars sticker book more than life itself.
The new Steven was out here every afternoon until nightfall,
sweating in dirt, eating mouldy sandwiches, prodding feebly
at the ground with a rusty spade, and seeking death.

For three years this had been his life. Three years! He felt
like a man who's just heard a sentence passed down. The
thought of three wasted years stretching out behind him was
as shocking as if they were still to come. What had happened
to him? Where had he gone?

Hot on self-pity's heels came an anger so intense that it
struck Steven an almost physical blow. He threw up an arm as
if he could ward it off. The anger was blinding. In a single
violent motion Steven rolled on to his knees and tore at the
heather and grass, ripping up great handfuls, gouging the soil
with his fingernails, slapping the sodden turf. He beat and
flailed and kicked and pounded as the heather flicked rain at
him. A high whining sound in the back of his throat was
punctuated by little mewling breaths that kept him alive for
this one purpose – to assault the very planet.

When Steven next had a conscious thought he was kneeling with his forehead on the ground, prostrate before nature.
There was scrub in his fists and in his mouth, as if he'd tried
to chew through the Earth.

He sat up slowly and looked at the feeble inroad his

hysteria had made into the moor. A few scattered clumps of uprooted grass; heather torn from its stalks, now dying on the ground, a couple of small muddy exposed patches fast filling with water. It was nothing. Less than nothing. An Exmoor pony pawing for winter grass, a deer calf lying down to sleep, a sheep squatting to shit, would have left more of a mark than Steven had in all his fury.

He stood up shakily into the white sky. His spade was where he had dropped it aeons ago; his lunchbox and map nearby – alien artefacts that had no meaning for him in this end-of-the-world fog.

He turned to go but had no idea where he was. Ten feet in any direction was as far as he could see, and then there was nothing. Something far back in his ordinary boy's mind stopped him from stumbling blindly into the swirling void. He had been caught on the moor before like this, enveloped by fog and wholly lost. This whiteness sneaked up on you, even on a sunny day out of a blue sky. Two years ago he'd sat beside an empty grave for three hours in total whiteout before summer re-emerged and he could find his way home.

The memory pulled Steven back to something like normality and he had the sense to stay where he was.

He was cold, but he'd been colder. He was wet, but he'd been wetter. He wasn't hungry – yet. He wasn't injured and, as long as he didn't walk stupidly into the fog, that should remain the case.

He glanced down at his spade and it seemed familiar to him once more. Not lovely, but at least familiar.

The rain was coming down again and Steven upended his lunchbox and put it on his head. The rain that was gently cushioned by the heather turned into a tin-roof rattle on his skull.

Being still would only make him colder. With reluctance, he leaned down and picked up the spade. He found the place where the first sliver of ground had been broken and dug the spade in again. It was a half-hearted effort, but his next strike was better and, by the fourth, Steven was back in a rhythm.

By the time the hole was half dug, Steven knew he would carry on, even when the point was not merely to keep himself warm.

Digging had given his life purpose. It was a small, feeble purpose and was unlikely to end in anything more than a gradual tapering off into nothingness.

But purpose was something, wasn't it?

A small, mean voice somewhere nagged that it meant nothing. It all meant nothing.

But there was another, stronger voice in Steven. It had no answers, only another question, but it was this question that kept him digging until well after an unseen sun set in the invisible sky.

If it all meant nothing, why did it matter so much?

13

'Steven! Breakfast!'

'I'm coming!' Steven's hands shook as he opened the letter from the serial killer.

Steven turned the page over with trembling hands and held it up to the light. Nothing. The paper was cheap and thin – no impressions could have been scored into it. He turned the toilet light on, but there was no mark on the reverse of the letter.

Steven frowned. What was the point of Avery writing back if he was not going to help him? Avery's previously neat and even handwriting had been replaced by an uneven script, dashed off carelessly, using inappropriate capital letters.

'STEVEN!!'

'COMING!!'

From his reading he knew that serial killers liked to play games – first with their victims and then with the police. They liked to show off. From what he could tell, that was how most of them were caught. If they were caught.

Maybe Avery just liked getting letters and was tempting him to keep writing.

But then surely he would make more of an effort to lure his correspondent into a reply this time?

Steven couldn't work out whether thanking him for his 'great letter' was sarcastic or not. He'd be the first to admit that his letter had not been top drawer stuff, but if Avery had found and understood the clue, then maybe he thought that *was* pretty great. Maybe that thing about time and tide meant Steven was right to be asking these questions right now. But if Avery had found the clue, why had he not responded in the same way with a map? Or—

Steven jumped as the toilet door banged open. His mother was red in the face from running upstairs.

'What the hell are you doing?'

'Mum! I'm on the toilet!'

Lettie looked down at him. 'With your trousers up? I've been yelling at you for ten minutes!'

She noticed the letter in his left hand.

'What's that?'

Steven reddened and folded it. 'Nothing.' He looked at his mother and saw an expression of flinty patience come over her face. She wasn't going to let it go.

'Just a letter.'

'Who from?'

Steven writhed under her stare.

'Give it here.'

She held out her hand.

Steven didn't move but when Lettie reached down and took the letter from him, he didn't have the guts to actively resist her.

Lettie unfolded the letter and read it. She was quiet for a lot longer than it could possibly have taken to read it, and Steven looked up at her apprehensively. Lettie was staring at the letter as if it contained hidden instructions on how she should react. She turned it over briefly and Steven thanked god that AA had not scored a map into the reverse.

After what seemed like aeons, Lettie suddenly handed it back to him.

'Come down right now.'

Steven was stunned. He followed her down the stairs and into the kitchen, where a bowl of Cheerios softened in the milk.

Nan folded her arms and glared at him.

'Where was he then?'

'In the loo.'

Nan snorted as if she knew what boys his age did in the loo and it had very little to do with what any decent person would be doing in there. Steven started to redden at the mere thought and Nan snorted again – her lowest expectations confirmed.

'Oh, leave him alone, Mum.'

Steven was so surprised that he bit down painfully on the bowl of his spoon. Davey looked up from his cereal, but was immediately intimidated back to it by Nan's scowl.

Breakfast passed in silence. Steven washed up his bowl and spoon and left for school with the killer's letter in his pocket.

The hoodies caught him at the school gates. They came out of nowhere, twisting his arms up behind his back and pushing his head down so that he stumbled and nearly fell. Vaguely he heard Chantelle Cox say, 'Leave him alone,' compounding the humiliation of the assault.

'Get his lunch money.'

'I don't have lunch money. I bring sandwiches.'

'What, Snuffles?' Someone pulled his head up by the hair so they could hear him, another was patting him down like a police academy graduate.

'I bring sandwiches.'

The boy holding his hair shook him; Steven gritted his teeth. He felt his backpack being unzipped and was tugged off-balance as they rummaged inside. He felt like an antelope brought down by wild dogs, feeling the pack starting to eat him alive. Books, papers, pens – all scattered at his feet as they tore at this thing still attached to him – still *part* of him. He felt sick.

Suddenly his lunchbox was under his chin, the lid peeled back. He could smell the fish paste and his eyes pricked with humiliation.

'No *cake*?'

They all laughed. Steven said nothing.

'Hungry?'

'No.'

'He's hungry.'

A grimy hand picked up a sandwich and rammed it at his mouth. He tried to twist away from them and keep his mouth shut, but a sharp pain in his leg made him cry out, and the sandwich filled his mouth like a fish-flavoured sponge, expanding, choking.

Steven coughed.

'*Fucking* hell!!' The boy with the grimy hands wiped wet bread off his face while his mates laughed at him.

'It's not fucking funny!' He ground the lunchbox into Steven's face – the apple hitting him in the eye, the other fish paste sandwich forcing its way up his nose and crushing his lip with the fake-Tupperware edges a surprisingly painful follow-up.

And suddenly the box clattered to the ground and they were gone, melting into the stream of children in their black and red jumpers as the vague figure of a teacher moved towards Steven.

He winced as the blood rushed back into his arms.

'Are you all right?'

Blood leaked saltily into Steven's mouth from his broken lip.

'Yes, miss.'

Mrs O'Leary regarded Steven. She knew he was in one of her classes, but she couldn't for the life of her remember his name. The boy looked like a fool. He was red in the face, with deep purple marks squared on his skin by the lunchbox. Half a sandwich stuck to his forehead and his cheeks were smeared with butter. He had a black eye coming and smelled of fish. It was this that made the connection for her. This was the boy who smelled like mildew. Any sympathy she'd had for him was now replaced by slight distaste. Mildew and fish. She became brusque.

'Pick your things up then, Simon. The bell's gone.'

'Yes, miss.'

She didn't know him.

It cut him to the core.

He was the boy who wrote authentic letters! *My grand-mother choked on your fillit! The Nintendo you sent was the best present ever! I won a trophy for being the most curteus soccer player!*

Steven wondered fleetingly whether Mrs O'Leary would remember him if he told her that he'd written to a serial killer for help in finding the corpse of his dead child-uncle. He swallowed the words miserably. She'd only remember him then as a liar – a macabre fantasist. Or worse, she'd believe him and call a halt to his correspondence. It was a no-win situation.

'Hurry now, the bell's gone.'

'Yes, miss.'

She stood over him impatiently while he picked his books and papers off the dirty wet tarmac. He was pleased to see his sandwiches had all but disintegrated, saving him the em-barrassment of picking them up. His apple, having blacked his eye, had rolled into the gutter, where he left it to rot.

It took him a couple of minutes to find the lid of his lunch-box under a car. He stood up again, his knees muddied, to see Mrs O'Leary holding the letter from Arnold Avery. He went cold.

'*Thank you for Your Great letter.*'

Steven said nothing. What could he say? He watched her face scan the scrap of wet paper, a little frown line appearing between her eyes.

Mrs O'Leary's mind turned slowly like the barrels on a rusty combination lock, and finally clicked into place. She looked at him and Steven felt his stomach drop.

'So you write great letters in your spare time too?'

For a split second he thought he'd misheard. But he hadn't. He felt the heat rising from his collar and creeping up his face.

'Yes, miss.'

She smiled, relieved to be able to muster some interest in the boy; she needed these little reminders that she had not wasted her life going into teaching. She held out the letter and he took it tentatively.

'Run now, Simon!'

'Yes, miss.'

Steven ran.

Geography.

Steven traced a map of South Africa. He transferred it to his exercise book and started to fill in the mineral wealth. Gold. Diamonds. Platinum. Such exotica. He snorted quietly as he thought of his home country's mineral wealth: tin, clay and coal were the only things that had ever been worth digging for on this tiny peak of sea-mountain called Britain.

Tin, clay, coal – and bodies. Bodies buried in the dirt, in the soil, in the turf. Bodies that had fallen asleep and quietly died, bodies of butchered Picts and Celts and Saxons and Romans; Royalists and Roundheads put to the sword in the sweet English grass. And as the coal and the tin and the clay industries died, so the industry of bodies had taken hold. Now the bones of Saxon peasants were pored over on prime-time TV as they emerged in careful relief from the earth. A rude awakening from centuries of hidden rest.

Bodies were as much a mineral wealth of Britain as gold was in Africa. The declined empire, shrunk to tiny pink pinpricks, had become withdrawn and introspective – tired and surrendered in conquest, now discovering itself like an old man who sits alone in a crumbling mansion and starts to call numbers in a tattered address book, his thoughts turning from a short future to a long and neglected past.

Britain was built on those bodies of the conquered and the conquerors. Steven could feel them right now in the earth beneath the foundations beneath the school beneath the classroom floor, beneath his chair legs and the rubber soles of his trainers.

So many bodies, and he only wanted one. It didn't seem a lot to ask.

As he carefully pressed the graphite into the clean page, Steven wondered how many of those ancient bones were in the ground because of serial killers. When Channel 4's Time Team prised femurs and broken skulls from the holding planet, were they contaminating a 2,000-year-old crime scene? Was the Saxon boy or the Tudor girl a victim? One of many? Would archaeologists a hundred years from now be able to link six, eight, ten victims and say for sure that they were murdered? And murdered by one hand?

Arnold Avery had been convicted of six murders. Plus Uncle Billy. Plus . . . who knew how many? How many lay undiscovered in shallow graves? How many through the whole of history? Did he crush their bones underfoot as he walked home? Did their eyeless skulls peer down at him when he explored the old mines at Brendon Hills? Steven shivered and prodded the map out of alignment. As he carefully covered Johannesburg with Johannesburg again . . .

'Oh!'

Kids around him sniggered and Mrs James looked up from marking papers.

'Something you want to share, Steven?'

But Steven had used the last of his breath to push out the exclamation, and had not yet been able to draw another.

The line Steven copied was even more crooked than it should have been. His hands shook; his whole body fluttered in a mixture of excitement and fear.

He pushed the *AA Road Atlas* away from him so hard that it slid off the old Formica kitchen table and broke its spine as it landed open on the floor. Steven didn't even notice. This was not the first time he'd used the atlas. Then he'd copied the outline of Exmoor on to a sheet of artist's paper to send to Arnold Avery. This time he'd captured it on tracing paper. The border was marked again, and Shipcott.

The TV was on in the front room but Steven still looked suspiciously down the hallway before unfolding Avery's letter and smoothing it down on the table. He placed the tracing paper over the letter, with the 'S' and 'L' of 'SincereLy' over the dot that was Shipcott. His heart thumped in his ears; Your Great, YG, and TiDe, TD, were both north-east of Shipcott towards Dunkery Beacon.

Avery was showing him the graves of Yasmin Gregory and Toby Dunstan.

He'd cracked the code.

14

Lettie Lamb cleaned the big house and thought about her elder son for the first time in a long while.

Of course, she thought about him every day. Why wasn't he up? Had he done his homework? Where was his tie? But it had been days, weeks – maybe even months, she thought with niggling shame – since she'd thought about *him*.

And almost as soon as she'd had the thought, she tried to wrestle it into submission. She couldn't think of Steven without thinking of Davey, and she couldn't think of Davey without the guilt of knowing that he was her favourite, and she could never feel that guilt without thinking of her mother – Poor Mrs Peters – and of how she'd loved Billy best.

This was a well-worn path – a wormhole linking time and people – so that when she thought of Steven, she thought of Billy. The two were so closely connected by her practised brain that they were almost the same person. Steven and

Billy. Billy and Steven. The fact that Steven was so close to the age that Billy had been when he disappeared only served to compound his sins. And although she loved Steven, she had to remind herself of that fact constantly when her resentment and guilt over Billy were so symbiotically tied to her own son.

Lettie rubbed at a water ring on the hall table. She tutted as if it were *her* precious mahogany.

It wasn't her fault. Everyone had a favourite, didn't they? It was only natural. And Davey would be anyone's favourite. He was so cute and chirpy and said funny things without meaning to. Why should she feel bad about that? How could she help it? Steven didn't help himself, with his isolated nature and that permanent little frown marking the middle of his smooth forehead. He always looked worried. As if he had anything to worry about!

Lettie felt that familiar flicker of anger at Steven. He always looked as if he had the woes of the world on his shoulders – cheeky little shit! She was the one who had to keep them all together; she was the one who scrubbed other women's floors so Steven could get batter bits at the Blue Dolphin; she was the one who'd been left to bring up two children alone, wasn't she? Not him! These were the happiest days of his life, for god's sake!

The ring wouldn't come out. Honestly, the more people had, the less they cared. She went into the kitchen and opened the larder. It was packed with the kind of impossibly exotic food that was beyond Lettie. All from Marks & Spencer. She barely even recognized it as food – there was no connection in her mind between what the Harrisons kept in their larder and the cheap, monotonous meals that appeared on Lettie's table.

Help yourself, Mrs Harrison always said. Of course, she didn't mean to the wild mushroom tartlets or the chicken in crème fraîche with baby corn and sugar snap peas. She meant to the snacks and biscuits she kept in what she called 'the children's cupboard'. Lettie had spent long minutes looking for something to eat in that cupboard but had never summoned up the courage to tear into the gift-wrapped chocolate biscuits, or to sully the foil on a pack of mature-cheddar and cracked-pepper savouries. Instead she took custard creams with her and ate them over the sink so as not to leave crumbs.

But she'd seen nuts in the larder – jars of Brazils and walnuts and almonds and macadamias. The Brazils were of such good quality that she couldn't even find a broken one; she had to cut one in half.

She rubbed the Brazil-half over the water ring, watching it fade.

That letter Steven had got. That was why she'd been thinking about him. She felt a little bad about reading it when it was so obviously private, but dammit, she'd been yelling herself hoarse for fifteen minutes! Didn't the boy have ears? Steven's ears stuck out at odd angles, always red at the tips, not like Davey's pretty, velvety little things.

The letter was curious. She'd wanted to ask him who it was from, but at the last second she hadn't. Some small, sleeping part of her had remembered being twelve and having Neil Winstone write 'Your hair looks nice' on the back of her English exercise book, and so she'd bitten her tongue.

Steven seemed too young, too detached – too bloody *miserable* – to have a girlfriend. But he'd obviously written at least one letter first. *Thanks for your great letter.* Lettie wondered what passed for a great letter in these days of text and email. More than two lines? Correct spelling? Or declarations of undying love?

Lettie was not happy for Steven. It was just another thing for her to worry about: how long would it be before some fourteen-year-old slag's mother was at her door demanding a paternity test? Lettie frowned, seeing a future where she and the slag's mother took turns to look after the baby while the slag tried vainly to pass her GCSEs; a future where she, Lettie Lamb, was a grandmother at thirty-four. Lettie suddenly felt physically ill and had to hold on to the hall table for support. She felt a sucking vortex tugging her towards death before she'd ever properly lived.

When was *her* turn?! When did *she* get a turn? How dare that little shit ruin her life. Again.

And then the guilt and self-pity ran together.

Her eyes burned and she jammed the heels of her hands into them before the tears could spoil her mascara. She still had two other houses to do before picking Davey up; she couldn't arrive looking a mess, dragging everybody else's day down along with her own.

She breathed deeply and waited for that crazy dizzy feeling to pass.

She was still holding the two Brazil-nut halves in her hands. Seized by sudden defiance, she ate them both.

15

SL was getting impatient. Arnold Avery smiled idly and held the letter over his face once more as he lay on the lumpy bunk that woke him ten times a night with its sharply shifting springs.

The letter was Zen-like in its simplicity.

SL wanted to know what he wanted to know. It amused Avery. And it also informed him. SL thought he'd been so clever keeping his identity secret, but here he was clumsily letting Avery know – or at least make educated guesses about – the kind of person he was.

For a start, thought Avery, SL was not a person who'd ever been in prison. If he had, then he'd have understood that in prison almost everything happens very, very slowly. The days pass slowly, the nights slower. The time between breakfast and lunch is an age; between lunch and dinner, an aeon, between lights out and sleep, an eternity. So the six or seven weeks since his first letter that obviously meant so much to SL meant nothing to Avery. To Avery, the longer this pleasurably mnemonic correspondence went on, the better.

He was surprised and a little disappointed by SL's weakness. He had thought of SL as an intellectual equal, but now he realized he was less than that – far less. To recklessly show his impatience like this was the mark of someone who had not thought things through properly.

Avery got a pang as he remembered the day he'd waited for Mason Dingle to return with his car keys. If only he'd been patient. If only the second child had not skipped into the playground and clambered on to a swing right next to him. If only he could have mustered the control . . .

Of all the thoughts he held about his career, these thoughts of Mason Dingle were the ones that plagued him like chicken pox scabs. They came unbidden and unwanted once, twice a week, and made him feel stupid and feeble.

He was a different man now. Stuck in this echoing stone and iron tomb he understood the meaning of patience. Polite conversation with Officer Finlay could only be achieved through the utmost patience. Standing in the line for food for almost an hour, just for a smirking ape to tell him that the only lasagne left was the burnt bits from the bottom of the pan, took patience and control.

But it was all too late. The dagger twisting in his guts was that now, finally, when he had mastered patience and control, he had nothing over which to exercise his mastery.

That was why this petulant, demanding letter gave him more pleasure than anything since SL's first careful missive. It showed a chink in SL's armour. A clumsy revelation of desire that gave Avery something he had not felt in a very long time. It gave him power.

16

Arnold Avery hadn't written back and Steven felt the absence of a letter like something physical. Sometimes he got an itch in his ear – or in his throat. Between his ear and his throat. And it didn't matter how far he stuck his finger in his ear, or how many times he made a coarse, rasping sound in his throat, neither could reach that point that made him want to cry with frustration. No reply from Avery was like that – an itch so deep inside him that he wanted to throw himself to the ground and roll and squirm like a fleabag dog in a senseless bid to scratch it.

It had been more than four weeks, and the heather on the moor had already started to bud.

Steven was a wiry boy, but those weeks had seen his features sharpen further, and little bruised hollows of insomnia darken under his tired brown eyes. The vertical frown-crease that had no place on the face of a child deepened on his forehead.

He had stopped digging.

The thought made him feel sick and weak every time he looked out of the bathroom window at the moor rising behind the houses. It crowded him, nudged him, stood over him in judgement at his puny efforts – and frowned at their cessation.

He had felt close – so close – to finding out the truth from Arnold Avery that his own random scratchings on the moor seemed increasingly laughable.

There was a man who knew where Uncle Billy was buried. Steven had made contact with that man.

That man had understood the rules Steven had created for them to play by and had joined the game.

And so Steven had given up his other game – a game that had no other players, no rules, and no realistic prospect of being won.

His admission that, alone, his was a hopeless task was the most shocking and painful moment he could remember in his young life. It had left him reeling and apathetic to the point where even Lettie had noticed.

'Not off with Lewis today?' she'd finally asked, and he'd just shaken his head mournfully. Lettie didn't ask any more. She hoped his newly pinched features were because he'd fought with Lewis, and not because he'd got her hypothetical slag up the duff. *Thank you for your great letter.* The words swirled uneasily about in Lettie's mind – too disturbing to mention, too disturbing to forget.

She hoped it was Lewis. Anything else, she didn't have the time to care about.

Now, while the rest of the class took turns to read a page each from *The Silver Sword*, Steven frowned into the middle distance of the whiteboard and wondered what would happen if Arnold Avery never wrote back. Could he accept it and go on as he had before? In his head, Steven insisted 'yes', but immediately blushed at the lie he was telling himself. The truth was, he'd come to rely on Avery. He'd hung every hope he had on the hook of the cat-and-mouse game they were playing.

For only about the millionth time in his short life, Steven wished he had someone to confide in. Not Lewis, but someone older and wiser, who could tell him where and how he'd gone wrong and how to put it right.

He cursed himself silently, hesitantly using the worst word he knew, which was 'fuck'. He was a fucking idiot. Somehow his last letter had pissed Avery off to the point where he'd picked up his ball and gone home – and Steven was sharply reminded that it *was* Avery's ball. With a sinking feeling he realized that if he – Steven – wanted to continue to play, he'd have to be the one to make the effort to be friends again, even if he didn't mean it. The stubborn streak, which had kept him at his gruelling task through three long years, made him bristle at the idea of making overtures of peace to the killer who'd very likely murdered his uncle Billy.

But – like a rat trained to behave by the application of electric shocks – the stubbornness was instantly curtailed by the horror of possibly never knowing. The jolt was so intense that his whole body spasmed and his wrist jerked against his desk with a loud, painful bang, propelling him back into the classroom with dizzying speed.

'Lamb, you bloody spazmoid!'

Everyone laughed except Mrs O'Leary, who admonished the hoodie weakly – too afraid of failing to eject him from her class to even attempt it. Instead she demanded that he read the next page and the boy glowered and started to stumble painfully through the text.

Steven sighed, and wiped a sheen of sweat from his fore-head. He knew he couldn't go on alone any more. As with the Sheepsjaw Incident, he'd glimpsed the pinprick of light at the end of the tunnel and without the help that only Avery could give him he knew he was lost in the darkness. This was not a momentary fantasy sparked by a false hope; this was real progress he'd made over months of careful planning and execution. Avery was a one-shot deal. Steven knew that if he blew this, he'd never get another chance. Either he would permanently have to stop the search that gave his life mean-ing, or he'd go on ad nauseam, possibly until he was old, like the tattered old man who dug about in other people's rubbish – but with Uncle Jude's rusty spade his companion instead of a stolen Tesco trolley.

Steven sighed as he realized he had no choice.

He was not a boy who had ever had much to take pride in, so swallowing a bit of pride now would be sour, but not impossible.

Just like Uncle Jude, he'd worked out what he wanted and the only way he knew how to get it.

Now – just like Davey – he'd have to be Frankenstein's friend.

17

Arnold Avery liked to think of the benches he made as his tickets to freedom.

From the first day of his incarceration, Avery had had a single goal in mind, and that was to be released as soon as was legally possible.

Life did not mean life any more. The petulant cry of *Daily Mail* readers everywhere was sweet music to Arnold Avery. He'd known life did not mean life when he was arrested and he reminded himself of it again in Cardiff. Still, he'd been surprised at the sick sucker-punched feeling in his gut when the judge actually said the word.

But by the time he'd reached Heavitree, he had already determined to be a model prisoner so that he could get out while he still had hair and teeth to speak of. While he was still young enough to enjoy himself.

In whatever way he saw fit.

Anyway . . .

Model prisoners wanted to be rehabilitated, so Avery had signed up for countless classes, workshops and courses over the years. He now had assorted diplomas, a GCSE in maths, A-levels in English, art and biology, a bluffer's knowledge of psychiatry and a certificate of competence in first aid.

And it was all paying off. Two years earlier his first parole review had approved his transfer from the high-security Heavitree to Longmoor Prison on Dartmoor. Even Avery had been surprised. He had hoped but never really expected that his apparent devotion to rehabilitation would achieve the desired aims. It was shocking really, thought Avery at the time. If he'd been anyone but himself, he'd have been up in arms about it. Of course, a recommendation that he could be trusted not to escape from a lower-security prison was not the same as the parole board actually approving his release after his twenty-year tariff had been served. But it was a very good start.

Compared to Heavitree, Longmoor was a holiday camp. The segregation unit was freshly painted, the guards noticeably less oppressive and the opportunities for reintegration activities were even better, so he'd done a course in plumbing too.

He'd really surprised himself, though, with a natural aptitude for carpentry.

Avery found he loved everything about wood. The dry smell of sawdust, the soft warmth of the grain, the near-alchemic transformation from plank to table, plank to chair, plank to bench. Most of all, he loved the hours he could spend sanding and shaping with relatively little input from his brain, which therefore left him free to think, even while he earned kudos for working his way to rehabilitation, parole and nirvana.

In the two years that Arnold Avery had been taking carpentry, he'd made six benches. His first was an uninspiring two-seater with ugly dowel joints; his most recent was a handsome six-foot three-seater with bevelled struts, curved, figure-hugging backrest, and almost invisible dovetails.

Now, as he worked on his seventh bench, sanding patiently, Avery let his mind drift gently off to Exmoor.

Avery could almost smell the moor. The rich, damp soil and the fragrant heather, combined with the faint odour of manure from the cattle and ponies and sheep.

He thought first of Dunkery Beacon, where all his fantasies centred, before spreading like bony tendrils across the rounded hills. From there he would almost be able to identify the individual gravesites – not from prurient newsprint graphics but from actual memory, the memory that had sustained him throughout his imprisonment and which still held the power to feed his night-time fantasies. The thought alone brought saliva to his mouth, and he swallowed audibly.

Dartmoor was very different. This moor was grey – made hard and unyielding by the granite which bulged under its surface and frequently broke through the Earth's thin skin to poke bleakly up at the lowering sky.

The prison itself was an extension of the stone – grey, blank, ugly.

There was little heather on Dartmoor, just prickled gorse and sheep-shorn yellow grass. There was no gentle beauty and purple haze.

Dartmoor was not Exmoor, but Avery would still have liked to watch the seasons change from his narrow window.

But his window had been blocked on the orders of his prison psychiatrist, Dr Leaver, who theorized that even visual contact with the moors would be counterproductive to his attempts to purify Arnold Avery's psyche.

Avery's bile rose in his throat along with the hatred and fury he now reserved exclusively for Dr Leaver and Officer Finlay.

It amazed him that Leaver couldn't understand that this was Dartmoor, and so held nothing but a passing aesthetic interest for him. The fact that both were moors was apparently sufficient reason for Leaver – a cadaverous man in his fifties – to decree the blocking of the window, which left Avery depressed and mopey, even in the summer months.

The terrible Catch-22 he faced was that Leaver was half right. While he was mistaken in thinking that Avery gave inordinate weight to the moor he might have seen from his window, Avery would only have been able to convince him of that fact by revealing the truly awesome weight he gave any idea, sight or mention of Dartmoor's smaller, prettier, more gentle cousin on the north coast of the peninsula.

If Leaver – or anyone else – had had any idea that merely hearing someone say the word 'Exmoor' could give him a day-long erection, his paltry privileges would have been suspended faster than Guy Fawkes from a rope.

Avery had never killed an adult but he knew he could kill Dr Leaver. The man's monstrous ego was fed by the power he held over the inmates he counselled. Avery was not empathetic, but he recognized his own sense of superiority in Leaver within five minutes of settling in for their first session together. It was like glimpsing his own reflection in a mirror.

He knew that Leaver was clever. He knew that Leaver liked to show off how clever he was – especially in an environment where he had every right to feel that way. After all, any con who was smarter than Leaver had, at the very least, to concede that they'd fucked up badly enough to get caught.

Avery had no problem with Leaver flaunting his intellect. A man who had a talent should use it; a footballer played football, a juggler juggled, a clever man outwitted others. It was Darwinian.

In Leaver's presence, Avery was a bright man who had flashes of intellectual connection that made him a cut above the run-of-the-mill burglar cum bar-room brawler. Clever enough to interest Leaver but *never* clever enough to alert him or threaten his ego.

He asked Leaver's advice and always deferred to Leaver's decisions, even if they had an adverse effect on him. The boarding up of his window was a case in point. When Leaver had suggested it might help, Avery had suppressed the urge to tear the man's throat out with his teeth and had instead pursed his lips and nodded slowly, as if he was examining the idea from every conceivable angle, but with the best of intentions. Then he'd sighed to show that it was a regrettable necessity – but a necessity nonetheless.

Leaver had smiled and made a note that Arnold Avery knew would bring him closer to the real life waiting for him outside these walls.

The benches were another step on the freedom ladder. But the benches were enjoyable to make. And had the immense added attraction of the nameplates . . .

Avery stroked the wood under his dry hands and reached for a shiny brass plate with a screw-hole in each corner.

'Can I have a screwdriver please, Officer?'

Andy Ralph eyed him suspiciously – like he hadn't used a screwdriver a thousand times before without running amok – then handed Avery the Phillips-head screwdriver.

'Flat-head please, Mr Ralph.'

Ralph took back the Phillips and gave him the flat-head, even more suspiciously.

Avery ignored him. Idiot.

He looked down at the plate in his hand and smiled as he remembered the scene of what had been – until SL's letters – the greatest power trip since his incarceration . . .

'I hear you're building benches, Arnold.'

'Yes, Dr Leaver.'

'How do you enjoy that?'

'Good. I like it. It's very satisfying.'

'Good. Good.' Leaver nodded sagely as if he were personally responsible for Avery's upped satisfaction quotient.

'Thing is . . .' started Avery, then stopped and licked his lips nervously.

'What?' said Leaver, suddenly interested.

'I was thinking.'

'Yes?'

Avery shifted in his seat and cracked his knuckles – the picture of a man struggling with a great dilemma. Leaver gazed at him calmly. He had all the time in the world.

'I was thinking . . .' Now Avery dropped his voice so it was almost a whisper, and looked down at his own scuffed black shoes as he continued haltingly. 'I was thinking maybe I could put a little brass plaque on my benches. Not the shitty one I made first, but some of the other ones. The good ones.'

'Yes?'

Avery scraped a match under his fingernails, even though they were already clean.

'With names on.'

His voice disappeared in the whisper and he dared not

look at Leaver, who now leaned forward in his seat (to give the illusion that he was part of a conspiracy – Avery knew the moves).

'Names?'

'The . . . names . . .'

Avery could only nod mutely, staring at his lap – and hope that Leaver was even now imagining that tears filled the killer's eyes – and that he had cottoned on to what he was trying to say.

Leaver slowly straightened up again, clicking the top of his Parker pen.

Avery wiped his sleeve across his bowed face, knowing it would add to the illusion of a man in personal hell, and Leaver fell for it, hook, line and psycho-sinker.

The fucking moron.

Avery screwed the brass plate to his best bench yet and stood back to admire his work.

In memory of Luke Dewberry, aged 10.

Oh, his benches were his ticket out of here all right. But they were also tickets to previously unimagined pleasure while he was still stuck in this grimy hell-hole.

Now his benches graced the yard and walkways that already evidenced the work of other prisoners, with their foolproof flowerbeds and neat verges. And every time he was allowed out for exercise, Avery made a beeline for one of them.

Other prisoners made benches. Other prisoners now started to put little plaques on them, most with the names of their children or lovers or mothers.

But Avery had no interest in sitting on other benches. He luxuriated against the plaque *In memory of Milly Lewis-Crupp*; he pressed *John Elliot, aged 7* with a thumb he'd rubbed dirty just for the occasion and, on one memorable afternoon, he rubbed himself discreetly against the back of a bench while staring at the brass words: *In memory of Louise Leverett.*

And while he did, a large part of him savoured the delicious irony. He was way too smart to show Leaver just how clever he really was.

Or how angry.

Or how desperate to hear from SL.

Despite his new-found control and patience, Avery could not help wondering whether he'd done the right thing in not replying to SL's last demanding missive.

For the first two weeks after he'd received the bald 'WP?', he'd enjoyed knowing that SL was waiting for something that he, Arnold Avery, wasn't going to give him. That had been satisfying and empowering and Avery had been energized by the experience.

The next two weeks had been more difficult. While his self-satisfaction continued to some degree, he also missed anticipating SL's reply to any letter he might have sent. He had to keep reminding himself that he was doing the right thing. But his resolve was tested and he started to wonder if SL had given up. People had no staying power, he worried. Avery had staying power, but he was exceptional. SL had been impatient, so maybe he had also been angry or frustrated or just tired of the sport. The thought that SL might not realize that he was now required to make a concession to appease Avery scared him.

SL's first communication had heralded the most interesting four months of Avery's entire incarceration, and he was loath for it to end. Every missive had been a reminder of his heyday, and everyone likes to be reminded of their finest hour, he reasoned.

Week five of Avery's unilateral moratorium brought despondency. SL was tough. Avery lay awake at nights and worried. He resented it bitterly; his nights had become oases of pleasure since SL's first letter had allowed him to re-examine his memories in fresh detail in a way he'd thought was long gone. But now he lay awake, unable to recapture those baser feelings and fretting instead over practicalities like the unreliability of the postal system, or the thought that SL might have concocted the correspondence as a kind of sick hoax to bring about the very punishment he was now experiencing.

It was this last thought that finally raised the anger in Avery that kept him strong. Anger was an emotion he had rarely given in to since his arrest. Avery knew that anger was counter-productive to life inside, which required resignation above all else.

Resignation had been his constant companion for years, with his anger at Finlay or Leaver never being allowed to break the surface, although he could feel it boiling in his guts whenever he saw either of them.

Now, in the pitch-black cell which did not even shed the light of a half-full moon on his darkness, Avery mentally added SL to his short but heartfelt list of fury, and resolved that his erstwhile correspondent would get nothing from him – not a word, not a symbol, not a carefully folded piece of Avery's shit-stained toilet paper – until he'd said sorry.

It was five weeks and four days since SL's last letter before Avery received the next one.

There was no map, no initials, no question marks, just the single word:

SORRY

Avery grinned. It had more grudge than grovel about it, but it would do. SL had learned the lesson and had realized that he was not in control in this game, and that Avery should therefore be accorded due deference. With that single word he had acknowledged Avery's power.

Now Avery sat and wondered how best to wield it.

18

If Arnold Avery had realized how Steven had struggled to write that single word, he would have been more appreciative of it.

Once he'd recognized that he'd offended and needed to make peace, Steven had written a dozen letters and posted none. They ranged from a rambling litany of the reasons he was so desperate for knowledge, through a sycophantic plea for guidance, to an angry rant at the callousness of the distant prisoner.

MY NAN IS AN OLD COW BUT ITS NOT HER FULT.

EVERYTHING WILL BE MUCH BETTER IF I WE HAD BILLY'S BODY

> IM TIRED SO PLEASE PLEASE PLEASE CAN YOU
> HELP ME
>
>
> HOW WULD YOU LIKE IT IF I DID THAT
> TO YOU?

So it had gone on. A rollercoaster of emotions that lasted for weeks and left Steven's mind sick with pleading and dizzy with anger. In short, he had found it a lot harder to swallow what little pride he had than he'd thought he would.

Finally – going with the brevity that had brought him the genius of 'Sincerely' – he simply wrote 'Sorry', hoping that Avery would read into it whatever underlying motivation would best serve Steven's purpose. He could do no less, but he was not prepared to do more.

Another week passed, during which Lewis claimed that Chantelle Cox had a crush on him.

It was not the first time Lewis had been convinced of the power of his own sexual attraction. Last summer Lewis had casually told him Melanie Spark had let him touch her tit. Steven had been stunned and it was only his careful and insistent probing that revealed that it had been through a cardigan *and* a blouse, and had really been more of a rib, and that fickle Melanie had immediately elbowed Lewis in the throat for it. When Steven hesitantly suggested that – just maybe – Melanie Spark hadn't been an active participant in the tit-touching episode, Lewis had merely grinned at him pityingly and revealed that women always changed their minds about sex; that it was what they were known for.

But apparently Chantelle Cox had not changed her mind;

at least Lewis had no fresh bruises to indicate that she might have.

'Lalo and me were the snipers and she ran round the back of the shed and I went after her—'

'Where was Lalo?'

'He was too scared. Last time he chased her round there she hit him with the hose. But I went round cos I knew Dad had used the hose to wash the car yesterday and it was out front. And she was just standing there, so I shot her, but she wouldn't fall down cos of that muck, you know?'

Steven knew. He'd died into the muck round the back of Lewis's shed a few times.

'So I says, if you don't fall down, I'm taking you prisoner, so she says, OK then, so I put her arms behind her and tied them with my jumper, right?'

Steven nodded. He'd also been tied with Lewis's jumper on a number of occasions. It didn't hurt and wasn't hard to get out of.

'And then she kissed me, right on the lips.'

'*She* kissed *you*?'

'*She* kissed *me*.'

'With tongues?'

'Tongues?' Lewis looked puzzled.

'Yeah,' said Steven. 'Did she put her tongue in your mouth?'

A look of revulsion flashed across Lewis's face. 'That's disgusting!'

Steven flushed. Somewhere he'd heard that that was what girls did, but now – flustered by Lewis's instant disapproval – he couldn't remember where he'd heard it and whether the source was reputable. His natural deference to Lewis in all things worldly was an integral part of their friendship and now he felt that not only had he stepped out of line but he'd stepped out of line into a bog, and he needed to turn around fast and get back on to solid ground.

He shrugged and looked apologetic. Lewis scowled at him.

'Did you touch her tit too?' Steven thought that handing Lewis the opportunity to brag would be his path back to terra firma, and he wasn't wrong.

Lewis looked glazed for a moment and then nodded enthusiastically. 'Yeah, both of them. At the same time. I got a stiffie and everything.'

Steven knew it was a lie. Not all of it. He was sure Chantelle Cox had kissed – or been kissed by – Lewis. But he could always tell when Lewis left his own path and strayed haphazardly and inexpertly into the minefield of lies. A tiny shifty look in his eyes preceded any such deviation, as if his inner eye were scanning the horizon for the possible pitfalls of his imminent dishonesty. Steven always let it go. It was like the good half of a sandwich. What was the point in arguing?

And besides, he thought with a sudden rush of unfamiliar maturity, just last week he'd apologized to a real-life serial killer; allowing Lewis his imaginary stiffie behind the garden shed seemed paltry by comparison.

Plus, kissing Chantelle Cox *was* something to boast about. She wasn't that pretty, and she was a tomboy, but she definitely had little breasts, although she never teased boys with them the way Alison Lovacott did. Apparently. Steven had heard that Alison Lovacott had flashed her boobs to John Cubby in the lunch queue. He could hardly believe it, but if it had happened to anybody it would have happened to John Cubby, who captained the Under-16s soccer team and was plainly the best-looking boy in the school.

This reminded Steven that it was John Cubby he'd

overheard about the tongues and that it was therefore almost certain to be true. Too late now – he'd already backed down over that. The thought of Chantelle Cox putting her tongue in his mouth didn't disgust him though. In fact, the idea sent a little shiver through him that was not at all unpleasant. He blushed. Maybe he was not normal. Not normal the way that Arnold Avery was not normal. He frowned, disturbed by the thought, and wished it had never entered his head.

'What's with you?' Lewis was staring at him quizzically.

'Nothing,' he knee-jerked, and looked up to see they were almost at Lewis's house.

They said goodbye and Steven walked on to his house alone.

He smiled at Nan in the window but she just pursed her lips at him as if he'd done something wrong merely by walking home from school.

Davey had spread every toy he owned in the hallway behind the front door. Something cracked under Steven's foot as he entered and he looked down to see a broken pink jack. He kicked it skittering towards the skirting board.

'Steven?'

His mother's voice sounded strained and Steven stood motionless, wondering whether he could still back out of the front door without her knowing he'd ever been in.

'He's just come in.' Nan's voice was sly.

Steven couldn't keep the wariness out of his voice: 'What?'

'Could you come in here please?'

He looked up to see that Nan had come to the door of the front room to enjoy his heavy walk to the guillotine of the kitchen.

His mother was sitting at the kitchen table holding a letter from Arnold Avery.

Steven felt his bladder clench in terror and almost doubled over as he barely managed to stop himself pissing down his legs. It was the Lego space station all over again.

Lettie looked at him coldly.

'You got a letter.'

He couldn't find words. Couldn't remember *how* to find words. He felt the back of his neck prickle and burn. His life was over.

Lettie looked down at the letter and cleared her throat.

'A photo would be nice,' she read.

'A photo! Disgusting!' Nan was standing behind him. Now she pushed him aside so she could cross to Lettie, and tried to take the letter from her hands. Lettie kept it from her.

'It's all right, Mum, I'm dealing with it.'

Nan snorted. They all knew the snort. It meant she knew best.

While their attention was momentarily elsewhere, Steven glanced at the brown envelope. As before, there was nothing on it to indicate where it had come from. He knew the notepaper Avery used had no prison markings on it. It was cheap schoolbook paper. It could have come from anywhere. Avery always wrote his prison number along the top of the page but, without context, that meant nothing.

The fact that the envelope and the notepaper were anonymous gave Steven hope, and hope gave him courage.

'Can I read it?'

Lettie and Nan both looked at him as if he'd asked for new underpants made of pure gold.

'It is mine. Isn't it?' He even managed to inject a very small note of anger into the words and suddenly Lettie was on the back foot. She'd opened a letter that didn't belong to her.

Whatever the circumstances, that was difficult to justify.

But she tried.

'It may be your letter, Steven, but if this is from some girl, then the business of it is mine too. I have a right to know if you're about to knock some girl up and leave me holding the baby, understand?'

Steven's mind raced to catch up along the path his mother's had long since travelled. Finally, after an agony of mental confusion that made him want to slap some sense into himself, he got there. His mother thought the letter was from a girl. A secret girlfriend. A girlfriend he might actually have had sex with.

Steven almost laughed out loud. He was so far from having sex with a girl that he wasn't even sure whether tongues was real or a sick joke. The closest he'd ever got to having sex with a girl was listening to Lewis's fantasies about tits and stiffies.

If Steven Lamb had been the boy he was at the beginning of spring, he *would* have laughed out loud. But the Steven Lamb who had written to a serial killer in a secret quest for a dead body saw the opportunity – and took it.

He held out his hand firmly but casually. 'I don't know who it's from until I read it, do I?'

His calm tone and her burgeoning guilt made Lettie hand him the letter even as Nan ground her teeth behind her.

Steven only needed a brief glance.

A photo would Be nice.

That was all there was. Not even Avery's initials. Nothing

incriminating. Nothing he even understood yet, but he would. He was sure now that he would understand it. The D and the B were capitalized, but the initials DB meant nothing to him off the top of his head. No victim's name started with DB. No matter. He'd seen the letter; he understood the code. He'd work it out.

And – more importantly – his mother never would.

'Is it from that AA?'

With a coolness that made him question his own basic honesty, Steven shrugged.

'It's just a girl, Mum.'

'A girl wanting a photo of you!' Lettie tried hard to re-capture her suspicion and anger but Steven's openness had taken the wind out of her sails.

He only shrugged again, at the same time as he slid the letter back into the envelope and shoved both into the back pocket of his black school trousers.

'Not my fault if I'm gorgeous.'

It could have gone either way but, for once, it went his way. Lettie's face relaxed and she smiled at him, then slid her arms around his waist while he wriggled half-heartedly not to be kissed on the cheek.

She won that battle and they both laughed and Nan turned away to the sink but not before Steven had seen her face relax at his joke and – for a single blissful moment – Steven remembered why he'd been digging.

For this.

For moments like this – when a reminder that they could one day be a real family suddenly burst through the crust of pain and resentment and poverty and left him feeling happy and achingly sad all at once.

He stopped wrestling and let his mother hold him in a way

she hadn't for many years, allowing himself to relax his head on to her shoulder while she stroked his back as she might a tired toddler.

'You will be careful, won't you, Steven?'

'Of course, Mum.'

'I'm only worried you'll get hurt.'

'I know. I'll be careful.'

'Ask him about protection,' said Nan, who'd reverted to type faster than he'd ever have thought possible.

Lettie let him go and scowled up at her mother. The moment was gone, and Steven straightened up a little reluctantly.

'Don't give me that look, my girl. I wish I'd done it for you and then you wouldn't have got yourself . . .' She tailed off but jerked her head meaningfully at Steven.

He flushed – partly with anger at his nan – and his mother slipped her hand around his.

'You know about protection, don't you, Steven?'

'Mum!' He flamed with embarrassment but a very small part of him felt rather smug that his mother and nan could entertain the possibility that he, Steven Lamb, could be desirable enough for somebody – at some indeterminate point in the future – to consider having sex with him.

It was a bit flattering.

But mostly it was just embarrassing.

He stepped away from his mother, feeling the heat coming off his head in waves.

He saw the worry in his mother's eyes, though, and – because she'd held him – he eked out an answer of sorts.

'Don't worry, Mum.'

'Don't make me, OK?'

He nodded and withdrew, although he could see from her face that Nan thought he'd got off lightly.

He took the stairs two at a time. It was a stretch, but Lewis had tried it and failed, so Steven figured he might as well practise it if Lewis thought it was worthwhile. It left him breathless at the top.

DB. DB. None of the children was called DB. Was Avery revealing another murder to him?

Once in his room, he studied the letter carefully in the dull light of the window. There were no other marks on it that he could see. He got out the map of Exmoor he'd used for his correspondence with Avery, and pored over it. The letters were not positioned anywhere in particular on the piece of paper, so Steven didn't bother trying to line them up with anything.

A photo woulD Be nice.

Avery wanted a photo of DB. But who was DB?

Three nights later, Steven jerked awake with the answer.

He could feel it in his gut.

DB was not a 'who' but a 'what'.

It was the highest point of the moor, and close to where all the bodies had been found.

Arnold Avery wanted a photo of Dunkery Beacon.

19

It took Steven well over an hour to walk to Dunkery Beacon, even though his way was speeded by not having to carry the spade.

The spade.

Now that he'd stopped digging, just thinking the word 'spade' made him squirm with the guilt of potential failure.

Still, he was faster without it, allowing his arms to swing freely, working up a rhythm and a slight sweat as he trudged uphill – always uphill – on to the moor. He hadn't even bothered with sandwiches, just a bottle of water and the camera making bulges in his old anorak.

The camera was Davey's; a cheap disposable – one of a pack of three he'd got for his birthday. He'd wasted the first photographing feet, ceilings and blurred people. He'd dropped the second in the bath while photographing the epic sea battle between Action Man and a plague of off-worldly beings in the shape of coloured bubbles of bath oil. Too late, Davey realized the colourful capsules melted in the hot water, leaving just a white oily slick, a scrap of fruit-gum-like gel – and him open to the wrath of his luxury-rationed mother. In his panic he'd dropped the camera.

The third camera had gathered dust on the bedroom windowsill until Arnold Avery's letter arrived, then Steven stole it without compunction.

He needed it, Davey didn't.

Dunkery Beacon was not only the highest point on Exmoor, it was also the coldest, thought Steven, as the wind whipped his cheap anorak around him, flicking his thighs painfully with the metal zip. He zipped it up to avoid further injury.

Because it was pretty much the only thing to look at apart from the non-existent view, Steven briefly considered the plaque that commemorated the gift of the Beacon, an area of outstanding natural beauty, to the nation in 1935. The names of the benefactors were carved in stone and Steven couldn't help snorting: they should see the natural beauty today, he thought.

From Exmoor there was often a view of the Bristol Channel and sometimes of the Brecon Beacons, rising across the channel from the foreign land of Wales, but today the white sky with its relief of scudding grey clouds left the horizon fuzzy and bare. He turned and looked back down the rough track that had brought him here, to the small level patch of gravel that constituted a car park. There were two cars there. It wasn't unusual – people liked views but luckily people also liked walking, and nobody could enjoy both at the same time unless they got out of their cars.

Steven glanced around but couldn't see anyone. It was

astonishing how quickly people could disappear on Exmoor's seemingly featureless hills.

Dunkery Beacon was not entirely featureless. Here and there were the stone humps of ancient burial mounds. He tugged the blue plastic camera from his pocket as he turned a slow circle, wondering which angle would be best.

All too quickly, he knew, and felt sick for knowing.

Avery would want the angle that showed the best view of that part of Dunkery Beacon where he'd buried the bodies.

Steven hadn't been thinking of the bodies when he walked up here, but now he realized he was standing within 500 yards of three of the shallow grave sites.

Yasmin Gregory.

Louise Leverett.

John Elliot.

With a feeling of uneasy voyeurism, he scanned the ground around him to see if he could spot any evidence, even after all these years, of the excavations that had been made during the search. The burial mounds – markers denoting respect and honour – became mere backdrop as his memory imposed three sets of red biro initials on to the windblown gorse and his killer's eye made shallows in the turf, scars in the heather. But his ordinary boy's intellect reasserted itself. It had been a long time. Grass, gorse and heather would have crept back by now, recolonizing the exposed soil, softening the harsh, gaping wounds of little families and the whole nation. He knew there would be nothing to see unless one knew exactly where to look, and even then imagination would have to play a part.

And so he imagined, and peered through the dirty little viewfinder across a part of the moor that he thought had held one of the graves and clicked the shutter. It seemed to be over rather quickly and easily, considering his long walk up here, so he moved around a little and clicked the shutter again before trudging back down the Beacon.

As he crossed the car park, Steven peered idly into the cars. Sometimes people left dogs in their cars on hot days. Steven dreamed of finding a dog in a car on a hot day and being forced to smash the window to rescue it, then taking it home with him, secure in the knowledge he'd saved it from stupid, undeserving people.

But today wasn't hot, and most people who brought dogs to Exmoor had brought them there with the express purpose of walking them, not leaving them in the car. Steven sighed and realized he'd have to live near a supermarket to have a decent chance of making his fantasy a reality, and there was no super-market in Shipcott.

He turned and looked back at the Beacon, brown and ugly under the louring sky.

The angle of the light made the ancient burial mounds stand out much better from down here. What had seemed flat from the summit was relief from the car park. It would make a better picture from this angle, he reasoned.

So, with fingers turning numb from the cold, Steven prised the camera out of his pocket once more, pointed it back up the rising ground and clicked the shutter.

Then he turned and started the walk home.

He was at the fork in the track that would lead him down into Shipcott when he saw the hoodies coming towards him, their heads down as they made heavy weather of climbing the steep hillside from the village.

Steven stood stock-still. He looked round briefly as though a rock, a bush, a tree might suddenly emerge from the almost featureless moor and afford him somewhere to hide. He knew it was pointless. He knew he could drop out of sight right here in the deep heather beside the pathway. He and Lewis used to hide that way from Lewis's dopey dog, Bunny, when Bunny was still alive. They would wait until Bunny loped off after a rabbit, then throw themselves into the heather and whistle. They would snigger and peer and whisper as they heard the Labrador-cross blundering about the moor around them – and always get a shock when he finally found them with his big wet nose, his lolling tongue and his excited yaps.

But that was from a dog's-eye point of view.

Steven knew that if he lay in the heather now, when the hoodies came to within ten feet they would see his frightened form flattened in full view against the flowers, like a stupid ostrich with its head in the sand, and then he would be humiliated as well as chased and roughed up.

For a moment he just stood there, waiting for one of the panting boys to glance up at the path ahead and see him, while he decided on the best way to run.

The camera.

The thought popped into his head. If they caught him, they would take the camera. Or break it.

Quickly he pulled it out of his pocket, chose a place, and dropped it into the heather. He tried to imprint the location on his brain. Two pale mauve heathers with a sprig of yellow gorse between them, next to that stone shaped like a jelly bean.

He looked back at the hoodies at the very moment one of them looked up and saw him, and realized that dumping the camera had lost him the distance he so badly needed to turn and run.

They were on him in a second.

'Lamb,' said one – the tallest one.

He said nothing and they seemed momentarily at a loss for what to do with him.

'Got any money?'

'No.'

Rough, careless hands tugged at his clothes anyway, pulling his pockets inside out, his water bottle dropping to the stony track with a hollow plastic slosh. They found 34p in his jeans, and Arnold Avery's letter folded in his back pocket.

The smallest boy shoved him in the chest, making him take half a step backwards, even though it was uphill.

'You said you din't have no money.'

Steven shrugged. The tall boy unfolded the letter.

'*A photo would be nice.* What's that mean then?'

'Nothing.'

The tall boy glared at Steven and the letter, wondering whether he gave a shit or not. Finally he just tore it into bits and sprinkled it across the heather. The smallest boy pushed Steven again, this time in the shoulder. He could feel them itching for him to push back – wanting the challenge so they could justify their own actions. When he didn't react, the middle boy yanked his anorak off his shoulders. Now Steven did resist, bending his elbows to keep it on.

'Gimme, you divvy.'

Steven didn't trust his voice. He didn't want to tell them that if he went home without his anorak his mother would go nuts. It was old and not completely waterproof, but he knew it was nowhere near the end of its useful life as far as she was concerned. He wouldn't be able to tell her it had been stolen, in case she tried to complain to the hoodies' parents – and then his life might as well be over. But the thought of having to tell her that he'd left it on the moor or lost it at school made his eyes suddenly hot with tears as the middle boy jerked harder, pleased he was resisting.

Steven bit his lip to stop himself begging, as the insistent pulling on his arms made him lose his balance and stumble sideways. Immediately the middle boy saw an opening and shoved him that way, sending him to his knees in the sharp gorse. His right wrist twisted as it was caught in the cuff of the anorak, momentarily taking his full weight as he fell, then wrenched free of the nylon, releasing him to tumble to his side.

He felt the spiky prickles on his arm, the side of his face, and even through his jumper and jeans; he jerked his head up to save his face, and heard the hoodies laugh.

'Get his trainers.'

The anger that had started to rise in Steven when the boy grabbed his anorak now made him kick at them as they tried to take his shoes. New last Christmas. His mother had been angry they were muddy; she would kill him if they were gone.

The boys gripped his flailing legs and he curled his foot up in an effort to hold the left trainer on, but it was wrenched from him.

His tears now were furious helplessness. He wanted to kill them; he wanted to yank them by the ears and smash his knee into their grinning faces; he wanted to pick up the stone shaped like a jelly bean and beat their laughing mouths until their teeth were jagged, bloody stumps.

Instead he cried while they took his right shoe too, and walked off laughing.

He waited and cried, wincing at the pain of the gorse pricking into him, but too scared to follow too closely behind them.

Finally he got up, flinching his way back on to the path. One of his socks had been pulled halfway off his foot. They were his favourite socks; his nan had knitted them for him for his birthday two years before and he kept them for special so as not to wear them out. Grey marl and ribbed, with a cleverly turned foot she called a French heel that made them hold their own shape, like cartoon socks. They'd been big for him when he got them, and they were small for him now, but he still wore them for special. Today had been special because of the photo of Dunkery Beacon. Now he'd remember today for other reasons too. He began to cry again, making it hard to find the jelly-bean stone through the blurring, but he managed it eventually and then found the camera and started back down the path. It was slow going and painful and – by the time he reached the stile that led through the backs of the houses to the road – both his socks had holes in them.

'What do you mean, lost?' Lettie was not furious yet, but she was well on the way and Steven knew she'd get there before long.

'I'm sorry.'

'How can you lose your anorak *and* your shoes? And not know where?'

'And ruin his socks.' Nan chimed in. 'Took me weeks to knit those with my arthritis. Doesn't appreciate anything.'

'I *did* appreciate them!' he said, angry that she could think otherwise. Hadn't she seen how he'd kept them for special? The thought made him start to cry again and some part of his mind sighed wearily at that. He was so fed up with crying today; he could hardly believe he had more of it left in him.

'Stevie's crying, Mum!' Davey was intrigued.

'Fuck off, Davey,' he snapped.

'You *dare* use that word in this house!'

Lettie slapped the back of his head – not hard, but

stunning him anyway, and shocking them all into a horrible, ticking silence.

His mother *never* slapped his head or face. She'd lash out at his arms or legs occasionally, but the head was off limits on the unspoken understanding that only drunks and council tenants slapped their children there.

Steven wanted to apologize. He wanted it so badly. He wanted his mother to hold him again the way she had the other day. He wanted to lay his head on her shoulder and be a baby again and not have to worry about his socks or his shoes or his anorak or the hoodies or the spade or bodies or serial killers. He wanted to curl up in bed with hot milk and sugar and have someone sing him to sleep while they stroked his hair.

He was so tired of his life.

But she'd slapped his head.

So, instead of apologizing, he yelled: 'Fuck you too!' then pushed past his mother, ran upstairs and slammed his bedroom door so hard that she came pounding up the stairs in a fury.

He knew he'd gone too far.

If she hadn't been so angry Lettie would have seen how scared he was – standing by his bed, eyes wide, hands splayed before him in surrender, no longer sure she had any control.

'Mum, I'm sorry!'

But it was too late and she slapped his head again – and then again, and hit his arms and hands and ears and, finally, rained slaps and weak, side-fisted girl-punches down on his back as he cowered over his bed with his head between his elbows.

It was Davey's hysterical screaming that brought Lettie back to her senses at last. She gathered her favourite son into her arms and shushed him gently.

'You see how you've upset Davey!' she shouted at Steven, in a voice shrill with guilt. 'Now come down for tea.'

'I don't want any tea.' His voice was muffled in the bed-spread.

'Fine,' said Lettie, hefting Davey higher on to her hip. 'Don't have any then.'

Steven heard them leave and go downstairs. He heard Lettie's voice, low and gentle with Davey, and some part of him understood that she was trying to make up for what she'd done – even if she wasn't making it up to him.

He sniffled and hitched and started to feel the places where his mother's ring must have caught him – his left ear, his left wrist, a stinging on his shoulder blade. He put his finger to the ear and found a little spot of blood. His ears also rang a little and his right cheek burned from a slap. He crept on to the bed, turned to the wall, and curled a bit more tightly into a ball. He hugged himself, suddenly cold but not want-ing to move again to get under the covers.

The touch of something soft on his shoulder startled him. Nan had picked up the bedspread behind him and folded it over him. He met her eyes briefly, but she straightened up and turned to leave.

'Nan?'

He expected her to stop and look back at him, the way it happened in the movies, but she kept going, disappearing down the hallway.

His voice was cracked with crying, but he spoke anyway, as if she was listening to him; as if she cared.

'I did appreciate the socks. I kept them for special.'

Steven thought he heard her pause at the top of the stairs, but he couldn't be sure.

20

The photos were crap.

The ones he'd taken from the top of Dunkery Beacon were blurred by wind-shake and the one he'd taken from the car park had the front wing of a car encroaching into the left-hand side of the frame.

But because he'd spent the last of his pocket money on getting the film developed – and because it was at least in focus – that was the one Steven sent to Arnold Avery.

21

Prison Officer Ryan Finlay enjoyed confiscating photos sent to prisoners and today was no exception.

Usually the photos were blurred, scuzzy shots of prisoners' wives and girlfriends lying on unmade beds wearing mismatched lingerie. Sometimes the pictures included some small careless domestic detail that shattered whatever shaky fantasy was being offered. A tabby cat; a grubby child peering through the bars of a cot; Kentucky Fried Chicken boxes on the bedroom floor.

Sometimes the prisoners got their photos and sometimes they didn't. In this respect, Ryan Finlay was god.

Total nudity meant immediate confiscation, as did any lewd act or simulation of the same. Those photos were supposed to be destroyed and, if the prisoner's wife was a dog, they were – although not before much passing round and disparaging remarks in the staff canteen. The prisoner concerned would merely get a tag on his letter, if one had been enclosed, which said 'Contents Confiscated'.

Sean Ellis had never had a letter without a tag. His wife was so hot and so uninhibited that the photos she often enclosed formed the backbone of Officer Ryan Finlay's personal collection, and the bank robber who'd shot two tellers in the face at a small branch of Barclays in Gloucestershire had probably entirely forgotten what his wife looked like under the demure beige mac she always wore to visit him. Ellis never complained, and that made Finlay and the others laugh. The poor bastard probably thought his missus was sending him pictures of the family mutt.

Today Finlay and PO Andy Ralph sat at the Formica desk in the post room, carelessly ripping open envelopes addressed to prisoners.

'What do you think?' Ralph held up a photo from a freshly torn envelope. It showed a small blonde girl with no front teeth, dangling a docile cat down her chest.

'Who's it for?'

Ralph glanced at the envelope. 'Karim Abdullahai.'

Finlay shook his head. 'That pervert's as black as the ace of spades. Doesn't look like a relative to me.'

Ralph – whose own skin tone was a shade away from coal – tossed the photo aside and put a tag on the letter without comment.

Mrs Ellis's photo was relatively tame today – her face blank as she lifted up a pale blue tank top to expose her perfect breasts.

'Jesus, would you look at the tits on that.'

Ralph peered over and grinned.

'Double fucking handful.' Finlay sighed. It had been years since he'd had a nice firm double handful. He'd have needed a cardboard box to cart his Rose's stretched, wrinkled tits about in.

The photo was hardly lewd and, if it had been any other wife or girlfriend, Finlay would have passed it on without hesitation, but he couldn't have Ellis realizing that all those photos he'd never seen might look very much like this one and starting to make a fuss, so he slapped a tag on the accompanying letter and stuffed Mrs Ellis in his pocket.

They worked in silence for a few minutes, struggling to read barely legible letters, sorting photos and tiny gifts – six safety-razor blades, a dozen Trojans, *Origami for Beginners*.

Ralph looked briefly at a photo of a tired-looking redhead holding a pizza box, and read from the accompanying letter: '. . . *at night I think about you fukking me up the arss* . . .'

He sighed. 'Misspelled fucking *and* arse.'

He took the censoring black felt tip and corrected both spellings before putting it on the 'go' pile and picking up the next letter, which was addressed to Arnold Avery.

There was no letter and the badly composed photograph barely warranted a glance. It certainly did not warrant seeking the permission of the senior screw. Andy Ralph was well able to discern what was lewd, what was inciting, and what was fetishistic. He didn't need anyone to tell him that a photo of a car and a rainy hillside was none of the above. Least of all Ryan Finlay.

The racist Paddy bastard.

When Arnold Avery saw the photo he felt faint. He thought he might collapse with the sheer erotic charge of it. He immediately wanted to cry that it was not night, not dark, even though his cell was always gloomy because of the board across the window. Well, Leaver might have blocked the view of one moor through the bars, but he held the view of another in his hand that was even sweeter.

His killer's eye had found the spot immediately. Yasmin Gregory. There she was. Or there she had been until some time after his arrest when the forensics teams had moved in and Exmoor had started to give up its grim secrets. They hadn't allowed him back on the moor, even to point out the bodies. They knew too well it was what he wanted – one more chance to feel the holding soil between his fingers; one more peer into the filthy holes he'd dug out of the heather – and they cruelly denied him that even when they finally had to call off the search for more victims. But they couldn't erase his memories. Couldn't then, and couldn't now, as they washed over him like a spicy balm.

He had parked in this place. Close to where the car was in the picture SL had taken. He had carried YG up that narrow track towards the summit of the rounded hill. He could feel her now, light in his arms, and remember how she'd felt under him when she was still warm and hurting.

He shook himself like a dog. Not now! Not now! This was too good, too intense a feeling to waste in daylight. He had to stop looking at the photo. He had to do something to distract himself until lights out.

He slid the photo under his pillow and opened the book he was reading. It was a good book – *The Black Echo* – and until SL's photo had arrived, it had been gripping him. But no longer. Now the book held no interest, and a dozen times in the next hour Avery had to put it down and steal a hand under his pillow to touch the photo.

Lunch was a small relief, although his leg bobbed nervously throughout.

The afternoon dragged horribly; supper brought more brief

respite. Lights out was at 10.30pm but at 8.30pm Avery took the photo from under the pillow and studied it anew, storing up the image for when he was alone in the dark.

Avery guessed SL had used a cheap camera. Everything seemed to be in focus; anyone even half competent with a better camera would have adjusted the focal length to blur the foreground and highlight Dunkery Beacon. Despite this his eyes were drawn inexorably to the patch of ground where YG had been – between two burial mounds that lumped the heather either side of it, about three-quarters of the way to the summit.

Emotion and memory washed over Avery.

The day had been clear, not grey like in this photo. The sky had been pure blue, and there were many walkers around, so Avery had had to wait until after sunset before his car was alone on the gravel patch; before he could take her from the boot and carry her up to her final resting place.

A bitter knife twisted in his guts as he thought of her taken from the place he had made for her and buried somewhere else – somewhere not of his choosing. Even worse, somewhere he didn't know. He was sure the location of her new grave had been in the papers, but those papers had been kept from him. All he had left of Yasmin Gregory was the memories. And this photograph.

And he might have been able to see the grave of John Elliot too, if only SL hadn't blocked his view with that stupid car. John Elliot was not his favourite. The boy had pissed on him. Avery shuddered at the memory. John Elliot's squeezed-shut eyes, his runny nose blowing desperate bubbles of snot because he couldn't breathe through his mouth any more. That had been bad enough but then, right before he killed him, John Elliot's bladder surrendered in sheer terror, leaving urine on Avery's good trousers. He'd made the boy pay, but he'd had to throw the trousers away; and the shoes. Hush Puppies, they'd been – not cheap – but the thought of the boy's fluids on them made him sick. Even now that thought made his flesh crawl.

Avery shook the memory from him; it was spoiling this moment. He turned his attention back to the photograph. Yes, the car was in the way. It was a pain. Another reason he knew SL was no photographer – poor framing.

For the first time since receiving the photo, Avery turned his piercing gaze to the car, as if he might be able to see right through it to the moorland behind.

All he could see of the car was the front wing, the wing mirror and part of the door. It was dark blue and Avery couldn't tell what kind of car it was, only that it was infuriatingly solid and in his way.

It was in his nature to feel cheated, and cheated was exactly what he felt. He glared at the car angrily, projecting fury that could not be completely assuaged by his eyes straying inexorably to the gravesite of Yasmin Gregory.

And then Avery's eyes widened and he brought the photo up so that it almost touched his nose.

A single sharp gasp escaped him and then his breathing stopped altogether.

If he hadn't been obsessing over the car he might – would – never have seen it! A river of ice ran down his back at the thought of what he'd have missed.

Neatly caught in the wing mirror was the small but in-focus reflection of the photographer.

And although the image was tiny, everything changed for Arnold Avery at that moment. The feelings that seeing Exmoor again had sparked in him shrank so small that they were swept away in an instant by a tsunami of stunned, choking, old-familiar excitement that sent blood rushing to his groin and saliva flooding his mouth.

SL was a boy.

The thought spun and careened crazily around his head like a firework in a small room.

A boy.

Just a boy.

His eyes stung and his racing heart pounded in his ears as he stared breathlessly at the image.

A boy. Maybe ten or eleven. Skinny. Dark hair tousled by the wind. Blue jeans, grubby white trainers. The image was tiny and the face obscured by the camera . . . but if there was one shape that Arnold Avery's brain was hard-wired to recognize, it was that of a child.

Avery sucked in a new breath with a shuddering whimper of sharp desire.

SL was a boy.

A boy who'd shown him possibilities.

A boy who'd handed him power.

A boy who – by cleverly inserting his own image into the seemingly innocent photo of Dunkery Beacon – had issued to Arnold Avery the very clearest of invitations . . .

22

Uncle Jude came back.

One day they were just four and the next they were five.

Steven was in his room struggling with 3x–5y and all its mystifying variations, when he heard a creak in the passageway and Uncle Jude's voice ask: 'How's the vegetable patch?'

Steven looked round in surprise which he quickly tried to conceal. It wasn't cool to look too happy to see someone.

'Tomatoes are rubbish,' he shrugged, 'but the potatoes are great.'

Uncle Jude grinned. 'Well, any fool can grow potatoes. Look at the Irish.'

'You're Irish!'

'That's how I know.'

He wandered into the bedroom, poking about at Davey's things, the grin never leaving his face, and Steven realized that Uncle Jude wasn't trying to hide how happy he was to see him, and that made him ashamed that he had. He swung his legs off the bed and threw his arms around Uncle Jude's waist, feeling the big man's hands on his back, patting him hello again after too long.

The sudden urge to tell Uncle Jude everything rose in him like a madness.

Let Uncle Jude take over the making of decisions; let Uncle Jude visit Arnold Avery in prison and beat a location out of him; let Uncle Jude dig up Billy and get all the glory – Steven didn't care any more, he just wanted it to be over.

He opened his mouth—

'I see your nan's trolley's still going strong.'

Steven nodded, suddenly unsure of his own voice.

'See her out and about with it. Pleased as punch.'

Steven hesitated then nodded. He didn't want to spoil this good subject. He knew Uncle Jude was not just being nice; Nan loved her trolley and took it out with her even when she wasn't going shopping. Her hips played her up and the now sturdy trolley was also a means of support for her odd, rolling gait.

'Look how tall you got.'

'Yeah. All my trousers are too short.'

'I hear ankle-whackers are the next big thing.'

Steven snorted and they parted.

'Where have you been?' He tried to keep the accusation out of his voice, but it still came out whiney.

'About.'

'Why didn't you come to see us?' Once again, Steven could have kicked himself. Uncle Jude was not his father. Why should he come to see them if he was no longer going out with his mother?

But Uncle Jude just spread his hands and sighed. 'You know how it is, Steven. Relationships.'

Steven felt a little swell of pride that Uncle Jude would say that to him – as if he knew how relationships worked. Coming hot on the heels of his mother assuming he knew how sex worked, it made him feel like both a grown-up and a fake.

'I suppose so,' he said.

The question he was desperate to ask stuck in his throat, and he was grateful for that.

Asking Uncle Jude how long he'd be staying would only be tempting fate.

Nan was tight-lipped at supper, shooting disapproving glances at Uncle Jude's nails, but Lettie was girlish and had released her captive ponytail, and Davey prattled on and on and on, bombarding Uncle Jude with his questions, opinions and statements of semi-fact that made them all smile.

'I'm going to grow a sausage tree, Uncle Jude!'

'Why haven't I got a beard?'

'Uncle Jude? Did you know hedges are made by hedgehogs?'

Steven sighed to himself. No wonder his mother preferred Davey; he was so entertaining.

By staying silent, Steven gathered the information that his mother had bumped into Uncle Jude in Mr Jacoby's shop and that he'd been invited for tea – although there was some teasing dispute about exactly how he'd been invited, or whether he'd asked himself to tea.

It didn't matter. Uncle Jude was back at the kitchen table and as he softened Nan up, chaffed Lettie and indulged Davey, Steven felt an unaccustomed sense of optimism settle on his shoulders.

He asked to be excused as soon as he'd hurried his baked

beans, and ran hell for leather in his cheap new trainers to where he'd left his spade six weeks before.

It was there. It was the same.

He jogged back with it held loosely in one pale hand, and went round the back of the house. Just like Uncle Jude, his spade had come home.

Steven surveyed the back garden and in his ordinary boy's mind he saw where the tomatoes should go, and the lettuce. The lettuce could be planted in pots and placed up high to deter slugs. The potatoes would take most of the room but there was space for a few strawberries to make his mother feel all upper-class come Wimbledon. Mr Randall had grown melons last year. He'd given them one and even though it was bland and cork-dry, Steven had been stunned that something so exotic could come out of the staid English soil. Maybe he could grow melons – the ones with orange flesh.

He hefted the spade better into his hand and thought of it biting into the earth to give life, rather than to seek death.

Out of nowhere, he was glad his mother had bought new knickers in Banbury's. He hoped with all his heart that this time they would be enough.

Steven leaned the rusty spade against the back wall and smiled to himself.

This was what normality felt like, and it was good.

23

Arnold Avery had never considered escaping. Not in any realistic sense.

Sure, the first few months he was in prison he had lain awake and thought about things he would do once he was free again. But the concept of escape was not uppermost in his mind. He assumed that he would be paroled at some point and that that point would be no closer than the twenty-year tariff the judge at his trial had recommended.

It seemed fair. Apart from being a child killer, Avery was a law-abiding man who voted Conservative with a capital C, and who thought most prison sentences were woefully inadequate and that the early release of some prisoners was a disgrace.

And so when he found himself facing a minimum of twenty years inside, Avery did not whine and complain and appeal against his sentence, citing previous good character and taxes paid. Instead he took the conscious decision to do his utmost to ensure that he was a prime candidate for release on licence as soon as he became eligible.

When the three men raped him in the showers, Avery allowed the screws their pleasure at his humiliation and never complained or retaliated.

When improving, rehabilitating lessons were offered, Avery signed up and exerted at least the modicum of effort it took to be top of every class.

When Dr Leaver ordered his view to be blocked, leaving him in permanent half-darkness, Avery thanked him.

And when the question of the other missing children came up, Avery swore blind he had not killed Paul Barrett, William Peters or Mariel Oxenburg. They might be dead, but those three children had the power to extend his stay at Her Majesty's pleasure, and he would never allow them to do that to him, however much it might ease the pain of still-grieving relatives.

Avery knew it was far from a foregone conclusion that he would be paroled after twenty years, but he knew he'd given himself the best possible chance, and was therefore content to wait another couple of years to find out. Within twelve months he could be in a programme at an open prison in Northumbria that claimed to prepare inmates for release. Everything was going just the way he'd planned it.

Until he found out SL was just a boy.

A boy he'd built trust with.

A boy he shared secrets with.

A boy who wanted something from him so badly that he might be inveigled upon to do . . . just about anything.

And if he wouldn't, then that wasn't a problem either.

But it had to be *now*. Not two years from now, when his

parole might possibly be granted. By then the focus of a boy on a quest would have given way to the clumsy distractions of a teenager on another kind of mission entirely. And certainly not if he was released to some crappy halfway house up north, far away from his beloved Exmoor.

Arnold Avery had spent eighteen years watching and waiting, knuckling down, doing his time . . . Eighteen years without fresh memories of just how exciting children could be and, hard though he'd tried to preserve his memories, the old ones had inevitably staled with overuse.

The photo of SL had been a supernova illuminating the dusty recesses of his mind. It had pierced his logic and good intentions like a laser through a magnifying glass. Now his brain was constantly burned and tortured by want – by desperate want and possibilities. Just as Steven had put his eye to the crack in the door and seen a future of summers and skating, so Avery saw that his future – his *immediate* future – could be similarly filled with astonishing pleasures. Something chemical had been released in Avery's brain – something that sharpened his lust and dulled his more sensible senses. The same chemical change had once seen him abuse one boy even while waiting for the police to arrive at the behest of another. All he could think about was SL. He knew where he lived. He had a rough idea of what he looked like. He could guide him, tease him, direct him.

Misdirect him.

At will.

The prospect of control was delicious. The prize was precious. The boy was his for the taking.

Suddenly all the time in the world seemed like too much slack to Avery.

Anything could happen!

SL could move; he could die; he could just lose interest. Avery had to write to him. Had to give him hope that the corpse he sought was a heartbeat away. He had to keep him on the hook.

He resented the subtle shift that had made him needy and dented his new-found power. But he knew a sure-fire way of regaining it. If he had to relinquish a little more power now to achieve complete control and sublime enjoyment later, then that was a bargain he was prepared to strike.

So it was with a brief acknowledgement – and immediate dismissal – of regret, that Arnold Avery concluded that he had to escape from prison.

And he had to do it very soon.

This sudden sense of urgency could have made another man careless, reckless, stupid.

It made Avery Superman.

He had woken from hibernation, rejuvenated and cocky and with all his senses heightened.

He knew he was clever, and he hadn't used his cleverness for a very long time. SL's letters had prodded his slumbering IQ but now that he was properly awake he could feel his neurons firing like buzzy outboard motors, and intelligence coursing through him like brandy on a cold night.

Every day now was an opportunity he didn't want to miss. He understood the need for caution and planning but he also recognized that unexpected openings had to be exploited. It was a two-pronged attack of intellect and he felt alive with the challenge.

Once he started to care, Avery noticed things in a never-ending stream of information that flowed through his mind.

Every bit of it was assessed, catalogued and stored away for future reference.

He had always known that Officer Ryan Finlay was a fucking idiot but now his calm, pale eyes saw that Finlay was a fucking idiot with a big bunch of keys of which he took very little care.

The keys were attached to Finlay's belt and were also supposed to be tucked safely out of sight in the little black leather pouch on said belt. Prison authorities knew that even the glimpse of a key could make an indelible impression on the criminal mind in a way that honesty and morals never had. Within hours a prisoner could fashion a key from the covers torn from paperbacks, or the ends of cereal packets; it wouldn't be durable, but it would only have to work once.

For this reason, officers were supposed to keep their keys concealed at all times. In reality, unlocking a door, putting the keys in the pouch, walking ten feet and having to take them out again to unlock a second door was not conducive to following the rules.

Officer Finlay didn't follow the rules. Arnold supposed that in his small, fat way, Finlay considered himself above petty rules, just like he did. Except, of course, when Finlay broke the rules it meant playing fast and loose with a bunch of keys. When *he* broke the rules, it meant choking the life out of a helpless child.

Everything was relative.

Arnold noticed now that Officer Finlay did not even like his keys banging against his not-inconsiderable hip. Instead he liked to unclip them from his belt entirely and twirl them on his fingers as he jingled up and down the echoing hallways. As Officer Finlay was the antithesis of athleticism and hand–eye co-ordination, sometimes he dropped them and, when he did, he took a shuffling age to pick them up – sighing and creaking down to the floor and back up again. Once upright, he'd blink dizzily for a few seconds as if the effort of bending double had knocked all the orientation out of him.

Avery watched him. Watched him come on to the block; watched him go out; watched the keys that he chose from the bulky ring to do those things with. The key on to the block was long and old-fashioned. Simplistic, almost. The keys he used to unlock the cells were Yales. That was harder. Apart from the Yales and the block key, Avery counted seven other keys on Finlay's ring. He didn't know what they opened but he had the feeling that seven keys would be more than enough to get an enterprising man out to the wall, or very close to it.

Avery was not fool enough to think he could just pick up the keys and let himself out of the prison, but it was something he mulled over; it was information catalogued.

The walls of Longmoor prison – at a mere twelve feet – were the lowest in the country. However, any man who managed to get through the fence, scale the wall and avoid breaking both ankles on the other side was faced with a far tougher obstacle: Dartmoor itself.

For over a century, the prison authorities had relied on the spacious confines of the moor to keep prisoners inside. On the few occasions escapes had been made, prison officers only bothered patrolling the roads, confident that they offered the sole realistic route to freedom. Prisoners who struck out across Dartmoor were doomed to suffer the vagaries of the moor's own brand of captivity – a malicious and unpredictable micro-climate. Even in mid-year, if the heatstroke didn't exhaust absconders on the treeless landscape, the weather could perform a spectacular U-turn and send a blanket of damp, cold mist down on them within minutes, chilling their bones as they stumbled blindly off house-sized granite boulders, through slippery rills and into sudden, gripping bogs that tempted the unwary with mirages of wiry grass growing almost hydroponically across their surfaces.

The moor was almost always the winner in the game of escape.

Now, with prisoner numbers rocketing and a nosey public's demand for efficiency, a sturdy chain-link fence had been erected fifteen feet inside the perimeter stone wall. This was still only twelve feet high, but had the added deterrent of rolls of razor wire on top. There were four locked gates in the chain-link fence, as if there was a need to pop through and retrieve an errant football or something.

The wall alone would have been enticing. The wall and the chain-link and the razor wire were a daunting prospect.

Even so, Avery softened a bar of soap in warm water and kept it in his pocket at all times, suffering the scummy residue it left in his jeans by repeatedly telling himself that soap *could not* be dirty; it was the antithesis of dirty – the embodiment of clean – and that therefore he could and should and *must* bear the constant greasy weight of it on his person. What he would do if he ever managed to press a key into the soap, he wasn't quite sure. He would cross that bridge if he came to it and felt something useful lay on the other side.

Avery also considered the walls of his cell. They were made of stone but the mortar between the blocks was naturally vulnerable. The enemy of escape through the walls was time, of which he had too little, and light, of which he had too much. Although his cell was gloomier than most because of the board at the window, the electric lights went on at 6.30am and stayed on until 10.30pm. Avery started scraping at the mortar around a stone under his bunk at about 11pm, using the handle of his toothbrush.

Three hours later he had made a vague indentation in the mortar and a very sharp toothbrush. He gave up on the wall, but kept the toothbrush under his pillow. This was prison and nothing was to be wasted.

Two nights later he used his sharp toothbrush to prise the board away from his window. The mortar around the bars was softer than that in the walls and, by the time the sky started to lighten, he had exposed two inches at the base of one of the bars. It was tampering that would have been spotted almost immediately in any cell in the prison. Any cell, that is, that had not had its window boarded up on the express orders of Dr Leaver. In two years nobody had ever removed the board and Avery saw no reason why they would start now.

Avery did not place any great faith in his own plans. He understood that disappointment was proportionate to the gulf between expectation and realization. He didn't like to hope – didn't even like the word, which implied some sort of help- less kowtowing to the whims of fate. He preferred to call what he had 'options' and, as his desire for escape grew into a burn- ing need, he took pains to leave no option unexplored.

Always one to stay in his cell when he was not required to shower or eat, Avery now started to lean on the railing opposite his door, like the scum did, to observe prison life. Of course, the scum smoked while they did this and Avery didn't. Filthy habit. He saw their yellow-stained fingers and shuddered. God knows what their toilet habits were like.

Avery wished he hadn't thought of that. It made the bile rise in his throat. The thought of being dirty made him shiver, but actual bodily functions and fluids had the power to make him clammy and nauseous, and the feeling of nausea – with its implicit threat of vomiting – could force him into a self-fulfilling prophecy.

He breathed deeply and focused on the man nearest to him, who happened to be Sean Ellis – he of the hot wife and the stolen photos.

Avery glanced at Ellis's fingers and found them a healthy pink, so – more to allay his own nausea than anything else – he nodded briefly at the man and raised his eyebrows in a neutral greeting.

'All right,' Ellis returned, indicating to Avery that he was new enough to Longmoor not to know what he had done, or bad enough not to care. Avery hoped it was the latter; he was mightily sick of having stupid, common criminals look at him as if he was shit on their shoes. He didn't want or need their friendship but – even after eighteen years – he was still genuinely uncertain as to why some killers got respect in prison while he was vilified. It fed his feeling of having been cheated out of what should have been his due – awe in deference to his crimes at the very least.

Ellis was certainly new to the Vulnerable Prisoners Unit. Avery wondered idly what he had done which required that he be protected but he also knew that information would seep out eventually – however hard a nonce or a snitch tried to keep it to themselves.

'Fag?' offered Avery.

'Nah, don't smoke. Thanks.'

Avery appraised Ellis quickly. He was a tall, powerfully built man with the squashed nose of a gangster but careful brown eyes with incongruously lush lashes. Avery did not know or care that they were the last eyes two bank tellers had ever looked into. He only knew that his first attempt for several years to speak to a fellow con as an equal had started rather well.

'Dirty habit.' He shrugged. 'Only keep them to be sociable.' It was the truth. Three days after seeing SL's photograph, Avery had bought half a pack of Bensons from Andy Ralph, just in case he needed a way into the kind of conversation he was now embarking on with Sean Ellis.

Ellis nodded then turned his idle attention back to the game of ping-pong clattering on three floors below them, watched through a criss-cross of safety netting designed to thwart the long drop of murder or suicide.

Under normal circumstances, Avery would have been happy to end the interaction right there. He didn't crave company or conversation. But now he had a purpose, he knew he needed to make more effort.

And suddenly it *was* an effort. For what seemed like forever, Avery scoured his brain for an opening gambit that would not seem forced. Or suspicious. Or queer. Finally Arnold Avery – serial killer, outsider, freak of nature, observer of no rules but his own – turned his face to the dirty skylights that let grudging daylight into the wing and observed like a commuter: 'Fucking awful weather.'

Ellis cocked an eyebrow at him and then glanced upwards, bemused by the observation. 'To be out in,' quipped Avery, breaking into a smile.

Ellis got it, thank god, and snorted a small laugh. 'Lucky we're in here then,' he said, and Avery grinned some more to let Ellis take ownership of the joke. The great ox.

Ellis was new on the block. He might know what to do with the impression of a key made in soap. He might *not*. But he might.

'Arnold,' he offered, extending his right hand like a lawyer at a conference.

'Sean,' said Ellis, his big, rough hand squeezing Avery's smaller one. Avery didn't like that – being made to feel small and weak – but he smiled through it.

'Food here is shite,' said Ellis, giving Avery free information. That information was that Ellis hadn't been here long (which explained why Ellis was speaking to him in the first place) and that Ellis hadn't been *anywhere* for too long, because prison food was shite wherever you were and that was just a fact. Arnold Avery had stopped mentally whining about prison food so long ago that it was a surprise to him that anyone didn't have this knowledge knitted into the very fibre of their being like the autopilot of breathing, or of their own sexual preference.

'Shit on tin,' he agreed sociably, happy that Ellis was now leading the conversation. 'You got money for the shop?'

The shop sold biscuits and chocolate and fruit at inflated prices that meant a day's work might yield an overripe banana if you were very lucky.

'Yeah,' said Ellis, 'my wife sends me cash.' He reached into his back pocket for a fold of clear plastic laminate which held a photo. He held it out proudly, openly inviting and plainly expecting compliments on his choice of mate.

Avery took the photo from him and studied Mrs Ellis looking up from an ugly but expensive-looking flock couch. Doe-eyed, pale skin. Early thirties. She would have been stunning twenty-five years ago.

He heard Finlay approaching. Those flat feet, those careless keys.

'What have we got here?' said Finlay with mock-camaraderie.

'Photo of Sean's wife, Mr Finlay.'

'Let's have a look then.' Finlay took the photo from Avery's hand without waiting for permission and squinted at the woman who now starred in his most lurid fantasies.

'Very nice, Ellis,' he said carefully.

'Breathtaking,' added Avery, trying but failing to keep a touch of irony from his voice.

'Yeah, she is,' said Ellis.

Finlay handed the photo back to Ellis and Avery watched the big man's dark brown eyes soften with a chimp-like quality as he stroked a callused thumb across his wife's face before putting it in his pocket.

'Later, mate,' said Ellis as he turned away and wandered off down the walkway with a slump to his broad shoulders.

'Later,' said Avery, although he despised the ungram-matical.

He didn't know love but he had a hound's nose for vulner-ability, and he added that to the small but growing collection of information that he'd started hoarding like trinkets.

Finlay winked at Avery. 'Wonder who's nailing her now . . .'

Avery shrugged and Finlay changed tack – regarding him through what he fondly imagined were cunning eyes.

'Not like you to socialize, Arnold.'

'Just fancied a change, Mr Finlay.'

'Your shrink'll be pleased.' Finlay laughed at his own joke, and Avery raised his eyebrows in apparent appreciation. 'You ever give your mate that old computer?' The oaf twirled his keys, unaware of how tenuous his grip on personal safety really was.

'Not yet, Mr Finlay.' Avery gave a very small smile. 'But when someone keeps asking for something, you know that eventually you're going to have to give it to them.'

'That's very true, Avery.'

The keys clanked to the floor and he drew in a deep breath as if preparing to dive to a reef to retrieve them.

Avery moved swiftly to scoop them up. He saw a flicker of panic in Finlay's eyes in the moment before he casually handed them back and turned to gaze down through the safety netting, as if the action had barely registered on him. Beside him he heard Finlay clip his keys to his belt. It didn't worry him; Finlay was a lazy bastard and the caution wouldn't last.

'Thank you, Avery.'

'My pleasure, Mr Finlay.'

24

Miraculously, it took Steven and Uncle Jude only hours to clear years of vegetation and rubbish from the back garden.

Both were stripped to the waist and sweating – Steven wiry and pale, Uncle Jude broad and nut-brown.

Steven blew his cheeks out in satisfaction, sweat dribbling into his eyes; he wiped it away, happily aware that he'd left dirt in its place.

Lewis was unimpressed. 'What about snipers?' he whined. 'There's nowhere to hide now!'

True to form, Lewis had come round at ten to help clear the back garden, and had proceeded to direct operations through mouthfuls of Lettie's cold leftover spaghetti Bolognese which he spooned straight from the Pyrex dish.

Uncle Jude winked at Steven and Steven grinned. Lewis clattered the spoon back into the empty dish.

'I don't know why you don't just *buy* some fucking carrots.'

Steven said nothing. Buying carrots did seem like the more sensible option. He felt stupid but also angry with Lewis, so he just kept on digging.

Lewis slid off the low wall. 'See you later,' he said coldly.

'Aren't you going to help dig?' said Steven appeasingly.

'Nah,' said Lewis, 'you're doing it all wrong anyway.'

He disappeared through the back door and Steven frowned after him.

'Don't mind him,' said Uncle Jude.

So Steven didn't.

He and Uncle Jude drank from the hose and laughed about stupid things, and when his nan refused to let them in for tea so grubby, they stripped down and marched into the kitchen in bare feet and underpants, making Davey and Lettie laugh. Nan turned away but Steven knew she wasn't angry – or even mildly annoyed – by the way she didn't purse her lips or bang the spoon as she dished out the stringy grey stew.

By nightfall he was aching and exhausted but there was a patch of newly turned, newly weeded black earth in the garden, seeded and marked in neat rows with string, and protected from cats and birds by a canopy of chicken wire.

As he drifted off to sleep, Steven thought that his spade had never felt so right in his hands as it had today, and that Arnold Avery and Uncle Billy and the Sheepsjaw Incident seemed like a bad dream he had once had as a very small and distant boy.

25

When Sean Ellis's hot wife burst into tears he was shocked, then embarrassed by the outburst. He was not a man who liked to show emotion in public. Even when the judge had sentenced him to a minimum of sixteen years, he'd maintained his composure, and had turned to wink reassuringly at his wife as he was taken down to the cells.

Now, as she bawled, his first look was around at his fellow cons to gauge their reactions. When he saw only mild interest, he turned his attention back to his wife, whose name was Hilary.

'Hilly,' he said softly, 'what's up, baby?'

Hilary Ellis bawled harder into her clenched fists, her face becoming hot with emotion, her cheeks streaking with mascara.

'You don't want me any more.'

'What?'

'You don't want me any more!'

Sean Ellis was confused. He adored his wife. He missed his wife so badly sometimes it hurt. He wanted her – had always wanted her – and had never wanted anybody else since he met her. The torture of being in prison was not his confinement, but the fear that she would gradually drift away from him; that she would start to leave longer and longer gaps between visits; and that one day he would receive not a visit from his hot wife but divorce papers from a cold lawyer. The near-expectation of those divorce papers had kept Sean Ellis awake at nights for two long years in a way that the faces of a couple of surprised bank tellers had never managed to do. The terror of losing her had even led him to turn in his drug-dealing cellmate – a betrayal that had earned him two years off his sentence, and a swift trip to the VPU, where he might have a chance of completing his time in safety.

And here she was, crying that *he* did not want *her*!

Sean Ellis was as confused as it's possible for a man to be – which is very.

'Sweetheart, how can you say that?' He grasped her hands and looked with love and amazement at her red, blotchy, black-streaked face. 'I love you! I want you! Of course I do! Are you nuts? Who wouldn't want you?'

'But the pictures!' she wailed. 'You don't like the pictures! You never say anything about them! You think I'm a whore!'

Conveniently within earshot, Officer Ryan Finlay twirled his keys nervously. Fuck.

Ellis pushed tear-dampened hair from his wife's face and cupped her cheek. 'What pictures, baby?'

He listened to her hitching, halting, hiccuping description

of the photos she'd been sending him every week since his incarceration, and felt himself move grindingly from confusion to cold, cold fury.

26

When Arnold Avery's latest letter whispered silently on to the doormat, Steven was not there to pick it up.

Lettie said she'd make tea and slid quietly out of the warm bed.

She looked in on the boys as she passed the half-open bedroom door. In the flat grey of dawn, Davey was a crooked splay of arms and legs, while Steven was pressed against the wall, flat and out of the way in the too-small Spiderman pyjamas she'd bought him for last Christmas. They were halfway up his shins, and the top and bottoms no longer met, exposing a pale slice of skin and the vague knobs of the base of his spine. The sheet and duvet were in a haphazard bundle at Davey's feet.

Only the kitchen clock kept company with the sound of the two boys' quiet breathing and Lettie felt a small electric tingle pass through her like the ghost of love.

At the foot of the stairs she picked up the post, mentally sighing at all the little windows.

Nan was in the kitchen pouring the last of a pint of milk over two Weetabix.

'I didn't hear you,' said Lettie, unreasonably put out that she was no longer alone.

'Couldn't sleep,' said Nan.

Lettie put the kettle on and sifted through the bills. The only envelope without a window was a flimsy brown one addressed to SL, 111 Barnstaple Road, Shipcott, Exmoor, Somerset. Must be for Steven.

She felt her mood sour further and checked the postmark. Plymouth. She didn't know anyone in Devon. *They* didn't know anyone in Devon.

The slag.

'What you got there?'

'Only bills.'

She ripped opened all the windowed envelopes as she waited for the water. The low rumble of the kettle mercifully rose to mask the sound of her mother dripping milk back into the bowl from her spoon.

She left the brown envelope unopened on the counter, staring down at it as if she could divine its message through some psychic gift.

SL. Steven Lamb.

Secrets. Codes. Intrigue.

Something meant only for Steven's eyes and not for hers.

To Lettie, there was no such thing as a good secret. If something was good, you didn't keep it a secret – you told everyone and bought Mr Kipling French Fancies for tea.

She frowned at the envelope and stacked it on to the pile

of bills, then poured the water on to the bags and went to the fridge.

'Did you use all the milk?'

Nan spooned sodden cereal into her mouth.

'Milkman will be here soon.'

Lettie thumped the fridge door shut and poured the tea into the sink, bags and all – banging the mugs down on the draining board.

Nan shrugged. 'These Weetabix suck it up like sponges.'

It was too much.

Lettie grabbed up the brown envelope and tore it open. Nan eyed her carefully.

'Is that a bill too then?'

Lettie scanned the page. A meaningless number at the top; not the date. The same as the other two letters. And a brief message.

Good news arriving soon!

Good news for whom? Her? Unlikely. Steven? Just as unlikely.

If this was from that girl. If that girl was pregnant. If the baby was due ... Only a stupid slag in expectation of a council house could possibly think *that* was good news.

Lettie almost squealed with the unfairness of it all. Just as things were looking up! Why could nothing go right and *stay* right for any of them?

She almost called Steven downstairs, but the thought of confronting him about something like this while he stood all tousled and sleepy-eyed in his little-boy pyjamas was more than she could bear.

After a few seconds of brooding, Lettie lit the gas ring and – ignoring her mother's tutting – burned the letter.

Arnold Avery's trinket box was full to overflowing. In a few short weeks he had stuffed it with careful observations of casual slips, sneaky short cuts, skirted regulations and the failing fabric of the very walls around him. He was almost spoiled for choice.

The keys were the most attractive option – stolen from Ryan Finlay or pressed furtively into his disgusting soap, he could make a mould. Into that mould he would pour wood filler of the type used to repair nicks and chips in old furniture; there was some in the workshop. A coat of varnish to seal and strengthen and he would have the means to stroll from his cell, from his block, from . . . who knew where? He had narrowed it down to two keys – one opened both the double doors on to the block, the other unlocked one of the four gates in the chain-link which lined the prison wall. Two keys might be enough. One on one side of the soap, one the other. Avery spent long hours practising little other than the sleight of hand he might need to complete the task – pressing his toothbrush into the bar, gauging the exact degree of push that would yield a workable mould, and rewarding himself with glimpses of the boy reflected in the wing mirror. He rarely allowed himself more – even when he got two perfect impressions in under five seconds. Time – of which he'd once had so much – now seemed precious and fleeting, and Avery kept himself from SL's photograph as much as possible. He knew that whole days might be lost in the fantasies he wove around the picture. Whole days that it was now vital to spend getting out of prison and replacing the fantasy with the real thing.

He continued to work on the bars of his window at night – his oh-so-versatile toothbrush exposing ever-increasing inches of metal, but with no end in sight either literally or figuratively. Avery didn't care. His prison-nurtured patience was refined and he continued to work on the window because every grain of grey mortar dust that coated his fingers symbolized potential progress to a goal so desirable that he finally understood what the hell Buddhism was all about.

Avery made a couple more forays into engaging other cons in conversation. Careful ventures which nonetheless earned him one swift 'Fuck off, nonce,' and one kick so close to his balls as made no difference, in that it left him curled on the lino, hoarse with fear and hatred – before Andy Ralph stepped between him and his assailant.

So he returned to Ellis, but found there had been a change in the big man's demeanour. From calm to twitchy; from open to brooding and irritable by turn.

Something had happened.

He had no time to waste waiting for Ellis's fugue to be over, so he enquired and Ellis told him. Simple as that.

Hilly had been sending Ellis photos and he hadn't been getting them. Now Hilly thought he didn't love her any more. And if Hilly thought he didn't love her any more then why would she wait for him? In Ellis's mind, the chances of him getting those divorce papers had increased a thousand-fold. And if Hilly divorced him there'd be nothing to hope for at the end of this soulless, harsh incarceration – no Hilly waiting for his return with a hot kiss, no surprising him at the door in the baby-doll nightie she'd got from Ann Summers; no evenings in front of the telly with a bottle of white, no tasting the strawberry lip gloss she wore just for him. He'd never find another woman like Hilly and, if she divorced him, they might as well hang him.

By the time he said it, he was close to tears: 'They might as well hang me.'

Avery had to keep from laughing. Truly. The melodramatic twit. Hang him! Over lipstick and knickers! People like Ellis *deserved* hanging. He'd happily tighten the knot around the man's neck himself just to be rid of the self-pitying, lovelorn whiner.

For a moment Avery indulged a sweet fantasy where he looked into those chimpy little eyes all shiny and brimming with monkey emotion, before springing the trapdoor and watching the big man's dumb head pop off his shoulders.

He wanted to tell Sean Ellis that his whore of a wife wouldn't have been sending him photos of her tits if she didn't want them masturbated over by anyone who laid eyes on them.

Instead he told him conspiratorially: 'He reads everything you know. Steals whatever he likes too.'

'Who?' enquired a puzzled Ellis.

'Finlay,' he shrugged.

It never hurt to plant a seed of hatred.

Ryan Finlay had never had occasion to speak to Dr Leaver. 'Mollycoddling' was a word he and his fellow guards tossed about with practised ease when speaking of their charges, and Finlay felt without thinking that what Leaver did fell neatly into that category along with television privileges and a vegetarian option at mealtimes.

So when Finlay passed Dr Leaver outside his office door, staring down the corridor after Arnold Avery as the prisoner was led back to his cell one afternoon, it was with no small degree of sarcasm that he enquired: 'Another one cured, doc?'

Leaver flicked his eyes quickly at Finlay, then returned to watching Avery's disappearing form – flanked as it was by Andy Ralph and Martin Strong, who were charged with keeping him alive on the short journey between blocks.

'Treatment is their right,' he said, a little stiffly.

Finlay snorted but Leaver didn't look at him. This irritated Finlay. He was used to being listened to at work. Obeyed. Not ignored.

'Those kiddies he killed had rights too, didn't they?'

Ralph and Strong had reached the barred door at the end of the block. Strong unlocked it while Ralph looked idly at his fingernails. Avery stood to one side – a slight, inoffensive figure beside the two beefy guards.

Leaver finally answered: 'Those children were not my patients.'

Fucking bleeding-heart! And *still* the man didn't look at him! Finlay felt like shoving Leaver hard in his bony chest; roughing him up a little. Make Dr High-and-Mighty Leaver give him the respect he deserved.

'So someone like that gets sent to a cushy nick like this and he does a bit of woodwork and you write your little reports and block up his window and he keeps his nose clean and says, "Yes, Dr Leaver," and "No, Dr Leaver," but at the end of the day it all means nothing because we're like a fucking hospital. We just have to patch 'em up and kick 'em out because we need the beds.'

Hoping to prod Leaver into a response, Finlay had only succeeded in getting all red in the face. He glared at Leaver now but the doctor calmly watched Avery until he'd disappeared from view through the double doors. Then for the first time Leaver turned and looked directly at Finlay – and for the first time the prison officer looked into the eyes that had sought light in the black souls of a thousand twisted killers, and felt a chill straight out of a bad horror film.

'Oh, we'll always have a bed for Arnold Avery.' Leaver smiled emptily. 'He's going nowhere.'

27

Father's Day in Lewis's household was not a big deal. Lewis often forgot and when he did, his mother would produce a random card for Lewis to scribble in and present along with a fumbled, jumbled mumble of awkward feelings. Sometimes she had to scribble in it herself because Lewis forgot. Sometimes *she* forgot too – and then when the day came round, it had to be enough that the thought counted. Even if that thought rarely came before mid-morning when Radio 2 would start to play Father's Day dedications and Lewis's dad had to pretend it was enough for him just to be at home with his wife and son.

Lewis went straight to the magazines while Steven looked over the paltry selection of Father's Day cards in Mr Jacoby's shop. If he were going to buy one – which he wasn't, of course – which would it be? Racing cars? Pints of foaming beer?

Dirty cartoons? There was one with a flower pot, a spade and a carelessly discarded pair of gardening gloves, but Steven thought it looked like an old man's card and Uncle Jude was not an old man.

He also wasn't Steven's father.

The thought brought with it a sad pang, poorly concealed by a hurried jab of faked carelessness that felt tinny and hollow in his heart.

'You getting a Father's Day card?'

Lewis looked up at him vacantly from *BMX Monthly*, even though he didn't have a BMX and was an over-cautious rider of the smart new bike he *did* have.

'Shit. Suppose so. Chuck one over, will you?'

'Which one?'

'Any one.'

Steven eyed the cards again more carefully. None of them seemed to suit Lewis's dad. There wasn't a card with a crossword or a cardigan on it. He finally decided on the foaming beer because he had once seen Lewis's dad going into the Red Lion and because he could remember opening Lewis's mother's well-stocked fridge to get them each a Kit Kat, and seeing a six-pack of Bud Light. It had stuck in his mind because it had seemed a very American thing for Lewis's dad to drink. Very sporty.

'This OK?'

'Yeah,' said Lewis, not looking at it. 'Lend us two quid, will you?'

'I haven't got two quid.'

Lewis looked at the price on the back of the card.

'One twenty then. My mum'll pay you back.'

Steven only got two pounds a week pocket money. Sometimes not even that if the gas meter needed feeding.

He sighed and rummaged in his pocket. Over the years
Lewis had borrowed what felt like hundreds of pounds from
him and never paid a single penny back. Steven had brought
it up once and Lewis had told him not to be so tight.

'I've only got one fifty.'

'That'll do.'

Lewis paid Mr Jacoby and pocketed the 30p change.

Avery had no idea it was Father's Day until an excited ripple
came back down the breakfast queue that they were having
kippers.

The news reached the man ahead of him, who turned
around, saw Avery was behind him, closed down his face and
turned back towards the steaming trays and the echoes of
metal on metal. And so the chain of information broke right
there and all the men beyond Avery were deprived of the
anticipation of a rare treat.

'What's up?' said Ellis with no great interest.

'Use your nose, Ellis!' Ryan Finlay laughed at his own joke.
He had to because no one else did.

'Kippers,' said Avery.

'What?'

'We're having kippers.'

'What for?'

'Father's Day.'

Ellis had already picked up porridge at the first serving
counter. Now Avery observed Ellis watching Finlay as he
strolled down the line. As usual, Finlay twirled his keys on his
porky fingers like a doomed gunslinger, then turned and
headed back towards them.

Avery's pale eyes flickered with interest between
Ryan Finlay and Ellis, who had taken to focusing his slightly

vacant gaze on Finlay whenever he caught sight of him.

Ellis had been a waste of time as far as the keys were concerned. In fact, even the soap was giving up on the plan, and had shrunk to the point where it was more scum than solid matter. Avery was seriously considering abandoning the soap moulds as a failed experiment.

Anyway.

Since all that hoo-ha with his slag wife, Ellis had done nothing but brood. Avery had done his utmost to jolly him out of it but the man was stuck in a loop of wondering about Ryan Finlay. Did he take the photos? Did he keep them? Would he give them back? What did Avery think he did with them? Should he demand their return? Avery regretted ever having said anything to him about Finlay stealing the photos. All it had done was make the only con who would speak to him useless, boring and time-consuming. As with the soap, Avery was about ready to give Ellis up as a bad job.

But now, with nothing to do but shuffle towards his promised kippers – and with Finlay almost level with them once more – he thought it might be fun to poke the bear with a stick.

'You got kids, Sean?'

Ellis looked vacantly at Avery. 'What?'

'Father's Day,' said Avery slowly, as if to a child. 'Have you got kids? You and Hilly?'

'No,' said Ellis.

Something started to swell in the ocean of Ellis's brain.

'Shame,' said Avery.

'Yeah,' said Ellis, frowning into his porridge but not seeing it.

Avery sighed heavily and then spoke carefully into the silence between them.

'Probably never will now.'

And suddenly, the fact that he'd been in prison for two years – and would be for at least another twelve – hit Sean Ellis like an anvil in the heart and sucked all the air from his chest like two-year-old shock.

For a moment he swayed slightly, his eyes blank and his mouth slack, holding up the breakfast line.

Ryan Finlay twirled his keys and said: 'Hurry it up, Ellis!' – blissfully unaware that it was the last thing he'd ever say.

Sean Ellis swung his tin tray into Finlay's face. The tray was not heavy and the porridge bowl was made of plastic, but the power of Ellis's sheer fury behind it felled the officer like a dumpy tree, blood jetting from his nose like water from a trick flower.

There was a second – not even that long – when it could have gone either way. Men could have stood and watched Sean Ellis beat Ryan Finlay with his tray, porridge flying like mud, until the other screws pulled him off.

Or all hell could have broken loose.

And – after the briefest of moments – that was the way it went.

The prisoners abandoned kippers, broke ranks and dived on to Finlay. The dozen guards, who – just moments before – had been picking their noses in boredom, ran to help, batons flailing – like a poorly trained pub football team losing its shape because they were all chasing the ball.

Some prisoners turned on them, others turned on each other – seizing the opportunity to settle old scores fast and hard and without the tiresome exchange of tobacco and sexual favours.

Whistles were blown and screams of 'Lockdown! Lockdown!' rang out in panicky voices as the sound of hatred, clanging trays and overturned Formica tables echoed through the building.

Avery adapted so fast he'd have blown a hole straight through Darwinism. Before Ryan Finlay even hit the ground, his thoughts spun from kippers and Ellis to the image of SL captured in tiny focus in the wing mirror of a car. As the other cons piled on top of Finlay, he dropped his tray over the keys which had tumbled docilely from the officer's hand.

Nobody saw. Nobody cared. Everybody else was fighting.

You see, thought Avery calmly, this is why I don't belong in here with all the stupid people.

Then he bent to pick up his tray, sweeping the keys along with it until he was beyond the melee, and stooping casually to scoop them up.

Despite all attention being focused elsewhere, and his own calm exterior, Avery knew he had to act fast. At any moment the guards could regain control of the kitchen and the opportunity would be lost. Even worse, the guards might not regain control of the kitchen.

Child killers were considered by the scum of the earth to be the scum of the earth, and if the violence escalated Avery knew that a good proportion of it would be directed at him and others like him.

Although he understood that speed was of the essence, Avery took a moment to look around. The civilian kitchen staff had disappeared behind the serving counters and through the KITCHEN STAFF ONLY door.

Avery swung himself over the counter and dropped down behind it to give himself another moment of contemplation.

He'd never been behind the serving counter. He glanced around him and saw he'd landed in a small pool of porridge, which had spattered his shoe. It was only a prison-issue black shoe, but Avery kept his stuff nice and irritation stabbed through him at the mess. He looked around for a cloth and saw old chips and bits of carrot under the counter. He grimaced; if he'd known how filthy this place was he'd never have eaten anything they gave him.

He grabbed something white from a low shelf under the counter, which turned out to be a chef's tunic.

He was genuinely torn for a second between putting it on and wiping his shoe with it, but finally pulled off his grey Longmoor jersey with its royal blue stripes on the ribbing and dressed in the tunic.

Moving the tunic had revealed a box of chocolate bars on the low shelf. Twix. Avery wasn't a chocolate person but he grabbed a half-dozen bars and jammed them into the pockets of his jeans.

He also noticed another little pile of whiteness. Hats. Nasty paper hats that made the men and the women serving behind the counters all look like hairless, sexless cancer victims. Made them all look the same . . .

Quickly he pulled one on, yanking it down low on his face before sliding it back to drag his hair off his forehead. He peered into the dull stainless steel cupboard door and saw a dough-faced nobody looking back at him. The dough-face broke into a brief, tense grin.

Then, before standing up, Avery used his jersey to wipe the porridge off his shoe.

He stood up, staying low so that anyone glancing in his direction would see only the top of the white hat above the counter-top, and slid swiftly through the KITCHEN STAFF ONLY door. He was surprised to find it unlocked. This was a prison, for god's sake! Did they really think a sign saying 'Kitchen Staff Only' was a deterrent? If that had been the case then half the population of Longmoor would probably be free men, never having contravened a single 'Trespassers will be prosecuted' or 'We always shop shoplifters' sign. Christ, if it were that simple, they'd all have kept off the bloody grass and this place would be empty.

Despite his predicament, Avery couldn't help smiling as he considered what effect might have been produced on him if his neighbourhood had been posted with signs reading 'Do not kill small children'.

He turned round and doused his smirk as he saw the terrified civilian cooks and porters huddled against the far wall by the exit door, looking at him with scared suspicion. Immediately he turned against the door he'd just come through, seeking a lock and finding none.

'Where's the lock?' he said urgently.

'Doesn't have one,' said an acne'd boy whom Avery strongly suspected of snotting in his mustard pot. The boy didn't look so smug now, thought Avery happily. His acne had flared with terror and his bottom lip trembled.

'Help me block the bloody door before the whole lot come through it!'

Avery grabbed a metal tray trolley and slid it against the door. He knew it was useless but this was just for show. A chubby middle-aged woman whose name tag read 'Evelyn' bustled over, apparently having made the decision that Avery was to be helped on the basis that her enemy's enemy was her friend.

Together they tugged and strained to move a chest freezer across the doorway. Halfway through the task, four or five of the dozen or so staff hurried over to help.

Once the freezer was in place, there was a pause, and Avery knew they were suspicious of him all over again.

His mind raced and pinged for the way to play this, and he was grateful it had been recently exercised.

He had three things on his side: first, civilian kitchen staff was a revolving-door job, he knew. He could only remember seeing Zit-boy and Evelyn before today – the others had not been at the prison long enough to register on his consciousness. Secondly, he was an unremarkable-looking man, and would not stand out in any crowd, let alone a crowd of men all dressed in grey and blue jerseys. And even if they did know him because of who he was, the tunic and, more importantly, the hairnet-cum-cap were a disguise that neutralized the features of anyone who wore them.

The final point in his favour was that, apart from Zit-boy and an elderly man so bent that he looked like a circus monkey in his baggy checked trousers, they were all women. And fuck women's lib, he knew that women were still less likely to challenge a man than most men were. Clinging to these truths, he puffed out his cheeks in mock-relief and looked them all in the eye.

'Nice day to start a new job!'

'Yeah, shit,' said Zit-boy shakily.

The others looked only slightly mollified. They were exchanging guarded looks and Avery realized he was going to have to keep moving if he wanted to get through this.

He produced the keys. 'Anyone know which one opens that door?'

There was a ripple of relief.

'Where'd you get those?' asked the monkey suspiciously.

'One of the guards. Told me to get everyone the hell out of here.' As he spoke, Avery walked to the exit door and started trying the keys.

'What happened to him?' said the monkey, jerking his head back towards the sound of the riot.

'God knows,' said Avery with feeling. 'I'm only interested in what happens to all of us.'

It was a masterstroke. The kitchen staff still didn't trust him, he could tell, but they now clustered around their only chance of escape like eager day-old chicks, prepared to risk following him as long as it was away from the sounds of mayhem that rang in their ears. The lesser of two evils, Avery thought with a little smile. It might be the only time in his life that even that derisory title would be accorded him.

The fourth key turned the lock with a satisfying click, and Avery stood back politely to let everyone else through first. Now they started to nod at him and mutter 'thanks' as they passed. Only the monkey still looked chagrined at being released.

A thump on the door behind them hurried them all through, and Avery locked the exit door.

Evelyn was bustling ahead and as he hurried to catch up a half-dozen guards hurtled past them. Avery recognized all of them, but their eyes slid over him in his white kitchen tunic and hat as though he were invisible.

He knew that the kitchen staff would not allow him to walk out of the front gate with them. Once they were safely surrounded by guards who were not panic-stricken and running, someone – probably the monkey – would voice his suspicions.

That was why, as they passed A-wing, Arnold Avery quietly slipped off the back of the group, stripped off the tunic and hat, stuffed them behind a large flowering shrub that he didn't know the name of, then headed for the chain-link fence.

Rumour had it that the chain-link was under such high tension that a spade jammed into it with enough force would split it open like a popped paper bag. Avery didn't believe that rumour. And he didn't have to. He had the keys to the kingdom.

Just before D-wing he passed *In memory of Toby Dunstan*. Two screws were hurrying his way and Avery knew that trying to hide anything from a screw was the quickest way to get stopped, questioned and searched. So he made sure that they'd seen him clock them before he picked up the bench and – with difficulty – hoisted it on to his shoulder.

'Stealing that, Avery?' said one as they hurried by, their suspicions allayed by the boldness of his move.

'Yes, sir, Mr Priddy!' he replied smartly and snapped a salute.

Both men laughed but didn't stop.

There were no alarms. Alarms only stirred up the other prisoners. Escapes, riots, fights – all these were only evidenced by crackling radios, red, sweaty screw-faces and the unusual sound of running feet as reinforcements flooded the affected area.

Avery set the bench down fifty yards away beside one of the four gates.

He walked – although he wanted to run – to the back of E-wing where Yasmin Gregory's bench was. He passed two other benches on the way, but they weren't his. He knew it was stupid and that he'd blame himself if he failed, but he wanted – needed – to do this.

He staggered back to the gate with the YG bench and, with a surprisingly steady hand, he pulled Finlay's keys from his pocket.

The first one worked, and Avery knew that fate was smiling down on him.

Two benches, each six feet long. One wall, twelve feet high.

It was meant to be.

He dragged the benches through and locked the gate behind him, then put Toby on top of Yasmin and tentatively tested their balance and strength by shaking the tower of wood.

Toby had been the second bench he'd made and was not as strong as Yasmin, which was the fifth. But both were strong enough.

After a couple of false starts when his weight threw the balance off and he teetered dangerously, Arnold Avery scaled the wooden tower named for his child victims, kicked them away without even glancing behind him, and then dropped carefully from the top of the wall on to the wide open expanse of Dartmoor.

28

Steven peeled off his socks and stepped gingerly into his cold wet trainers outside the back door.

It was 5.30am and he felt stupidly as if he was six years old again and waking up to a Christmas he thought would never come.

Steven grinned to himself. Christmas in June. He'd felt this way every day for the past week – sliding out of bed over Davey, who was spread out like a starfish caught in sheets, stepping over the creaky board outside Billy's room, holding on to the banister to control the fall of his feet on the stairs. Then shivering a little – partly as the warmth of sleep gave way to the cool new day on his skin, partly with excitement – as he padded quickly into the kitchen, where sunlight scattered shafts of golden dust through the window.

And all because of the tiny green shoots that had started to appear like little emeralds sprinkled in the dark loam of the vegetable patch.

The carrots had come first and Steven's throat had closed up to see them. He almost cried! Over stupid carrots! He didn't even much like carrots!

He tried not to show his excitement when he told Uncle Jude about the carrots but Uncle Jude had been excited all by himself, and had immediately got up from his bacon to come and see. Steven had felt like a man showing off his new baby. He'd felt the need for a cigar. Instead Uncle Jude had put a hand on the back of his neck, which was even better.

After the carrots, the beans made an appearance at the foot of the poles they'd tied into wigwams. Right now it seemed impossible that the helpless little specks of green could ever scale the heights of wigwam-land. Steven was filled with amazement that they would even try.

He'd wondered what would be next.

It was the potatoes.

But before that – three days after the first carrots appeared – Steven had come in from school and Nan had not been in the window.

Terror had clutched his heart but he tried not to run through the house shouting her name.

'Nan?' he'd called up the stairs. No answer. He'd gone halfway up and seen the toilet door was half open. She wasn't in there.

Nobody was home.

Steven hurried through to the kitchen and stood still in astonishment.

Nan was in the vegetable patch. She was peering at the shoots and poking the earth now and then with her stick. Not in a mean way, Steven realized, but in the same way he'd seen her poke at the all-terrain wheel on her trolley.

The same trolley that Nan now gripped for support as she rolled and swayed slowly back down the bumpy garden.

I'll make her a path, Steven had thought, a smooth path.

Then he'd run, back through the house and out of the front door, grabbing his schoolbag on the way.

A short while later he'd waved hello to his tight-lipped grandmother, motionless in the window, and let himself into the house for the second time in ten minutes.

This memory made Steven sightless until he was halfway up the garden, and then he stopped suddenly.

The beanpoles had fallen down.

He hurried the rest of the way, tamping down the unease that had started in his stomach.

The beanpoles hadn't fallen down. They'd been pulled up and scattered across the rest of the vegetable patch.

Or what was left of it.

Something large and heavy had trampled and gouged the soft black earth, kicking up little seedlings that now lay scattered like bodies on a battlefield, their bright green uniforms failing to cover the naked, spindly limbs beneath that should never have been exposed.

Steven wanted it to be a fox. Or a cow. He even looked about the garden for an escaped cow. A cow would be bad, but not as bad as the bald fact that a person had done this. Person or people.

The hoodies. The hoodies would do this. In his mind Steven could imagine them stomping and laughing as they mashed the tender shoots underfoot, their shadowed faces twisted with stupid humour.

But even as he tried to convince himself of that, Steven knew that the hoodies didn't care enough to do this – or know him well enough to think *he'd* care.

In his plummeting heart, Steven knew it was Lewis.

29

Because of the disturbance in the kitchen, because Ryan Finlay had been rushed to hospital – and from there to the morgue – and because Avery had locked the gate in the chain-link behind him, it was almost an hour before he was found to be missing and not just banged up in the wrong cell or hiding somewhere for his own safety. And it was another twenty minutes before a screw spotted Toby and Yasmin and anyone realized that Arnold Avery had gone over the wall.

Since being promoted from his post as Assistant Governor at Newport Open Prison in South Wales, the Governor of Longmoor had lost four prisoners. Four in four years. It was not a shockingly high number. Longmoor was a training prison; a few select prisoners were even sent to work outside the walls on cleaning details or farm duties as part of their rehabilitation. Understaffing meant that on two occasions a couple of men had simply ducked behind a bit of machinery or wandered off into a thick mist. All four had been re-captured on the roads before any driver would stop for them.

But four escapes in four years had the unfortunate ring of a pattern to it. As if it might be five escapes in five years, six in six years, and so on, and that gave the Governor palpitations.

So, once Avery's escape was detected, every available officer was immediately dispatched on to the roads, and roadblocks were established to search cars leaving the area. It was assumed that – like those before him – this particular escapee would head for the nearest road, then flag down or steal a car. To do anything else was stupid and dangerous, even in summer.

Having taken this view, the Governor then took another: escapes reflected poorly on prison staff and that led to a lowering of staff morale.

The Governor was a good man, and wanted to keep morale as high as possible.

If only Avery could be recaptured within the next few hours. If only the fact that a formerly notorious child killer had gone over the wall could be kept out of the press until he was safely back within those very walls . . .

The Governor was a good man.

But he made a bad choice.

He didn't call the police.

Arnold Avery's first half-hour of freedom after eighteen years in prison was the worst thirty minutes of his life.

As soon as he straightened up from the twelve-foot drop, he panicked.

The feeling grabbed him by the throat and squeezed, and he ran blindly on to the moor, his terror making him whine with every snatch of out-of-shape breath. His legs burned, there were daggers in his lungs; even his arms ached from running – all within 400 yards of the wall. Years of sitting in his cell, thinking, had done nothing for his muscle tone.

He stumbled and panted and whimpered until his own self-loathing finally slapped the panic down and forced him to stop, regain control and take stock.

His panic was groundless. However many times he looked back, he saw no sign of pursuit. The prison itself had melted away behind him like a bad dream.

Built in a large natural hollow, Longmoor Prison was a village-sized stone monstrosity that was barely visible to the thousands of walkers and tourists who roamed the moors each summer. One minute they would be striding out with only short yellow grass and pale granite outcrops for company; the next they'd be gazing down on the huge dark grey wheel inside a crater, often only the pitched roofs and chimneys jutting up through the fog, as if the whole prison was sinking into a lake of dirty milk.

Out here now, with the prison disappeared and only the sunny moor around him, Avery felt his panic shredded and scattered by the bracing breeze. In its place he felt the sudden, laughing excitement of being free.

He had an almost irrepressible urge to throw his arms out and spin dizzily across the slopes.

Contrary to his forerunners, he had no intention of flagging down a car or going anywhere near a road if he could help it.

He would have considered stealing a car but he was a serial killer, not a common car thief, and had no idea how to hot-wire a car – or even to break into one unless it was with a brick through a window.

For the first time in eighteen years, Avery regretted his isolation from other prisoners. He could have learned so much. Too late now . . .

Avery wished he did not need a car at all. But he knew that the instant he'd started running, a clock had started ticking. Soon his face would be on TV screens. By tomorrow morning it would be on the front page of every tabloid.

He was wearing his blue-and-white-striped prison issue shirt and dark blue jeans. He wished he had kept his pullover because, although it was June, the sun had not yet warmed the air. He knew he would wish it even more fervently as night fell.

He passed two sheep lipping the vast, immaculate lawn of the moor. Neither bothered looking at him.

He walked calmly now, not noticing where, just regrouping as he moved forward.

His throat relaxed and cooled enough for him to properly appreciate the bright, fresh air that did not smell of today's dinner or yesterday's socks. It was heady stuff and he swayed as he sucked it into his lungs, feeling it pressing to his very fingertips as it replaced the stagnant prison fumes.

Having had no burning desire to escape until he received the photo SL had sent him, Avery had only the vaguest notion of what lay before him. He knew, for example, that the south and east of Dartmoor was dotted with tiny villages, some little more than a handful of houses around a pillar box or a bus shelter. He also knew that the north and west of the moor were even less populated. More than that, he only knew that somewhere between him and the northern edge of Dartmoor were miles of desolate and difficult terrain, rocky and boggy by turn. Coupled with the unpredictable weather, it was no wonder most escapees took the easy option of the roads, despite the increased likelihood of being caught, because of the decreased likelihood of dying.

But now that he had gone over the wall, Avery had

nothing to lose and everything to gain by avoiding recapture.

It had all changed. If he was caught now, he would lose eighteen years' worth of Brownie points for having been a model prisoner. His chance of parole was now precisely zero, and he'd languish for twenty-five or thirty years maybe, back in somewhere like Heavitree where he'd spent the first sixteen years of his sentence in fear and squalor.

He would rather die than go back there.

He realized with a little jolt that that was true, and then the jolt became a warm certainty. There was something steeling about having only one option left. It focused the mind.

'Nice morning!'

He turned to find a middle-aged man, and what Avery presumed to be his wife, just yards away. Both carried telescopic walking poles, day packs and map cases. Both wore khaki shorts over sun-wrinkled legs – his lean and hairy, hers stubbornly chubby.

Thank god he'd stopped that crazy headlong flight. They would have known for sure.

'Yes,' he nodded, in complete agreement.

'Going to be hot.'

'Yes,' he said again, feeling that he should be making more of a contribution to the exchange, but at a loss to know how.

'We're on our way to Great Mis.'

Avery noticed that now the man's eyes were sweeping him from head to prison-issue black-booted toe, looking for evidence that he was a walker, and starting to be suspicious that he wasn't finding any. Avery was temporarily happy that he'd ditched his pullover; the dark grey with the distinctive blue strip through the ribbing would have given him away in an instant.

'How about you?' the man continued pointedly.

Avery's newly exercised neurons fired gratifyingly fast.

'Oh, I'm not walking!' he said in a tone that might make them feel stupid for thinking such a thing. 'I'm just stretching my legs. On my way to a job in Tavistock and thought I'd take advantage of . . .' he swept out an arm '. . . all this. My car's just over that rise.'

They both glanced at the rise, then back at him and he gave them his special smile. The man didn't go so far as to smile back, although he nodded in acceptance, but his wife lost herself in his smile and beamed happily.

'Oh yes, too nice to be stuck in a car or an office today.'

They all nodded then, finally on common ground in every sense.

The wife cheerfully poked her husband with her walking pole.

'Get on then, Father!'

The man gave a small smile and raised his eyebrows at Avery before starting to move.

'You have a nice walk,' he called after them and they turned to wave at him.

He breathed a sigh of relief. That could have been awkward and – more importantly – time-consuming.

He knew that time was of the essence. There were things he needed to do – things he wished he didn't have to. He wished he could just head north and keep going, but despite his initial panic at being free, Avery had already devised a plan and now only had to stick to it.

He had to give himself the best possible chance of success. He had to make the most of his time on the run.

He had to send a postcard.

Avery walked for three hours before he saw the village and by the time he did, he was shivering. The sun that had greeted his freedom was now a sharp, pale disc in a white-smoky sky.

It was not a proper village, and he never knew its name, because he didn't approach from the road. He skirted the moor above the twenty-odd houses until he saw the shop and then dropped down between the houses to reach it.

The shop was tiny – just the converted front room of a two-up-two-down cottage with bulging walls and liquid glass in the windows. A billboard for the *Western Morning News* made him feel suddenly as if he'd been sucked back in time. The headline read: CHARLES AND CAMILLA VISIT PLYMOUTH. Poor them, thought Avery.

A rickety carousel outside the shop held yellowing postcards. Most were of Dartmoor, or sheep, or pretty rose-covered cottages, but there was one compartment that held several of the same card, showing Exmoor blanketed by purple heather. Avery's stomach thrilled at the sight. He took all six cards on the rack and stuffed them into his back pocket. Then he picked another card of a Dartmoor sheep and went inside.

Although the day had turned dull, his eyes still had to adjust to the gloom of the interior. There was a newspaper rack on one wall, shelves of goods on the other, and an ice-cream freezer in between. Avery could see that the shelves were crammed with a startling array of goods – spray cleaner, toilet paper, dog food, chocolate bars, curry-in-a-can, nails, Band-Aids, Coca-Cola, scrubbing brushes . . .

A glance into the ice-cream freezer showed him that most of it had been annexed for frozen peas and chicken portions. In the remaining corner he recognized a Zoom lolly but nothing else.

There was a small counter and an archaic till, but nobody

behind them, so he opened a plastic litre bottle of water and swigged down several gulps. There was a charity box on the counter – RNLI. Lifeboats. In the middle of Dartmoor? Who gave a shit? He shook it briefly and almost smiled: apparently, no one.

'All right?' A long, stringy girl of about fifteen slid into the room and slumped in a kitchen chair behind the counter.

'Hi,' he said. 'Do you have any postcards of Exmoor?'

'Postcards are outside.'

'Yes, I know. I looked. Couldn't see any of Exmoor though.'

The girl looked at him vacuously.

'This is Dartmoor.'

'I know. I want a postcard of Exmoor.'

She stared at the door as if a postcard of Exmoor was expected any second.

'Don't we have one?'

Avery breathed steadily. Control. Patience. Valuable lessons.

'No.'

The girl tutted and jerked to her feet. Avery saw she was wearing skin-tight jeans on the thinnest legs he'd ever seen. And stupid little ballet shoes. She slouched past him without a glance and went outside.

He watched her as she turned the creaking carousel on its rusty spindle, her slightly bulging blue eyes frowning at the cards, chewing a ragged lock of her mousey hair.

She was too old for him. Her innocence was lost, or well hidden behind boredom or stupidity. It made him hate her more as she stood, hand on hip, looking at the postcards he'd already looked at.

'Can't see one,' she said finally.

'No,' he agreed.

'Sorry.' She didn't sound sorry. He'd like to make her sound sorry – it would be so easy – but he didn't want to waste his time.

He followed her back inside.

'Can you see if you have any in stock?'

'I don't think we do.'

'Can you check for me?'

She tossed her hair by way of an answer. He mustered his reserves of self-control.

'Please?'

She made an irritable sound with her lips, and scuffed back through the interior door. He heard her ascending or descending some wooden steps, surprisingly heavily for such a thin girl. Letting him know she was put out.

He smiled, then leaned over the counter and hit the OPEN key on the dirty old till that was more like a fancy money box. There was £60 in tens; Avery took three of them and a handful of pound coins. When he'd last been in a shop there had still been grubby green pound notes.

He noticed a pale green cardigan slung over the back of the chair and stuffed it into a plastic bag.

He filled the rest of the bag with Mr Kipling cakes, peanuts, a couple of pre-packed cheese-and-tomato sandwiches and more water, then leaned out of the door to leave it just out of sight on the pavement. Then he picked up a chewed Bic pen from the counter and wrote on one of the Exmoor postcards.

He heard the girl stamping up or down the stairs again and slid the card of Exmoor back into his pocket as she reappeared.

'We don't have any.'

'Oh well, I'll take this one then, please. And a first-class stamp.'

The girl served him sullenly and he paid for the sheep card with a single pound coin, putting his change in the RNLI box.

Outside he tried licking the stamp, but found it was already sticky – an innovation he had to adjust to.

As he dropped the Exmoor postcard into the letterbox, he noticed that the collection time was a mere half-hour away. Avery was not crazy; he knew it didn't mean god was on his side. But he also knew it meant god really didn't give a shit one way or the other.

When he was a reasonable distance from the village he sat down on the sheep-shorn grass, ate three cherry Bakewell tarts and drank a third of a litre of water. The sugar suffused his blood and made him feel strong and confident. The sun came out and warmed him and he lay back and stretched like a cat on a car-port roof.

He lifted one hip, took one of the remaining Exmoor post-cards from his back pocket and unbuttoned his jeans.

Twenty minutes later, Avery stood up and focused on his surroundings once more.

He took no formal bearings. He didn't need to. He felt a strange, inevitable tugging in his chest and could do nothing but follow it.

With the sun now warming his back, Arnold Avery, serial killer, quickened his pace and headed north.

30

Because of the vegetable patch, Steven was late for school and so missed seeing Lewis before the bell rang. They were not in the same classes and then, at lunchtime, Lewis failed to appear at the gym door, which was where they always met.

Steven huddled out of the wind and ate his cheese and Marmite alone, not knowing whether to wait for Lewis or to go looking for him. Both options seemed pathetic and neither gave him any clue as to how he should proceed once he and Lewis came face to face.

His mother had put a Mars bar in his lunchbox; a real Mars bar – not some inferior generic copy of a Mars bar – and on any other day it would have excited Steven. The Mars bar meant that his mother was happy. Of course, it was Uncle Jude who was making her happy, not him, but they would all benefit in trickledown. Lewis was not there to admire the Mars bar, and that took some of the shine off it. Still, Steven ate it while appreciating the silver lining – if Lewis wasn't there to admire the Mars bar, at least he wasn't there to eat half of it.

But once the thick, caramel sweetness had left his mouth, the bitterness of a friendship betrayed was still there.

He saw Lewis at the end of the day, jostling other kids as he hurried through the throng at the school gates, glancing around nervously as if he might be pursued. Steven ducked behind the canteen bins and stood there, staring at his cheap new trainers, already scuffed and breaking apart from a combination of poor workmanship and overactive boy.

He knew Lewis was looking out for him, hoping he wouldn't catch him up on the way home. Steven still didn't know what to say to Lewis, so he gave him a long head start and then walked home so slowly that Lettie tightened her mouth at him for the first time in days.

'You're late.'

'I helped Mr Edwards put the gym stuff away. The door was locked and he had to go to the office for the key.' Steven had thought of the lie during the interminable walk home. It sounded just fine coming out of his mouth, and Lettie's lips loosened in acceptance, but Nan looked at him sharply and he felt himself grow warm about the ears.

Still, she didn't say anything, and Uncle Jude came downstairs, whistling 'There is a green hill far away' which was her favourite, and so tea unfolded without further incident, until Uncle Jude said: 'Did you see the patch?'

Steven nodded non-committally but didn't look at him.

'Any idea what happened?'

He shook his head and put fake butter on a piece of bread, hoping his silence made the lie somehow less sinful.

Uncle Jude shrugged and sighed. 'We can put the beans up again but we'll lose a lot of the carrots and potatoes.'

Steven nodded.

'Do it after tea, if you like.'

He nodded more vigorously. The evening was calm and warm and the thought of repairing the damage was an attractive one. He'd been afraid Uncle Jude would lose interest; that the vegetable patch was a one-shot deal and it was over now.

'Wondered if your friend would like to help.'

'Who?' said Steven warily.

'The one who's all mouth and no trousers.'

Steven flushed as he recognized Lewis, feeling laughter bubbling, but quickly tamped down with guilt and sudden nerves at ever seeing his best friend again.

'Why don't you go and ask him?' Uncle Jude was studying him now with a careful look in his eye. Steven saw him exchange a small glance with his mother.

Uncle Jude knew. Somehow.

Steven looked at his fish fingers.

'I don't think he'd like to. Digging's not his thing.'

He held his breath, waiting for Uncle Jude to make him, or argue with him, or expose Lewis. But he didn't.

'Just the two of us then,' he said instead, and Steven met his eyes for the first time today, and smiled.

31

Arnold Avery was right about the direction he should take, but he was wrong about the ticking clock.

Because the Governor wanted to keep morale up.

When Avery wasn't recaptured by 5pm, the Governor even got into his own two-year-old Mercedes Kompressor and cruised the drizzling moors, convinced that spotting Avery was just a matter of time and motivation.

And he was getting very motivated.

Every hour that Avery remained at large compounded his sin in not having called the police. And every hour that he didn't call the police increased his desperation to get Avery back in custody without anyone knowing he'd ever been gone.

When Avery wasn't captured by nightfall, the Governor's discomfiture at not having called the police earlier turned to twitchy foreboding and – shortly thereafter – blind panic.

It was in that condition that he staked his entire future on Avery's being in custody by morning.

Which meant that when he wasn't, the numb, soon-to-be-jobless Governor didn't call the police until 7.09am – almost twenty-four hours after Avery went over the wall.

32

Sixteen-year-old Private Gary Lumsden didn't like the army but – like his father before him – he did like guns.

The difference, thought Lumsden, was that his father had never been in possession of a gun quite as menacing as the SA80A2, with its thirty-round magazine, an accurate range of 400 yards and a muzzle velocity of just a shade under a kilometre per second.

Not that his father would have given a shit about any of the technical details, of course, thought Lumsden; Mason Dingle would only have wanted to know how cheap, and could it be traced.

But Gary Lumsden loved the technical details. Certainly, he wished the SA80A2 had a more glamorous name, like Colt 45 or Uzi. But it was the technical details that had kept his mouth watered through thirteen weeks of sweaty basic train-ing, and his fists at his sides as Second Lieutenant Brigstock

– all shiny and new from Sandhurst – bossed him about like a hated older brother.

The thought of the SA80 obsessed him. On drill his eyes swivelled illegally to watch other squaddies carrying their guns, and he felt rather than heard the dull metal-on-metal clicks and sharp slides of well-maintained weaponry. As he hung with screaming arms over a pit of mud on the assault course, his ears were attuned to the snappy cracks from the nearby range. At night, while the man in the bunk below his made them both shake to the rhythm of imaginary sex, Gary Lumsden's skin thrilled instead to the thought of cradling his SA80 in his left hand, while his right forefinger twitched on a phantom trigger.

And now he finally held the culmination of all those technical details cool and heavy in his hands, it was all Private Gary Lumsden could do not to stand up, spin on his heel and spray his platoon-mates with high-calibre bullets at a rate of 700 rounds per minute – just to see what it would feel like. He yearned to feel the weapon heat up in his palms, spit fire from his fingers, ring in his ears, commit distant murder.

Instead Private Lumsden breathed through his mouth as the moment of truth arrived.

The SA80 fitted him like another limb. They'd been separated at birth and now it was part of him again. He'd cleaned it and dismantled it and cleaned it and reassembled it and cleaned it again. He could do it blindfolded. Be good to your gun and your gun will be good to you. By that reckoning, Private Lumsden's gun should have gone down on him every morning and then cooked him bacon and eggs.

But now – finally – it was his gun's turn to pay him back.

Controlling his excitement, Private Lumsden drew a bead on a card target that didn't even have a human shape on it – it was just five bullseyes on a page. Fucking crap.

Still, he focused, relaxed, exhaled smoothly and squeezed lovingly, and the single round kicked his shoulder and the card rippled briefly to let him know he'd hit it.

'Well done, Lumsden!'

Lumsden didn't hear Brigstock. The shot had opened a gate of hot pleasure in him that made him wince. He had to bite his lip to keep from whimpering. Never in a million years had he imagined his gun would be *that* good to him.

In a rush, he thought of his father.

Lumsden's father shared his DNA but not his name. Thank god. Life had been tough enough for the Lumsden boys without the added encumbrance of a name like Dingle. No wonder his old man had had a short fuse.

That short fuse translated into quick fists for young Gary and his brother Mark. The boys did not complain; they had never known anything else. In just the same way, they had never had clothes on their backs that were not shoplifted, food on their table that had been legally purchased, toys they had not bought with stolen lunch money.

Even their mother did not really belong to their father – she was one of six on the Lapwing estate who had borne his children – the first offspring arriving just shy of Mason Dingle's fifteenth birthday. Gary and Mark had a half-sister they had nothing to do with, and knew who their half-brothers were by their quick tempers as much as by the angelic blue eyes they all shared.

The eight boys aged between six and seventeen prowled warily around each other on the estate – aware of the tenuous bond they all resented. There were long periods of uneasy quiet, punctured by flurries of sharp but generally minor violence. Their father flitted between families, staying only until everything wasn't going his way, then he'd move on and start again. He had no favourites – barely seemed to acknowledge the boys – and made no contribution other than drawing regular late-night or early-morning visits from the police.

Gary Lumsden was first taken into custody at the age of nine for stealing a tube of toothpaste from the corner shop. His mother had sent him for the toothpaste; she didn't give him any money and Gary didn't expect her to. The shopkeeper held his shirt so tight until the police came that Gary had red marks under his armpits for days.

He knew shoplifting was wrong, but only in an abstract way. At school it was wrong and at home it was all he knew. The thought of going to work somewhere, earning money and buying stuff with it was alien to him; he had no experience of anyone in his family doing such a thing – and would have thought them foolish to attempt it. Toothpaste was in the shop; all he had to do was transfer it to his mother's bathroom with the minimum of fuss.

The police came and took him home, instead of to the police station. The copper led him from the patrol car to the front door in a death grip that told Gary he'd like to do much more to him than this pointless exercise. Something inside the young Gary had understood that this wasn't just about him; that the policeman's rough handling had been primed by other, older experiences that Gary had no knowledge of. But for now he was at the sharp end.

His mother had been unable to muster the required sobriety to appear even vaguely interested in a policeman at her door and – apart from her later bitching about no toothpaste – that had been that. Given that Gary had been relieving the corner shop of its shabby stock since the age of four, his first brush with the law seemed a ridiculously small price to pay.

Mason Dingle occasionally 'went away', but he always came back and never seemed embarrassed, chastened or changed by the experience, and Gary and Mark had no doubt that they would one day follow him into the family trade.

Until they saw *Band of Brothers* on a pirated DVD. Then everything changed.

Suddenly Gary and Mark Lumsden were the good guys – staunch, courageous, noble – if only in their own minds. They stopped being famous footballers and gangsters and started being soldiers.

It wasn't all good. At first, soldiers meant they moved from sneak-thieving and shoplifting to all-out noisy attacks, using threats, diversionary tactics and confusion to cover their actions. Military strategy, they learned to call it.

There was a hiccup in their game when they found a dull black pistol in a box in the shed. It had MADE IN CZECHOSLOVAKIA down one side with the letters CZ inside a circle at either end of that. It was dirty and scratched and was the most beautiful thing either of them had ever encountered. For a heady six hours, Mark and Gary Lumsden held each other hostage, gunned each other down, pressed bruising rings into each other's temples and backs with the muzzle of the pistol in a barely suppressed excitement of violence.

Then their father caught them with it and beat them both black and blue.

Mark had no ambition anyway and the beating laid to rest any daring he possessed regarding the CZ, but slowly – with the memory of the heavy pistol in his small hands always fresh – Gary started to aspire to a gun.

A big gun.

A gun he could call his own. A gun he would not even have

to steal. A gun he could – possibly – fire at real people with minimal repercussions.

The British Army beckoned loudly, and Gary Lumsden was far from deaf.

He picked up leaflets, he called Freephone numbers; he learned that a criminal record would bar him from recruitment – and he cleaned up his act.

For seven years Gary Lumsden had talked and dreamed of little other than achieving that gun. He joined the army cadets and was the only boy who attended every week, come rain or shine. Intellect that had not been exercised in English or history classes was suddenly stretched by signals, rule-books, drill patterns, boot-polishing and uniform-pressing. He hated it all, but every shined button, every measured turn-up, every jealous insult hurled by other blue-eyed boys on the estate – each brought him a few seconds closer to the gun.

And everything he'd been through – the pain, the hard work, the humiliation, the fear, the poverty – everything had become worth it the second he pulled that trigger and felt the rush of holding death in his hands.

Although his turn to shoot was over for now, Gary Lumsden did not join his mates in shuffling into a more comfortable position on the wet grass, or in turning to watch his fanned-out companions pull their own triggers.

Instead, he drew another bead on his target and relaxed his breathing. His finger hardened on the trigger and – with difficulty – he took it away entirely, fearing a reflexive squeeze that would mean an unauthorized discharge of his weapon and all kinds of shit pouring down on his head once they were back in Plymouth.

He lined his sights up with one of the four small targets on the card, knowing he could hit it, waiting, waiting for his turn to come round again.

A crack, a zing, and scattered laughter to his left meant someone had hit something so off-target that it merited derision. Gary Lumsden didn't bother taking his eye off his card. Both eyes open – the way they'd been taught. Ignoring the left, using the right.

Something moved in his blurred eye's vision. Lumsden refocused and saw a man walking across the firing range – a long way behind the targets, maybe a quarter of a mile away, heading north.

Lumsden frowned, lifted his head minutely and glanced left and right to see whether anyone else had spotted the man. His nearest colleague, Private Hall, was twenty yards to his right, facing his own target, so he was turned slightly away from Lumsden. Hall was black, which meant he suffered at the hands of the bigots in the platoon. To his left he could see only the boots and wet camouflage fatigues of Private Gordon, who had red hair and so suffered at the hands of pretty much everyone else. Neither was looking towards the man.

Lumsden swung his SA80 so he could look at the man through the sights, but even then he was too far away to fill them. The man was walking but didn't look like a walker. Lumsden could see no stick, no backpack. Instead the man was carrying what looked like a plastic bag! Like he'd just popped down to Tesco's! The man didn't even have a waterproof jacket on – just a shirt that looked blue from this distance, and jeans. Jeans were the worst thing a walker could wear. Hot in the sun and cold, heavy and slow to dry in the much more frequent mist and rain. It confirmed Lumsden's first opinion that the man was out of his depth on the moor. For a start, he couldn't have checked the firing notices that were bread and butter to every experienced walker on Dartmoor. With a single call on their mobile phones they could find out when live firing was taking place on the ranges that covered the north-east quadrant of the moor. This man couldn't have checked. And if he'd seen the red-and-white warning signs, then he'd either ignored them or been stupid enough to cross them into the Danger Range.

Private Lumsden's finger slid gently back over the trigger of his own, personal SA80A2.

The guy was just asking to get hit by a stray bullet. Or a not-so-stray one.

Lumsden followed the man's progress under the crosshairs, his hands steady, his breathing calm.

If he were to pull the trigger now, he might even hit him, he realized with a thrill. He wasn't going to shoot, but the sensation of holding the man in his sights while the cold steel warmed itself under his finger was almost dizzying.

Off to his left, another crack and he heard Private Knox say 'Fuck' quite loudly, but he didn't flicker for a moment.

Every cell of his body was focused on the walker. Every ounce of his self-control kept his finger from squeezing the trigger the way it wanted to.

Discharging a round without authority was serious trouble. Discharging it in the direction of another person outside a war situation was grounds for court martial. Deliberately firing on a civilian out for a stroll on Dartmoor would almost certainly mean prison. And he'd battled so hard and so long not to follow his father and Mark down that road. There was no way he was going to blow it now – not now he'd finally got the gun.

Lumsden sighed inwardly – to sigh outwardly would have made his aim waver.

Four hundred yards. That was the range of his weapon.

The walker was probably beyond that. Despite the ease with which he held the man in his sights, Lumsden knew that the chances of hitting him, if he *were* to fire, were slim. Although the weather was good by Dartmoor standards, there was rarely less than a stiff breeze to contend with. After 400 yards, the round would begin to lose thrust, lose direction, become unpredictable.

The man disappeared behind some rocks and Lumsden gently moved his gun to anticipate his reappearance, feeling another thrill as the man walked straight back into his sights.

He was approaching a small tor about fifty yards ahead of him. If he reached it, Lumsden would lose him.

A sense of urgency made his finger tighten on the trigger and he had to make a conscious effort to relax it again. His breath hissed between his ears and, although the platoon were still firing at their targets, the shots sounded thick and distant to him.

Lumsden admired his own self-control. He was still young, but the basic training had knocked the remaining child clean out of him, hardened him up, shaped him into a man. He knew he was already a better person than his father or brother or any of his half-brothers would ever be.

Here in his hands he held the power of life and death. Gary Lumsden, the boy, would have fired; Private Gary Lumsden, the soldier, was tougher than that. He felt an unaccustomed swell of pride.

The man walked on, head down, through a patch of sunlight and Gary Lumsden held him in his sights, steady and careful. The tor was approaching, the kill-shot would be lost, but it wasn't about the kill-shot, he told himself; it was about being in control, doing the right thing, growing up and being a man.

The walker clambered on to the first of the big grey

rocks. Two more and he'd be lost from view behind the tor.

For less than two minutes, Private Gary Lumsden had been in possession of the power to inflict instant death, but had chosen instead to allow life to continue. It was godlike.

Lumsden's angelic blue eyes stung with heat at the thought of how far he'd come as he watched the distant, stupid man reach to pull himself on to the next rock. So small, so vulnerable, so oblivious to how close it had been . . .

Private Lumsden's entire being thrummed with the knowledge that this *meant* something; that this was pivotal; that he'd remember this moment for ever.

And then – in a sudden, sneaky triumph of nature over nurture – he pulled the trigger anyway.

Arnold Avery opened his eyes to a blank white sky, a wet back, and a sharp ache in his left arm.

His first fuzzy thought was that a bird had flown into him. A big bird. All he remembered was clutching at the fresh Devonshire air as he fell off the rock he'd been standing on.

He turned his head creakily to one side, and sharp grass pricked his cheek. There was a disc of pure white something with two red dots in it beside his head; it took him several blinking seconds to work out it was a Mr Kipling cherry Bakewell tart, spilled from his bag of stolen shopping. One red dot in the white icing was the cherry, the other was blood.

Avery groaned as he sat up and saw his left sleeve dark and red. He winced as he moved his arm. It hurt, but it wasn't broken.

He looked around and could see nothing and nobody. But then, nothing and nobody could see him; he'd fallen into a shallow dip behind the tor. He had no idea how long he'd been unconscious for, or what had happened to him. His bird theory was shit, he already knew, but he had no others. The moor stretched around him for miles, looking yellow-grey now under the louring clouds.

He pulled his arm from his sleeve, wiping away blood with the tail of his shirt, and saw the bloody crease through the top of his bicep, as though someone had dragged a forefinger through the flesh of his arm, removing the skin and leaving a bloody groove in its place.

It looked as though he'd been shot, although he knew that wasn't possible. This was England, after all, and the screws they sent to hunt down escapees were likely to be armed with little more than expense vouchers for their petrol costs.

He shook his head to clear it, and slowly started to gather his stolen goods together. There was no point in hanging about trying to solve the mystery of what had happened to him. He doubted it was relevant anyway. If it had been an armed, over-enthusiastic screw, then he'd be back in custody by now; if it had been a bird, there would be feathers. It didn't matter. What mattered was keeping going. He tried to find the sun behind the clouds but couldn't. It wasn't getting dark yet, but that meant nothing; it was June, and would stay light until well after ten at night.

Although he didn't know it, Arnold Avery had been unconscious only long enough to miss the very faint, outraged shouts of Private Gary Lumsden's military career coming to an abrupt but almost inevitable end.

33

Steven stared at the black ceiling he couldn't see, and listened to Uncle Jude and his mother arguing.

He couldn't make out words, but the tones alone made him stiff with tension and his ears prickled with effort.

She was cross. Steven didn't know what she had to be cross about. His mind raced, trying to assess the previous day, prodding it to shake loose the moment when things had changed. Something. Something. Something had happened. Must have! Because last night, he'd lain just like this, gazing into blackness, and heard them having sex. He recognized the sounds from a DVD he and Lewis had watched last school holidays. Something with Angelina Jolie in it. It had been under some sheets, so hadn't shed any useful light on the mechanics of the whole sex thing. He and Lewis had stared, flame-faced, at the screen, not daring to speak or look at each other while the scene played out. When it was over, Lewis had said, 'I'd give her one,' in a triumph of redundancy.

But the sex between Uncle Jude and his mother had been last night. Tonight was the row. Uncle Jude mostly silent, occasionally defensive; his mother sharp and cold. He felt a rush of pure fury at her; wanted to run next door and scream at her to stop. Stop fighting, stop hurting, stop being such a . . . such a . . . *fucking bitch*!

His fingers ached and he realized they were gripped too tightly around the top of his duvet, rigid and trembling – like the rest of him. He let his breath out and tried to relax.

'Is Uncle Jude leaving?'

Steven jumped. 'Shut up, Davey.'

'You shut up!'

Steven did shut up, wanting to hear how the row ended, but there was no more.

'I don't want Uncle Jude to go.' Davey's voice was whiny and tight with snot but instead of making him angry it infected Steven with the same feeling, so he said nothing, biting his lip and squeezing his hot eyes closed until he opened them and found that it was morning.

And that some time during the night, Uncle Jude had left.

Steven slouched downstairs on heavy legs and cold feet, despite the season.

Halfway down the stairs, he saw the purple oblong on the doormat.

By the bottom of the stairs his eyes realized it was a postcard and picking it up confirmed it was a picture of purple heather.

When Steven turned it over, his heart jumped into his throat and started pumping there instead, making his whole neck throb.

Compared to their previous communications, there was a cornucopia of information on the six-by-four-inch postcard.

There was the edge of Exmoor, reduced by familiarity to a single dashed line. DB was where it should be. SL was where he'd shown Avery. Between them was a strange circle of short radiating lines, like an aerial view of Friar Tuck's haircut, enclosing the initials WP, and the single word:

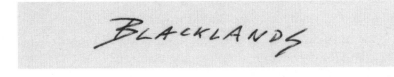

*

Steven couldn't eat. He'd never have thought such a thing was possible. It wasn't because he wasn't hungry; it was because his head was so full of thinking that the thoughts overflowed and pounded into his mouth, down his throat, into his chest and even as far as his guts – a raging river of swirling hopes and white-water fears that left no room for food.

His first thought on seeing Avery's directions was how quickly his own quest had faded from his mind. Uncle Jude's return, the vegetable patch, Lewis, the real Mars bar. These things – these normal things – had squeezed Uncle Billy out of his day-to-day consciousness and into a corner in the back of his mind.

But the postcard brought Uncle Billy bursting out again in a rush of old guilt and new anticipation.

In an instant, he was recharged, reinvigorated, focused.

He did not remember washing or dressing or doing his teeth, but they must have happened, because he arrived at the breakfast table without eyebrows being raised.

Davey was miserable; his mother cut their sandwiches with

a hard hand and a tight mouth, and Nan was uncharacteristically quiet on the subject of her daughter's love life. But Steven was only aware of these things in the most peripheral, hazy way.

I know where Uncle Billy is buried!

He almost thought he'd shouted it out loud when his nan fixed him with a neutral stare.

'Pass the butter to your brother.'

Steven passed the butter and was gripped with a sudden certainty that someone else would find Uncle Billy first.

Now that he had Avery's map, it seemed so obvious! Blacklands! Of course! So close he could almost see it from his own bedroom window!

Even Lewis had worked it out. *'Next time I come up to help, I'm digging at Blacklands . . .'*

What was to stop someone else working it out too?

Someone who didn't have to go to school today?

Someone who would beat him to it?

Someone who would push open the door of opportunity and whose life would be transformed by the discovery instead of his, leaving him trapped for ever between his nan and his mother and the dim, undersea room where his own piss still stained the carpet. Steven went cold and felt his middle empty as everything inside him pressured out towards his throat and his bowels.

He got up from the table with a loud scrape.

'Where are you going?'

'School.'

'You haven't eaten.'

'I'm not hungry.'

Lettie looked as though she was going to make an issue of it, then bound his sandwiches viciously in clingfilm and banged them into his lunchbox without a chocolate bar.

Steven didn't care. Chocolate bars were for children, and today he would become so much more than that. He might not know how sex or relationships worked, but by nightfall he hoped his family would be a whole thing, instead of this cracked, crumbling half-thing that left him nervous and sad.

Steven glanced round at his mother, Davey and Nan – all of them unaware of how he was about to change their lives.

He turned to go, but only got two steps before his mother said sharply: 'Wait for your brother.'

And so instead of digging up the body of a murdered boy, Steven had to wait for his brother and walk him to school and then go straight to double history, where Mr Lovejoy made them draw cross-sections of the pyramids, showing all the dark, secret ways the Egyptians employed to ensure that their ancestors remained undiscovered and undisturbed for thousands of years.

Steven had still not been taught the meaning of irony, but once more he could hardly fail to understand it when it reared up in front of him and smacked him in the face.

All day long, he felt like screaming.

34

Arnold Avery's arm bled on and off all day long on Friday.

Now and then he felt dizzy, but wasn't sure if it was because of the blood loss or the ebbing sugar rush of the cherry Bakewells.

He'd walked until it was dark on Thursday night, and then tried to sleep, but the cold was having none of it. After an hour of sitting hunched, teeth clattering, wrapped in the too-small green cardigan, Avery had got up and continued walking in the dark. It was slower going, but it was going, at least.

Could be worse, he thought. Could be raining.

He felt better for walking. He needed to get to Exmoor before his postcard did. The thought of SL finding WP without him made him feel sick and fluttery.

In the early hours of Friday morning – at about the same time as Uncle Jude had been picking up his truck keys and leaving quietly so as not to wake Steven and Davey – Arnold Avery had reached Tavistock and stolen a car.

It was surprisingly easy.

He'd found several parked cars with their doors unlocked in the driveways of various homes. That's the countryside for you, he'd thought as he ran his hands around their interiors and inside their glove compartments.

One driveway held a scuffed BMW parked behind a small red Nissan hatchback. The hatchback had the keys under the sun visor. The car started on the first turn of the key and, with the BMW blocking his reverse exit, Avery had simply swung the hatchback in a juddering L-plated arc across the front lawn and through the token fence.

In seconds he'd been driving north, hunched spider-like over the wheel in a seat that was adjusted for a very small woman, his knees banging the dash, his heart racing in time to the engine, which – for some panicky reason – he couldn't kick out of third gear.

In a layby he'd levered the seat into a more comfortable position and searched the car. On the back seat was a child's picture book – *The Weird and Wonderful Wombat* – and a box of tissues. There was a toolkit in the boot, along with a tow rope and a plastic bag of women's magazines. He took the magazines out of the bag and put the tow rope in it, along with the wheel brace. He almost closed the boot, then leaned in and picked up a copy of *Cosmopolitan*. He might have a long wait.

As he shut the boot, he was overcome by dizziness and fatigue. It took a huge effort to get back in the car and find the ignition with the keys, but he did it in the end. He turned the Nissan off the main road and drove jerkily down a series of haphazard lanes until he could pull into a field behind a hedge.

Then he crawled into the back seat and slept.

When he woke it was late afternoon and he felt a lot better. His arm still throbbed but had stopped bleeding entirely. His shirt-sleeve was stuck to his arm but he decided to leave well alone.

He drank more water, ate a cheese-and-tomato sandwich, and pissed with abandon into the hedge, enjoying the sensation of the gentle afternoon breeze caressing his penis. It felt like freedom.

Reinvigorated, Arnold Avery set off again, this time triumphing over the vagaries of the Nissan Micra gearbox. Without the scream of the straining engine, his heart slowed to the point where he could think clearly once more.

He tried not to think about what his immediate future held. It was just too distracting. Too exciting.

Instead he tried to concentrate on relearning to drive; on the smell of the hedgerows that slapped against the passenger window now and then; on the smooth black ribbon of road that presented mostly forgotten sights around every corner.

That was exciting enough.

For now.

35

Saturday dawned so still and shrouded in mist that it deadened every sound.

Steven was awake. Had been awake for hours.

He felt sick. He felt happy. He felt butterflies in his stomach, and prickles in his knees that made his legs jump with wanting to run. To run up the track to Blacklands and stake his claim to the body of his dead boy-uncle Billy.

He felt sick again – this time enough to go and bend over the toilet bowl and retch a little. Nothing. He spat into the bowl but didn't flush in case it woke anyone.

He dressed in his favourite clothes. His best socks were ruined – although he hadn't been able to bring himself to throw them away – but everything else was his favourite. The Levi's his mother had got in the charity shop, still dark blue with lack of wear, and the perfect weight on his hips; the red Liverpool shirt with the number 8 on his back and his own name in white over the top of that. It had been a birthday present two years ago. Nan had bought the shirt and Lettie had paid for it to be printed when they went to Barnstaple, £10 for the number, £2 for each letter. She had joked it was lucky that they weren't called Lambinovski and they'd all laughed – even Davey, who didn't know what he was laughing at.

As he dressed (clean underwear and everything), Steven was a little embarrassed to admit even to himself that these were the clothes he wanted his photo taken in for the newspapers when he revealed his find.

This was how he wanted himself to be for posterity.

He looked out of the window. The mist was down but he could tell that behind it the sun was shining. By mid-morning it would have chased the gloom away. Probably. He tied the sleeves of his new boot-sale anorak around his waist anyway. It was the moor; you just never knew.

Downstairs he made a raspberry jam sandwich, clearing up after himself with precision. He put the sandwich and his water bottle into his anorak pockets, feeling them swing against the backs of his thighs.

Outside in the garden, the air was thick, white and still. Steven could hear Mr Randall's shower and, seeming closer than he knew she was, Mrs Hocking singing something soft and off-key – the sound dampened by the moisture in the air but still carried easily to him over the hedges, fences and shrubberies of five gardens.

Picking up his spade made a musical scrape against the concrete that seemed clangingly loud in the motionless air.

Steven had planned to take his spade and go, but instead he went up to the vegetable patch. Walking up the garden made him sad as he thought of Uncle Jude being gone, but once he got there he felt better. Only a few days ago they had repaired the damage, and repaired it well. He could still see Uncle Jude's footprints in the soil's edges, still see the marks his fingers had made where he had pressed the dark earth back down on the rescued seedlings. The evidence of Uncle Jude was still here, even if he himself was not.

Steven realized the evidence of Lewis's betrayal now lingered only in his heart. He glanced automatically towards the back of Lewis's house – to Lewis's bedroom window – and saw movement there, as if a face had been rapidly withdrawn beyond the dark reflection of the glass. Lewis? Maybe. The mist made everything doubtful. Steven watched but nothing reappeared. He shouldered his spade with the practised ease of an old soldier and turned away from the vegetable patch.

As he walked back through the house, he could hear his nan stirring upstairs – the little cough she tried to quell behind her old-lady fingers, the creak of boards under her pale, slippered feet. The thought of leaving her like this – the way she had been for as long as he had known her – and returning to somebody new and wonderful made him ache anew for it soon to be over.

Careful not to bang anything with his spade, Steven left the house and pulled the front door quietly shut behind him.

He was almost at the stile when Lewis caught up to him.

Lewis was out of breath, and Steven was a little at a loss for what to say to him, so for several seconds they just stood and faced each other silently, squirming a little at the awkwardness of it.

Then Lewis glanced at the spade and said: 'Want a hand?'

Part of Steven wanted to shout 'No!' very loudly and with

feeling. But when he opened his mouth, he said: 'I didn't think digging was your thing.'

Lewis's blush deepened and spread to the tips of his ears and down under the neck of his T-shirt. For Steven it was a confirmation and an apology, and he accepted both with a shrug. 'You got something to eat?'

Lewis nodded eagerly and pulled a carrier bag from the pocket of his waterproof. It was folded around some square-ish thing that was probably a sandwich. Steven didn't ask what was in it and Lewis didn't volunteer; they both understood they'd have to work their way up to that again.

'OK then.'

Steven climbed over the stile, which was slippery from the mist, and Lewis followed.

The promise of the dawn faltered as the boys trudged up the hill on to the moor. Fifty yards above the village they broke through the mist briefly, then were enveloped again as the little breeze dragged more off the sea and over the sun.

It wasn't bad. Steven estimated they could see twenty or thirty feet ahead of them. He could tell that the air beyond the mist was warm. It had been an uncommonly clement season and heather and gorse were blooming in slow drifts of mauve and yellow.

Lewis hadn't bothered putting his sandwich away after showing it to Steven, and quickly ate the first, good half. He wrapped the bad half again carefully.

Two hundred yards further up the track, he ate that too.

At the fork, Steven turned left behind the houses instead of his usual right, and Lewis spoke for the first time since the stile.

'Where you going?'

'Blacklands.'

'Why?'

'To dig.'

'I—'

Lewis bit his lip with a squeak, but the words 'told you so' hung in the wet air. No matter. Steven appreciated the act of will it had taken for Lewis to swallow the jibe. They walked on in silence while the sky lightened and the tentative birds finally got the hang of the dawn chorus.

As they approached Blacklands, Steven saw the postcard again in his mind. He had it in his back pocket but he didn't want to get it out in front of Lewis and have to explain things.

He knew from geography lessons what the Friar Tuck hair-cut symbol meant – it marked a rise in the ground. And he also knew exactly where that rise was. It looked very like the burial mounds on Dunkery Beacon – just closer to home. That thought made Steven stop and look back down towards Shipcott. It was invisible – still covered in mist below and behind them.

Another fifteen minutes brought them to the mound at Blacklands and Steven turned again and looked down the moor to where he knew the village lay.

'Why d'you keep stopping?'

Steven didn't answer Lewis. He glanced above them at the mound, remembered the map, the positioning of those initials he'd been so desperate to see.

He started to skirt the rise, zig-zagging a little through the heather. Lewis followed him. The dew was thick on the flowers and their jeans were soaked in seconds.

Lewis shivered. Steven stopped and took his bearings.

Here. About here.

Steven could barely believe that after years of random

digging, he was about to bend to the task with real focus, based on inside information. Of course, there was still a big patch of ground to cover – probably half an acre – but compared to the whole of Exmoor, half an acre was a pinprick. This was the place. Somewhere here, Arnold Avery had buried the uncle he never knew and now he was going to start the task of finding him for real. Steven didn't care how long it took him. Nothing would keep him from returning Uncle Billy to his family.

Far from feeling excited and triumphant, the thought of succeeding suddenly made him overwhelmingly sad. Once more he looked down into the sea of mist and knew that – on a clear day – he'd be able to see his house. Uncle Billy had been buried within sight of his own back yard. His heartbroken mother, who had watched the searchers on TV prodding miles of heather and gorse, could have glanced out of the back bedroom window and seen her son's shallow grave.

Steven shivered and turned away from Shipcott.

'Cold?' Lewis regarded him with sharp eyes.

'Nah.'

'Where we going to dig then?'

'Here, I guess.'

Steven turned a slow circle to pick a spot – and stopped dead.

From a patch of white heather not twenty feet above them, a man was watching.

Steven flinched in surprise.

Then – before the flinch was even over – he felt his bowels loosen in shock as he recognized Arnold Avery.

36

Avery had arrived in Shipcott just after 5am.

Unlike the towns of Bideford and Barnstaple and South Molton, Shipcott had barely changed. No new road layouts, no mini-roundabouts, no one-way systems. The one in Barnstaple had stolen damn near half the night from him as he looped and reversed and came at the town square what felt like a dozen times from different directions.

Finally he'd stopped at a newsagent's shop, donned the green cardigan to hide the blood on his sleeve, bought a *Daily Mirror* and asked directions.

Then he'd gone back to the car and stared at the face on the front page under the headline: CHILD KILLER ON THE RUN. The photo was a small fuzzy thing he'd been used to seeing clipped to Dr Leaver's file. Dr Leaver himself had taken the picture at their first session, and Dr Leaver had been wise to go into abnormal psychiatry because his photography skills left a lot to be desired.

Not for the first time, Arnold Avery thanked god for incompetence, but felt a pang. Had he missed his chance? If he was on the front pages today, then surely he must've been yesterday? Maybe SL knew he was out, or had been warned not to leave the house.

He suppressed the desperation that that thought sparked in him and checked out his face in the rear-view mirror. He looked only vaguely like the photo on the front page of the *Mirror* and, even if it had been a dead ringer, most people were not observant. Avery remembered that from before – remembered all the times he could have been stopped, if only people had kept their eyes open, made connections, believed their guts.

Nobody did. Sometimes he felt invisible.

Circling North Devon in a confusion of new roads had run his petrol low and he pulled into a service station. As he wrestled increasingly stupidly with the buttons and hoses and multiple choices, he had prepared a cover story about being French. But the bleary-eyed boy at the Pay window barely looked at him, saving Avery a smile, a lie and a bad accent.

Once he was in Shipcott he knew exactly where he was going.

He drove past Mr Jacoby's shop and noticed that it was a Spar now. Globalization comes to Exmoor, he thought with a wry little smile. The shop wasn't open yet, and piles of bound newspapers lay outside, waiting to be sorted and sold so that the residents of Shipcott could hold his fuzzy face in their hands and be guarded against him.

He drove through the sleeping village. At the turning to a dead-end street he noticed that he was on Barnstaple Road and his heart started to race even as he slowed to a crawl, peering at the houses, their colours distorted to variations on peach by the sodium glow of the streetlamps in the dull grey of dawn.

Number 109 . . . 110 . . . 111.

Avery stopped the car without bothering to pull into the kerb, and stared at the house where SL lived.

Many years ago he had played poker. He hadn't known what he was doing really and was nervous of losing and making a fool of himself. But it was only when he picked up a pair of aces and saw another two drop on to the table that he'd started to shake. That was how he knew that the trembling that now coursed through his hands, over his shoulders and across his cheeks to his lips was a good thing. He held an unbeatable hand.

As the car ticked over, Avery stared at the black windows of the tatty little house and imagined SL asleep inside it; imagined creeping up the stairs and opening each bedroom door noiselessly so he could stare down at the occupants, until he found SL, lying unwary and weak and at his mercy . . .

Avery whimpered and jerked his imagination back from the brink. He was too close to reality to waste effort on speculation. If the worst had come to the worst and he was too late, then maybe he would have to return to 111 Barnstaple Road and take his chances. But for now . . . The spectre of the carelessness that had ended his divine pastime loomed large over Avery and kept him behind the wheel when he might otherwise have ventured on to the kerb, the narrow pavement, through an unfastened window . . .

That loss of control had haunted him for eighteen years. He wasn't going to repeat that mistake.

He left the village behind quickly and drove out to a farm access track a few hundred yards beyond it. It was so overgrown that he passed it three times before recognizing the dark tunnel through the hedge and turning in. The Micra bumped and squeaked across the grass and potholes and the paintwork squealed in protest as it was ruined by brambles and blackthorn.

When he could drive no further, Avery got out with his bag of new supplies, popped a bottle of water and several cheese-and-tomato sandwiches into it, and walked up on to the moor.

He was immediately hit by a sensory overload composed of sweet dew-sodden heather and the memory of the soft weight of a boy in his arms. The two-pronged assault left him momentarily faint with excitement and he had to stop and bend over with his hands on his knees until his breathing evened out.

He had to stay focused. Avery had no illusions about his future. He knew he could not stay on the run for long – especially after what he had planned. While he had worked so hard and waited so long for his legitimate release, he had no experience of – or desire for – the life of a fugitive. After the event, his life would effectively be over. His only objective now was to stay in control long enough to make his fleeting freedom worthwhile.

Slowly he felt the rush subside, and that control return to him. He knew he would have to be on his guard; the thrill of the moor alone was almost overwhelming. Coupled with the memory of this overgrown track and the possibilities that lay ahead, the sheer effort it took to remain calm brought Avery out in a sweat. His arm tingled and ached where the mystery groove had opened his flesh, and he felt a little light-headed but he ignored it; he thought it looked worse than it was and he didn't care if he was wrong; it wasn't going to stop him. Nothing would.

He started up the hill again. His thoughts battered noisily at the smoked glass of his mind, desperate to be set free and run on ahead like yapping puppies. Avery was almost deafened by the ruckus. He took a deep breath and started to count backwards from a thousand.

982 . . . 981 . . . 980 . . . 989 . . .

He stopped and started again from the top.

So, concentrating on getting the numbers right, Avery managed to stay in control all the way to Blacklands.

He found the mound easily.

There was mist in the valley below, hiding Shipcott, but up here the air was clear and might soon be bright.

The last of the night had faded and left a pale, blank sky into which the sun crept lazily from under the horizon.

Avery climbed to the top of the mound and looked down.

The excitement bubbled up in him and he clenched his knuckles white and ground them into his own thighs to stay sane for a little while longer.

He wasn't sure he could do it.

He whined and bit his lip. His breathing was jagged in his chest and his heart bumped loudly in his ears and sinuses.

Right here. He was right here. A place he thought he might never be again. Everything was worth it. If they rushed him now and dragged him off the moor on a bed of fire, it would have been worth it – just to stand here and smell the wet heather and the dank earth beneath it.

Avery tasted blood where his lip leaked into his mouth. He didn't know how he would stop his head bursting with need, but he knew he had to. He wanted this feeling to last as long as he could make it; knew it could get even better if he were very, very lucky.

But right now he had to keep a lid on things. He had to get a grip.

He squeezed his eyes shut to blot out the overwhelming visual stimulation.

Don't blow it.

Don't blow it.

Don't blow it.

Whining, sweating and trembling with effort, Avery slowly regained dominion over Exmoor and his own body.

His whining tapered, he stopped gasping for every breath; his fists loosened, leaving half-moon cuts in his palms like little stigmata.

He felt the dawn air filling him to bursting with life and self-possession. The sun made him shiver with anticipation, while the first skylark sang his praises.

When he finally opened his eyes, he felt like god.

Calm. Patient. Controlled.

Powerful. Vengeful.

He spread a plastic bag in a patch of wet white heather and sat gently, feeling the moor embrace him like an old lover.

And an hour later, when the boys rose up towards him through the mist, Avery's eyes blurred with the sheer beauty of it all.

They were like angels emerging from a cloud so he could welcome them into heaven.

37

'Hello,' said Lewis.

'Hello,' said Arnold Avery, serial killer.

Steven said nothing. What could he say? *Hey, Lewis, don't talk to him – he murdered my uncle Billy . . .*

Anything Steven said right now would require so much explanation, and so many questions from Lewis, that he wouldn't be able to think straight. And something told him that this was a point in his life when straight thinking was going to be critical.

He'd already nearly given himself away, but had looked across the heather just in time, before Avery could see the shock of recognition on his face.

Now, as he regarded the moor with eyes that saw nothing but dead newsprint children, Steven's mind spun in pointless overlapping circles. A Venn diagram of confusion. How could this be? This was impossible. Arnold Avery was in prison, not here. Here was where *Steven* was supposed to be, not *Avery*. Possibilities far crazier than mere escape raced through his head – a dream, a drug-induced hallucination, a Hollywood body-swap, a reality TV show to gauge the reaction of boys meeting their worst nightmare. It took half a second that felt like half a lifetime before he came to the idea of escape and settled there uneasily. It was the worst of the options.

Gradually the wild rush of adrenalin subsided to manageable levels. His breathing was still uncertain but at least he wasn't about to soil himself. He glanced back at Avery. It was definitely him. He questioned himself closely on this point – wanting to have made a mistake – but he was sure. Steven supposed that the context and the occasion had primed him to recognize the killer, even though Avery was the last person he'd expected to see.

Still, he had the advantage: Avery didn't know Steven and therefore had no reason to believe that Steven would know him. If he was to maintain that advantage, he had to act normal.

Taking a deep, shuddery breath, Steven forced his head back around and blinked at the sheer reality of the man who had filled his life for so long, right here, sat above them on a bed of less common white heather, his forearms resting casually on his knees, his jeans rising from his black work boots enough so that Steven could see his cheap blue cotton socks.

He stared at Avery's socks and felt an odd sense of wonder.

Socks were so normal. So mundane. How could someone who pulled on socks in the morning be a serial killer? Socks were not hard or dangerous. Socks were funny; foot mittens, that's what socks were. They made a knobbly hinge of your toes and became comical sock-puppets. Surely anyone who wore socks could not truly be a threat to him or anyone else?

Steven realized they were both looking at him while he stared at the socks. Lewis looked puzzled and Avery quirked an amused eyebrow at him, as if they shared a secret.

Which they did, of course.

Steven reddened. He had to act *normal*. If Avery had any idea he knew who he was . . .

Steven didn't finish the thought; it was too frightening.

The silence was a physical thing between them. Avery was used to silence and Steven was reluctant to puncture the still-ness until he had some idea of what he might say.

So it was left to Lewis to take the lead, as always.

'Nice day.' The perennial favourite of walkers.

Avery nodded slowly. 'So far.'

Steven shivered and Lewis frowned at him, like he was somehow letting the side down.

'We're digging,' offered Lewis, jutting his jaw at Steven's spade.

'Oh yes?' enquired Avery coolly. 'What for?'

Lewis had talked himself into a little corner. On any other day he'd have told the stranger, Steven knew. He'd have blabbed and then watched the stranger's reaction; if it had been awe, Lewis would have taken credit for the joint oper-ation; if it had been disgust, Lewis would have rolled his eyes and jerked a thumb at him.

But because this was their first time back together – and because a strange, unspoken shift had taken place in their relationship – Lewis seemed uncertain of whether to reveal their true mission.

Lewis looked at Steven and was surprised to see his friend was even more pale than usual. Steven looked sick. But still,

it was Steven who now picked up the conversational baton.
'Orchids.'

Avery only raised his brow again. This time Lewis almost
joined him. Steven ignored it. 'Sell them to the garden
centre.'

Avery eyed him carefully. 'Isn't that illegal?'

'Yes.'

Lewis shot a worried look at Steven and then at the man,
but the man didn't look too perturbed by the revelation.

In fact, he shrugged and almost smiled – just the tips of
prominent teeth breaking out briefly before being recaptured
by his ruby lips.

'Oh well,' he said.

There was another lumpy silence.

'Are there any round here?'

'Any what?' said Lewis.

'Any—' Avery cleared his throat politely, his fist in front of
his mouth. 'Any orchids.'

Lewis flickered a sidelong glance at Steven. He'd got them
into this – he could bloody well get them out.

'No,' said Steven, scanning the ground. 'We should go.'

'Don't.'

Both boys looked up at the man. Lewis thought that was
strange – saying 'Don't' like that. Most people you met on the
moors couldn't wait to have you walk away and disappear and
restore their illusion of splendid isolation. But this man said
'Don't' as if he really didn't want them to leave.

Lewis was not a sensitive boy, but he felt the first vague
itch that told him something was not quite right.

Arnold Avery had recognized SL immediately – the shape of
him – from the photograph.

Now SL stood before him with his anorak tied around his whippety waist, his bony arms projecting from a red T-shirt, his dark hair poorly home-cut, his body turned slightly away.

On the back of his T-shirt was the word LAMB. The boy's name was S. Lamb.

Lamb.

He had to keep from laughing.

Now S. Lamb and his more robust friend were both looking at him because he'd said 'Don't' in that stupid, needy way.

A flash of Mason Dingle and a bawling child. Avery was angry with himself, but controlled it so it wouldn't show.

He had to be careful. There were two of them. S. Lamb had a spade slung over his shoulder. They were older than most of the others. Bigger than he remembered children to be. He'd said 'Don't' and both of them had looked up in surprise.

He had to be careful.

He had to smile.

So he did, and saw the rounder boy's face relax immediately. He was not unattractive.

S. Lamb glanced at him but still looked pinched and wary. Understandable, thought Avery – a strange man on the moors; a boy *should* be on his guard. He was proud of SL's open suspicion, and felt a little better about the way he'd been played by a boy. At least it wasn't a stupid boy.

'I'm sorry,' he said, 'my name's Tim.' He looked pointedly at the bigger boy until he cracked and said: 'I'm Lewis. He's Steven.'

'Nice to meet you.'

Steven Lamb. Avery dared only a brief glance and nod at Steven Lamb because he did not want to telepathically transmit the images in his head – images of Steven Lamb's

dark eyes bulging from their sockets in terror; of his own
fingers around Steven Lamb's slender throat as the blood rose
like geysers in both of them, but for different reasons; of a
scant but ironic map of Exmoor with the initials SL forever
beside WP.

'I have sandwiches.' Avery reached past the tow rope to get
them and added, more casually: 'If you want.'

Lewis did want.

Of course.

Steven watched Lewis close the distance between himself
and Arnold Avery. He held his breath as Lewis reached for the
sandwich. His warning shout caught in his throat as Lewis's
hand almost touched Avery's.

Nothing happened except that Lewis got a sandwich.
Steven grunted in relief.

Avery looked at him now, holding out another sandwich.

This was it. This was the moment when Steven had to
decide. To take the killer's sandwich, or to fling aside his
spade, turn, and run back down the moor to home.

It was Barnstaple all over again. Without Lewis, he could
have run. Taken Avery by surprise and outdistanced him. The
man was fifteen feet away, and seated. Steven could have
thirty yards on him before he stood up and started running.
He was fast and had no doubt that fear would make him
faster.

But with Lewis? Lewis was eating the man's sandwich; if
he suddenly yelled a warning and turned tail, Lewis would be
confused. He wouldn't run. And even if he did run, he
wouldn't realize he was running for his life. The very act of
running would tell Avery that Steven had recognized him.

Even if Avery didn't catch *him*, he'd catch Lewis for sure.

And Steven couldn't leave Lewis in the hands of a serial killer.

Steven throbbed with guilt at his own stupidity. He had baited a trap for Avery and fallen into it himself. Now he felt wholly responsible for Lewis's safety as well as his own.

No, running was not an option.

So, Steven willed his legs to move, forced his hands to reach, ordered his lips to mumble 'Thank you' as he took the sandwich from the man he now knew planned to kill him.

38

The sandwich was cheese and tomato. Steven grimaced at the first bite but swallowed anyway, not wanting to provoke Avery.

Lewis's defences were down now that he was eating again. He told Avery about the moor – making up what he wasn't sure of – and Avery nodded and listened and asked pertinent questions.

Steven was dimly aware of Lewis swelling proudly under Avery's attention. Some part of him felt sick at the ease with which Avery made Lewis relax and open up to him.

But most of him – all the important parts – was churning with a million flashing images: biro crosses on a map; a single white pixel of buck teeth; the Lego space station in the gloomy blue bedroom; the smell of the earth; the taste of it in his mouth; the tooth wobbling in the sheep's jaw; running across the moor with his heart in his mouth; legs kicking through an open van window; his nan waiting. Forever waiting.

And this was the image that finally stopped the crazy spinning in his head. His nan waiting for Billy, and waiting for him. He'd wanted so much to put an end to her misery, but he was only going to make it worse. Arnold Avery was going to kill him and then his nan would be waiting for both of them for ever, and his mother would become his nan at the window, waiting as she had, even after Nan was dead.

And Davey? What would happen to Davey? Davey wasn't used to being ignored but he would be, and he had nobody else in the world who loved him. All of the people who loved him would be gone – or as good as.

Steven felt sick.

He'd fucked up. Fuck. He'd fucked up. He was a stupid fuck. Fuck.

Fuck was not a big or bad enough word for what he was, but it would have to do for now. What had made him think he could do this? He was so stupid he deserved to be murdered, but he felt bad for Nan and Mum and Davey and Lewis.

Then he remembered what he was here for. Why he'd started this in the first place. And why he couldn't leave now . . .

He shuddered at the horror of that truth.

'Cold?'

Steven jerked as Avery spoke, and realized he was shaking.

'Yeah.' He was also gripping his sandwich so tight that his fingers had gone through the bread and he could feel the hated wet tomato like slime on his fingertips.

'Want a jumper?'

Avery took off the pale green cardigan and Steven noticed

it matched his strange, washed-out eyes. The last eyes Uncle Billy ever looked into.

His throat closed and he made another attempt before he could squeeze out: 'No.'

Avery regarded him coolly and Steven looked at his messed-up sandwich, feeling his cheeks burn under the scrutiny.

From the corner of his eye, he saw Avery's right hand loosen from the cardigan and move towards him. He watched the goosebumps stand up on the flesh of his own arm, and then the gentle touch of the man's finger on his cheek.

'You have butter on your face.'

Steven's stomach rolled and he burped softly and remembered that he'd eaten tomato.

Remembered Yasmin Gregory's Tuesday knickers.

Remembered that what the newspaper referred to vaguely as 'bodily fluids' disgusted Avery.

Hand shaking, and already slightly queasy, Steven braced himself and took another bite of sandwich.

Avery withdrew his hand and licked the butter off his forefinger with a quick pink tongue.

'What happened to your arm?'

Lewis was staring at the blood on Avery's torn shirtsleeve which he'd exposed by taking off the cardigan. Avery looked down at it and felt another pang of self-loathing. He was so careless! What was he thinking? Being reminded of his arm also made him feel woozy and tired. He hadn't lost a lot of blood but the arm throbbed more now than it had yesterday. Perhaps it was becoming infected. It was bad, bad luck. Just when he wanted – needed – to be at the top of his game physically as well as mentally. And now the freckled boy was staring at it – only curious right now, but Avery knew that curiosity was a micro-step from suspicion and fear and flight.

Or attempted flight.

Inwardly he grinned at a slew of memories of attempted flight and gathered inner strength from those.

'Got it caught on barbed wire coming up here,' he told Lewis.

Lewis nodded slowly. The sandwich had made him forget that he'd felt uneasy about Avery, but now that his mouth had done its work his brain was re-engaging – and something about the barbed-wire story didn't ring true. Not least the fact that there was no barbed wire on the moor. Surrounding farms had barbed wire, sure, but he couldn't think of a nearby route on to the moor where anyone would have to negotiate any-thing more than a stone or wooden stile.

He got up and wiped his hands on his jeans.

'Thanks, mate,' he said. Then he looked at Steven: 'We should go.'

Steven chewed, hating every second, then swallowed big chunks, his eyes watering.

'You go,' he said.

'Huh?'

'You go,' he said quickly, before he could lose his nerve. 'I'll stay.'

Lewis gave a confused laugh and glanced at Avery, who was looking at Steven with an odd expression on his face.

Steven was white, with two burning patches high on his cheeks, his eyes fixed on his sandwich. Lewis noticed he was trembling. He also noticed that the sandwich Steven was eat-ing had tomato in it. As he watched, Steven took another bite and sloppily sucked a bit of errant tomato into his mouth.

Something was very wrong with his friend.

'C'mon, Steve!' He laughed again but it sounded so odd to

his own ears that he cut it short, leaving a strained silence in its wake.

He'd been engrossed in his own sandwich but now he saw that Avery was squeezing the green cardigan between his hands, twisting and crushing it, his knuckles white with tension. His vague sense of unease became an ache in his belly.

'C'mon, you divvy. I got to be back soon.' It wasn't true, of course, but Lewis suddenly felt the overwhelming need to be at home.

Steven hurled what was left of his sandwich at Lewis, hitting him in the chest.

'Just fucking *go*, will you! Just fucking *go*!'

Lewis's eyes were round with surprise. He took a step backwards.

Steven got up, shaking, and closed the gap between them. 'I know what you did to the garden.'

Lewis flushed deep red. 'W-what?'

'You heard me. I know what you did. Now fuck *off*!'

Steven shoved Lewis in the chest with the shaft of the spade, making him stumble backwards down the mound. Steven came after him and shoved again. Lewis fell on to his backside in the heather, and panic burst on Steven's face. He grabbed Lewis by the shoulder, trying to lift him and push him away at the same time. Lewis stumbled once, twice; Steven screamed over him: 'I hate you! I fucking hate you! Just piss off home! Just *go*!'

Bits of sandwich and spittle fell on to Lewis from Steven's furious mouth. He scrambled to his feet and Steven came at him again. This time Lewis skipped out of the way down the track.

'Are you nuts?' he yelled at Steven. 'Are you pigging crazy?' Again he glanced at the man – as if for support.

'He's nuts!' Lewis yelled, but the man was not looking at him. He was looking at Steven; his red, red lips had drawn back to reveal his sharp white teeth in a grimace of concentration. More than Steven's sudden attack, that sight made Lewis's insides lurch dizzily and suddenly he had to get away. Had to. Couldn't stay another second. Primeval fear gripped him and he cried out as if struck – then turned and ran.

Steven watched him go, feeling the thread of his life unravelling and trailing down the track behind his friend as if caught on his heel, leaving him with nothing but a black, hollow chest and bits of bloody tomato free-floating in his rolling gut.

He felt Avery swishing slowly down the hill behind him, wet heather stroking his ankles, a knife, a rope, a gun at the ready.

A shudder passed through him and he spun round on a sob.

Avery hadn't moved.

For a long moment they regarded each other. Steven pushed tears of panic out of his eyes with the heel of his hand, feeling how strange was the disconnection that allowed him to think that Avery would attribute them to his row with Lewis. It was almost as if his mind had unravelled a bit too far and was now able to consider his own actions from a little way off. The coldness of that scared him but he clung to it nonetheless – it was almost like having someone else in his head, someone else to make decisions – and it was the only thing keeping him from curling into a ball of pissing terror in the heather to await the inevitable.

'You OK?'

Steven nodded, biting his lip. There was more silence.

Avery stood up and brushed the seat of his pants carefully, then made his way down the mound.

Steven saw that the man's jeans were soaked to the knees and it made him aware that his own were the same, cold and stiff against his shins.

His nerve endings twitched, jumped, screamed to turn and run.

But he just stood there and waited for the killer to come to him.

Why?

The voice observing him demanded an answer. Steven didn't have one, just a buzzing jumble of words and images like the pieces of a jigsaw when the box was first opened. He knew that those random pieces made a picture – a country garden, sailing ships, puppies in a basket – but the pieces in his head were fragments and some were turned face-down and it would take more than a demanding voice to assemble them into something coherent. Something useful.

Avery stood so close to him now that Steven had to look up into his face.

'What was that all about?'

His voice was kind and his expression was sympathetic. His features were making all the right moves, but his eyes were elsewhere, thinking other things.

He put a cold hand on Steven's shoulder.

Lewis could not remember running; he could only remember being on the moor and suddenly being off it.

He had eaten the good half of too many sandwiches to be a fit boy, but adrenalin filled his lungs and squeezed his heart more efficiently than any conditioning that could have gone before or would ever come again.

The stile at the bottom of the track scraped his shins and tore his knee as he barely broke stride to clear it.

He turned left on to the narrow, still-misty street – the only one of any note through Shipcott – and wondered at the way his frantic footfalls smacked sharply and echoed off the canyon of bright, bow-walled cottages.

Lewis had no idea why he was scared, and so he worried about how to impart his fear to anyone who could help him. But he knew he would have to try, because instinctively he knew this was not a job for a secret agent or a sniper, or even a famous footballer.

This was a job for a grown-up.

It was early on a Saturday morning but the mist gave Shipcott a dead, eerie feeling and the street was unusually empty. He rounded the short curve in the road and saw why.

There was a little knot of people outside Steven's house, spilling off the narrow pavement and into the road.

Grown-up people. Thank god.

Lewis almost cried with relief.

Lettie was in the bathroom when the knock came on the door. At the first rap she frowned, wondering who it could be so early on a Saturday. But then she frowned because it wasn't really knocking; it was pounding. Pounding of the type Lettie had only ever seen on TV where the drunken husband goes round to confront his errant wife's new lover. Pounding like police.

It scared her, angered her and galvanized her all at the same time.

She hurried downstairs and opened the door a crack, her left hand holding her robe closed, not because she was afraid it would swing open, but to let the pounder know that she disapproved of his rudeness.

It was Mr Jacoby. Holding a newspaper.

Lettie experienced a second of complete disorientation during which she wondered whether they now had a newspaper delivered and, if so, why they had ordered the *Daily Mail*, and – even stranger – why Mr Jacoby was making the deliveries himself instead of leaving it to Ronnie Trewell, who seemed to have spent at least ten of his fourteen years trudging up and down in the rain with a Dayglo sack pulling him so badly off-centre that, without clearly marked pavements, he would have just wandered around in circles all day.

'Mr Jacoby,' she said neutrally so that she could smile or frown as the ensuing occasion required.

To her surprise, Mr Jacoby held up the paper in shaking, newsprint-blackened hands, opened his mouth as if to tell her something of great importance – and burst into tears.

Davey was surrounded by legs. It was nothing new; when you're five, legs are your constant companions. When you're five your whole experience of gatherings consists of pulled seams, rubbed crotches, bulging thighs, scuffed knees, trailing hems.

But this was extreme. He was on the pavement outside his house trying to stay at his mother's side as people pressed all around them to see the *Daily Mail*. Legs nudged him, bumped him, propelled him this way and that.

Now and then a hand would reach out to steady him and apologize, but nobody spoke to him or looked at him – everything in this jungle of legs was going on in the canopy over his head. He gripped Lettie's ratty blue towelling robe and felt her warm thigh under his knuckles.

His mother wasn't crying but Mr Jacoby was. Davey had never seen a man cry before – never imagined that such a thing was even possible – and found it so disturbing that he tried not to see or hear it but couldn't stop looking. Big Mr Jacoby in his green Spar shirt and his wobbly chest and his hairy arms, crying. Davey laughed nervously, hoping it was a joke – but nobody joined in. He gripped more tightly on to his mother.

People were talking grown-up talk very forcefully but very secretly and Davey could only catch fragments. The fragment he heard most often was 'It'll kill her.'

Kill who? thought Davey desperately. What will kill who?

'Can't keep it secret . . . has to know some time . . . don't show it . . . it'll kill her.'

And through it all, Mr Jacoby cried his strange, wheezing, blubbery cry, while Lewis's dad patted his shoulder, looking cross, but not with Mr Jacoby. To Davey it looked like Mr Jacoby was a giant toddler that someone had bullied off the swings and Lewis's dad was taking care of him while trying to spot the culprit to give him a good telling-off.

'Don't tell who what?'

They all looked up guiltily at Nan. Davey couldn't see her through the legs but knew it was her. No one said anything.

'Don't tell who what?' she said again, a little more suspiciously.

Davey thought someone was clapping. A slow, sharp slapping sound getting closer and closer, and suddenly the sound skidded to a halt as the people around him surged and parted to reveal a red-faced, wild-eyed Lewis.

Lewis could barely speak. He saw his father.

'Dad!'

'Quiet, Lewis. We're talking.'

'But Dad!'

'Lewis, go home!'

His father looked away from him and the gathering turned its back on the boy and reshaped itself, nudging him to its edge like an amoeba egesting waste.

Mr Trewell, Skew Ronnie's dad, was holding the *Sun* and Lewis saw the face on the front of it. It wasn't right, but somehow he recognized it. Those red, red lips gave it away. Lewis sucked air into his depleted lungs and shouted 'FUCK!' as loudly as he could.

The word skittered off the walls and everyone turned and looked at him angrily. He just jabbed the picture.

'That's him! That's the man who's on the moor!'

There was a stunned silence while anger turned to confusion, so he took advantage to explain further.

'With Steven.'

39

Steven flinched when Avery put a hand on his shoulder but he turned it into a shrug and thought he had got away with that.

He answered Avery's question with 'Nothing.' Then he turned away so he wouldn't have to look into Avery's strangely flickering eyes.

Instead Steven looked longingly back down the moor to where he knew Shipcott was hiding in the mist. Not being able to see even the church spire made him feel very alone.

As he stood with his prickling back to the killer, the jigsaw pieces in Steven's mind whirled and spun. Bits he recognized: a slice of Uncle Billy's wide grin; a shakily traced map; a dent made in the moor by the blade of a blunt spade; *on the box it said it was a fillit*. He wrote a good letter. The pieces floated and scattered; he didn't know where to start with them. So, like all good jigsaw builders, he started by finding a corner.

And that corner – to his utter surprise – was anger.

He'd thought his fear was all-embracing, but the anger was good. It anchored him and trumped fear for a moment and made him feel stronger.

Lewis was gone. Safe. Steven felt a pang that the last words he'd said to his friend had been harsh but shoved the pang aside. He'd done what he had to. This was his mess and so he'd taken care of Lewis.

Now all he had to do was escape the clutches of the psychopath who had baited his own little trap and then – in some crazy, nightmarish way – magicked his way out of prison and come here to kill him.

Harry Potter with a chainsaw.

Steven laughed and shuddered at the same time, and felt bile sour his throat.

He swallowed hard and felt weak. He knew that if escape was all he wanted, he'd have taken his chance by now. He'd started this thing; he'd set it in motion. Now it was moving too fast and out of control, but Steven still felt a burning, jealous need to keep hold of it. All the thinking; all the digging, all the planning; all the good letters he had written. He was so close that the thought of letting go now was at once un-conscionable and so alluring that it made him think of tongues and Chantelle Cox. It would be so easy to let go, feel his cramped fingers creak open and release the burden he'd picked up so casually and carried for so long without ever really having a good grip on it.

But the stubborn streak that had kept him soaked, sun-burned and callused on the moor for three long years elbowed its way to the fore, trampling the dizzy panic Steven felt at overriding every instinct he possessed.

Now that it was just him and the killer alone, one thread of thought separated itself and pulsated more urgently than any other: he'd tried so long. He'd come so far. He'd done so much. He was so tired and he wanted to know. He needed to know. He *had* to know.

Which meant that – instead of hitting him with the spade and running for his life – he smiled at Avery.

'Fuck him,' he shrugged. 'You got any more sandwiches?'

Steven watched the mist creep up the heather towards them. It was only forty or fifty feet below them now, moving so sluggishly it was almost imperceptible. By ten, it would be summer.

Avery had put down a second plastic bag for him to sit on – so close that their hips and shoulders were touching and he could feel the warmth of the man through his jeans and bloody shirt. It made him itch to move away, but he didn't.

Now Steven stared at the last bit of Avery's sandwich and knew that if he didn't speak soon, his chance would be gone.

'You live around here?'

'No. Do you?'

'Yeah. Down in Shipcott. Over there.' He waved a vague hand at the sluggish mist.

Avery made a grunt of non-interest, then looked round at Steven.

'I heard there's bodies up here.'

A jolt of pure electricity pulsed through Steven. His heart flared with it and he felt the tingles and crackles all over his skin.

Avery smiled with his mouth. 'You OK?'

'Yeah,' said Steven. 'Bodies. Creepy.'

He concentrated on a piece of tomato dropping out of the back of the crust and took his time stuffing it into his mouth, licking his fingers and chewing without tasting the watery mess. He waited for his heart to stop pummelling his chest, but it didn't slow.

This was what he wanted. What he'd been waiting for. And he hadn't even had to ask. Bodies. He was excited and terrified in equal measure.

'Yeah,' said Avery. 'I heard some nut killed some people – kids – and buried them out here.'

'Oh yeah. I heard that.' He wished his heart would stop pounding – he was scared Avery would hear it.

'He strangled them.'

Steven nodded, trying to stay calm.

Avery lowered his voice. 'Raped them too. Even the boys.'

Steven tried to clear his throat. Tomato stuck in it. 'Did they find them all?'

'No.'

Steven felt faint. Not 'I don't think so'; not 'I'm not sure'. Just 'no'.

'There's a few still out here, I reckon,' said Avery.

A few.

Paul Barrett. Mariel Oxenburg. William Peters.

'Yeah?' he said. 'Like where?'

Just like that, Steven asked the question. He felt giddy with anticipation.

Avery looked off towards Dunkery Beacon. 'Why do you care?'

Time slowed into a strange sucking vortex for Steven as the reasons why he cared nearly overwhelmed him. A spinning wheel of fortune and the suffocating press of frozen mud around a small boy's lonely bones.

'I don't care,' he said, and his voice cracked in his tense throat. 'I'm just interested in . . . I mean . . . if you were going to bury a body out here, where would it be?'

He'd hoped for casual but his question sounded horribly loud and desperate to his ears as it hung over them in the still morning air. He felt sick that he'd asked it. Sick and clammy.

Avery turned to look at him carefully and Steven met his eyes, hoping the man couldn't see through them into the dark pit of fluttering fear that lay behind.

The silence stretched out around them until Steven could swear he felt it creak under the strain.

Then Avery merely shrugged. 'Around. About. Who knows?' He smiled a little smile at Steven and dug about in the bag. 'You want something to drink?'

Steven wanted to kill him.

He jerked to his feet. He picked up his spade to go, but Avery gripped the shaft hard and looked up at him, his face suddenly cold and dangerous.

'I'm going to need that,' said Avery quietly.

And when he looked into the man's milky green eyes, Steven knew he'd lost the battle to keep the book of his mind closed – and Avery's ruby lips split into a crooked white grin as he read the boy like a billboard.

Steven cried out as if he'd touched something dark and slimy.

He let go of the spade, making it rebound hard into Avery's bloody arm.

Then he turned and ran.

As he hit the track, he heard Avery come after him – close, too close, he should've made his move before, when he'd have had a head start! – then he felt a sharp pain in his back and fell to the ground, winded.

He felt Avery grip the back of his best T-shirt and lift him like a bad puppy; his feet scrabbled for purchase as he almost staggered upright, then collapsed sideways to his knees against the man's legs.

Still gripping his shirt, Avery stooped to pick up the spade and Steven's remote brain informed him dully that that was what had hit him in the back. Uncle Jude's spade. Felled by his own weapon just as he'd been caught in his own trap.

Because he was just a stupid, stupid boy. Not a sniper, not a cop, not even a grown-up. He'd played at being a grown-up and this was how it was ending. Him dead on the moor in his best red T-shirt with Lamb on the back. And the papers reporting not his triumph but his pathetic, lonely, weak little-boy death. A death that would reduce him to initials on a map and a blurry old photo in a fading newspaper. Not even a good photo, he'd bet. Probably the one from school that Mum had on the mantelpiece, which made him look like a refugee. Not the photo he'd dressed for this morning when he still thought he could be a hero.

Fear, shame and nausea mingled inside him and he sagged against Avery's cold jeans.

Avery pulled him away and slapped his face.

'You know who I am?'

Steven nodded dumbly at Avery's black rubber-soled shoes.

'Good.'

He yanked Steven to his feet and half pushed, half dragged him back up the mound, wincing and cursing at the newly opened pain in his arm. Halfway up, Steven started to sob. He wished he didn't know about Arnold Avery. Knowing was worse than not knowing. Knowing what he'd done to the others. Knowing that he'd do that to him too. It didn't even seem possible – what Avery had done – but he'd read it in the papers so it must be true. He was about to find out. The thought drew fresh tears of fear.

'Shut up,' said Avery. 'And get down.'

Steven just stood, arms slack, head down, hitching with sobs.

'I said get down.' Avery shook him again and pointed at the patch of white heather where he'd been sitting, back when Steven had still had a choice; still had a chance of escape.

'Down?' Steven sounded confused. He *was* confused; the word 'down' seemed just a noise to him. It did not compute.

'Down. On your knees.'

Steven nodded stupidly but did not get down.

Avery leaned forward and put his lips close to Steven's ear, making him shudder.

'Get down or I'll make you.'

'OK.' But he still didn't move. Couldn't. Wouldn't. Shouldn't. Standing up was better. Getting down was worse. The lower he got, the less chance he had. He'd prefer to stay standing. These thoughts were simple and definite in Steven's head. Once he got down, he felt sure he'd never get up again.

'*Down*, I said!'

'OK.' He stopped sobbing on a soft burp that brought tomato-flavoured bile to his throat.

But he still didn't move. Maybe if he just kept agreeing to get down but didn't actually do it, Avery would get bored with asking.

Avery did get bored with asking. Steven only heard a small grunt of warning before the spade swung into the backs of his knees, making him roll into ball, clutching at his legs in agony.

'You little shit!' Avery clutched and grimaced at his own arm – wet with fresh blood.

Then once more Avery pulled him up by the scruff, positioning him carefully on his knees.

'Now stay there. Understand?'

Steven nodded and swayed but stayed where he was. He could feel a little trickle down his back and thought it must be sweat or blood where the spade had hit him when he tried to run. No sooner had he thought about sweat than he felt his face go tingly as sweat broke out on him. He swayed again; he wanted to lie down in the heather where it was cool and he wouldn't feel so dizzy. But kneeling was bad and lying down would be lower and therefore even worse. He had to try to hang on, although quite what he was hanging on for, he was afraid to examine too closely. He had to hang on, and he had to try to make Avery move as slowly as possible towards killing him. Not because he thought he could avoid it entirely, but because delaying his own death seemed the sensible thing to do.

His own death.

He was going to die. He had nothing left to lose, not even his life; it was a foregone conclusion. The thought brought with it a kind of perverse freedom.

'Did you kill my uncle Billy?'

'What do you think?'

Steven looked up at Avery in surprise. He hadn't expected to be asked his opinion.

'I think you did.'

'You want to know how?'

Steven didn't. He felt sick at the thought of knowing how. But it was another delay.

'Yes.'

Avery stood in front of him now and touched his hair with one hand, almost gently.

'He'd just come out of the shop. I asked him for directions. I had a map . . .'

He stopped and Steven looked up and saw the gleam of fond memory in Avery's eyes.

'I had a map. I asked him to show me on the map. And he leaned in the window and I . . . just . . . grabbed him—'

Steven cried out as Avery's hand tightened around a chunk of his hair.

'It was so easy. So fucking easy. And he was so scared. I had to hit him straight away to stop him screaming. You should've seen his face when I did! Like he'd never got a good smack before! It was very funny.'

He grinned at Steven then looked away across the moor of his memory again.

'I played with him, you know? I played with all of them first. Before I killed them. Just like I'm going to play with you.'

Steven twisted as the grip on his hair tightened again. He bit back his whimper of pain; he didn't want Avery to remember he was here, kneeling before him; the longer he was remembering Uncle Billy and the others, the longer he, Steven, would stay alive. But it was hard. The pain in his head was more than discomfort and he was still shaking and nauseous. But he had to do it. He had to stay still and quiet and keep hoping for a way out. There was only one alternative and Steven didn't want it. Didn't want to find out what it was like to be 'played with' and tortured and killed while he cried for his mummy. Just that thought made tears roll easily from his eyes again. Not crying with shame or fear; this time he really was crying for his mummy; but quietly – so as not to distract Avery.

'He wanted it. You know that? Your uncle Billy was a fucking little slut just like you. I could tell.'

Pure anger bubbled up in Steven in defence of a boy he'd

never liked even though he'd never known him. All his good intentions to stay invisible disappeared in an instant.

'You're a liar!'

Avery shook him by the hair, making Steven yelp in pain.

'You what?'

'You're a . . . *fucking* liar!' The tears were coming thick and fast, but now they were tears of fury, and fury made him feel stronger. He knew he was stupid to challenge Avery but he no longer cared, and that was liberating. He put his hands up to try and control the grip Avery had on his hair and Avery slapped them roughly away, but he kept trying to grapple free of the tight knot of pain. The tugging on his hair made him think of the way it pulled and twisted up inside the green living-room curtains while he and Davey waited for Frankenstein to come find them. Well, he'd tried to be Frankenstein's friend and he'd blown it, and the pain of his hair being pulled now was far greater, just as the hammering of his heart at the back of his mouth was so much more – so much bigger it seemed impossible. It was as if that vital organ was being squeezed up his throat by the sheer force of the terror that had exploded in his belly.

He flailed wildly with his hands and caught Avery on the bloody wound inflicted by the son of Mason Dingle. Avery yelped and, for a glorious second, let go of his hair. Steven almost fell with the release of his head.

Then the punch caught him unawares and knocked every bit of air and every bit of fight clean out of him.

He lay dazed, only aware that his face was in the cold wet heather, then – from a long way off – he felt his body being manhandled on to its back, floppy as a fish.

Hands tugged at his jeans.

A wave of blackness made his stomach clench – and he

doubled upright and vomited violently all over himself and Arnold Avery.

In the split second of still silence that followed, he noticed a chunk of guilty tomato on Avery's sleeve, before the man recoiled from him with a shout of disgust, flicking puke off his hands and scrubbing himself with the pale green cardigan.

'You little shit! You dirty little bastard! I'll fucking kill you!'

But Steven was running. Running before he even realized he was on his feet. Running downhill through the wet, slapping heather, stumbling over tufts and roots, missing the track! Where was the track? He turned right anyway and blundered on through the rough terrain. Heard nothing but a faint squealing sound which, he realized, was the noise that terror made in the throat of a boy running for his life.

Steven threw a wild look over his shoulder; Avery was above him and behind, but was catching up. He'd found the track and the running was easier there. He was faster; Steven couldn't go any faster. Not here; not in the deep purple heather.

He angled up again to try and rejoin the track, slowing still further in the process, Avery gaining. If only he could get to the track, he'd make it. He was sure. Fuck it! He turned sharply and bounded up the hill back to the track then skidded on to it and kept running.

Avery was only twenty yards behind him when Steven ran into a wall of fog so thick that he flinched. He hesitated momentarily, fought the instinct to slow down, and rushed headlong into the whiteness.

He could hear Avery behind him, cursing in breathy spurts. He sounded close, but everything did in the fog.

And then he heard nothing.

He stopped, panting and wheezing, and turned circles, ears

hurting with the strain of listening over the thudding of his own blood. Nothing.

Steven decided to keep running but then realized that stopping had been a terrible mistake. Before he'd been running the right way simply because he was running away from Avery. But now he'd stopped, he'd lost any sense of direction. He looked down at his feet and the ground around him. Heather barred the way he would have chosen. He shuffled sideways quietly and found only grass and patchy gorse with his feet. With a panicky tingle he realized he'd lost the track. He stood for a long moment, listening to his heart pounding in his ears, trying not to breathe and give himself away.

Steven sucked in his breath and held it as he heard a rustling sound. He couldn't tell where it came from or how far off. He turned. A quiet – strangely familiar – squeak and a bump. He spun the other way.

It was the wrong move.

His head was jerked back and he lost his footing and fell. Something soft around his neck; a knee in his ribs pumped the breath out of him and Avery was over him, on him, staring down into his face with his teeth bared and his eyes narrowed into glittering slits.

Something soft but tight was around his neck; Steven realized he was being strangled with the pale green cardigan. He could smell his own vomit on it.

He couldn't breathe. His head felt huge and about to pop; his lungs spasmed and screamed for air. He had to breathe.

He focused on Avery's eyes, inches from his own. *Please*, he said in his head, but his lips just moved silently; no air to form the sound of the word. He kicked feebly and tried to push the man off him but only had the strength to lift his fists against

Avery's denim thighs and rest them there, like the two of them were old friends and this was a game they played.

Please, he tried again, but there was nothing there.

This was what it felt like to die.

It seemed to take for ever, and it hurt even more than it scared.

Uncle Billy hurt like this. Uncle Billy looked into these same shiny eyes and hurt like this. Uncle Billy had left no clues, and neither had he, he thought distantly; he understood now about having no idea that this might be the last day of his life; he'd put on his favourite shirt to be murdered in.

The pain in his chest was unbelievable and his own blood squeezed through his eyes and started to blur his killer's face behind a misty red curtain.

Please.

He was unsure of whether he was trying to beg for his life or for his death.

He thought vaguely that either would be OK.

And the darkness covered him like a cold black wave.

40

There was breathing and feet, breathing and feet.

The moor did its worst.

Twisted roots tripped and tangled, wet heather slapped and gorse whipped and prickled. Mud gripped and slid.

The mist was a thick white veil. Or a shroud. It chilled the eyelids, slid up the nose and pooled in the gaping mouth – its damp fingers stroking the senses with a seaside memory of childhood and a portent of death.

But through it all there was breathing and feet, breathing and feet.

With a *purpose*.

41

There were voices and suddenly Steven could breathe. It wasn't dramatic; there were no gasps, just a ragged little whining sound as he started living again instead of dying. He stared up into the streaky pink sky, wondering what had happened to Avery. He thought vaguely of getting up and running again but his head felt like lead and there was a great weight across his legs, pressing him into the moor.

If Avery appeared and tried to kill him again, there was nothing he could do to stop it, he was that weak. He didn't even care really.

The cardigan still wound around his neck was warm and comforting now and he felt tired and floaty.

There were still voices. Close, but not that close. Not right over him. They were men's urgent voices – the kinds of voices people used in TV cop shows when something worrying had happened. Steven didn't bother working out what they were saying, but he did wonder why they weren't saying it over *him*. Maybe they thought he was dead. He wouldn't blame them – *he'd* thought he was dead. Maybe he *was* dead, although he didn't think he'd feel the prickly wet gorse under the small of his back if he were. Steven let his mind drift away from the question of his death. It was tiring.

'Steven.'

That was more like it.

Steven flickered his eyes to the right and found his mother bent over him in her old blue bathrobe.

Mum, he wanted to say, but couldn't – just felt his lips open briefly as he tried silently. She was holding his right hand, which made Steven feel five years old again. Having his hand held like Davey. He almost smiled at the thought. Then didn't bother. Tired. Too tired to bother. Maybe he'd sleep a bit.

But under the voices he became aware of a ticking whirr in his left ear. He made an effort and turned his head minutely and frowned. Right next to his face, an all-terrain wheel spun lazily against the sky, something dripping from it that was not water.

It was so out of context that he had to know more. Slow with pain and effort, he turned his head further to the left and found himself looking at a maroon slipper with a stout ankle in it.

It was his Nan, lying in the heather beside him – her trolley between them.

Lettie stroked his face, but all the voices were over Nan. All the activity was over Nan. Some men from the village were with her, one murmuring softly into her face and pressing his lips to hers like a public lover, another pumping at her chest with his arms straight; a third tucking his jumper around her legs.

The fourth – Lewis's dad – just stood, staring sightlessly, his expression blank and his freckles oddly dark against the sickly white of his face.

A little way behind them all, almost hidden by the thick fog, was Lewis.

But his friend's eyes didn't meet his. Instead they flickered between Steven's legs and his father's face, wide with horror – and a jolt of panic made Steven jerk his head up to make sure his legs were still there.

They were. But in the two seconds that Steven could keep his head raised, he took a mental snapshot that would stay with him for ever, however much he tried to erase it . . .

Avery lay on his back across Steven's legs, his hands curled into loose fists beside his head.

And what used to be his face.

Now it was just a face-shaped clot of blood and hair and splintered bone. Only the eyes gave a clue as to its previous form – dull green half-slits like those of a dead cat.

Steven's head lolled back in the heather as he felt his childhood drop away behind him, winking out in the darkness of the past, and he burned with the tears of suddenly being a grown-up. He knew now what was dripping off the all-terrain wheel, and why the freckles on the face of Lewis's dad looked so dark.

Steven watched the bloody sky pass bumpily overhead as the paramedics carried him off the moor.

He wanted to know how his nan was but speaking was beyond him. All he knew was that somehow she'd come up the track with his rescuers and that something had happened to her there because of it.

Because of him.

The thought brought red tears to his eyes and everything went kaleidoscopic.

He'd thought that him dying was as bad as this day could get, but he'd been wrong. Something had happened to his nan.

Because of him. Because of his plan. Because of his trap. Because of his good letters. *On the box it said it was a fillit.* Because he'd been a boy. Not a man, who would have done everything differently; everything better.

They were loaded into the same ambulance. His mother's hand squeezed his and she said she'd see him in a mo, and she was gone.

Inside, Steven could only see that his nan had an oxygen mask on, but so did he, so it meant nothing. Gave him no real clues.

Nan, he said with his lips, but sound was still unable to squeeze through his swollen throat.

Nan.

It was hard to see through the blood in his eyes so he didn't bother trying. He closed them and slipped away once more, still feeling sick because of the tomato sandwiches Avery had fed him.

42

Steven lay in Uncle Billy's bed and watched his grandmother knit.

They had moved him in here so he could rest without Davey bothering him – and so Davey could sleep without Steven's thrashing, weeping nightmares waking him up and making him grouchy all day.

The curtains were open, making everything strangely bright – even now when rain spat on to the window, blustered there by unseasonal little winds.

The bedroom looked wholly different from the bed. With his feet swelling the end of Uncle Billy's blue duvet, it suddenly looked like a normal boy's bedroom – as if a spell had been broken. Steven felt oddly at peace here, strangely completed.

The Lego space station had been pushed under the bed to allow the regular passage of feet bringing books, tepid soup and Lucozade.

The photo of Billy had been pushed to the back of the bed-side table, which now held an array of Steven-related items: half a dozen pill bottles, a glass with a bendy straw, a box of Milk Tray that Davey was assiduously working his way through, and a slew of Get Well cards.

There was another Steven-related thing in the room now that only he knew about. At night – after his mother and his nan and Davey had all looked in on their way to bed – Steven would roll carefully on to his side and use the point of a compass to carve his name deeply into the wall behind the bed. He knew it was a bad thing to do on one level – and Lettie would be angry when she found it. But on another level he never wanted to venture out of this house – or any house – again without leaving some clue that he had once existed and that he understood the transitory nature of life.

Everybody should make his mark.

Steven let his mind drift to his most recent missive – contained in a card showing a flower pot, a spade and gardening gloves.

Dear Uncle Jude

Thank you for your card. Lewis is taking care of the garden until I am better. He says he is good at digging but that culd be a lie. It probubly is. See you when you come again.

Yours Sincerely,

Steven

He had badly wanted to write 'Love from' but finally didn't. He didn't want to scare Uncle Jude. He didn't want to scare himself.

Now that Lettie had posted the card for him and it was too late, he wished he had.

But it would have to do. It would have to be good enough.

He sighed and looked away from the sky.

Nan knitted slowly in the chair at the end of the bed. Her fingers were gnarled and knotty and she stopped often to flex them. Steven blinked but said nothing.

She'd insisted. She was putting new feet on his best socks. Before she'd even left hospital she'd demanded Lettie bring the socks in, and painstakingly unpicked the old, ragged feet until by the time she came home – with new angina pills – the socks were just ankle-tubes with a lacy fringe of little loops around the bottoms.

'What colour do you want?' she'd asked.

Steven had leaned back into Billy's pillow with thought, and seen the Manchester City scarf over his head.

'Sky blue,' he'd answered.

Steven was living on the settee by the time Nan pressed the socks. She wouldn't let him help with the ironing board, setting it up in the bay of the window where she used to stand, and placing a crinkled brown paper bag over the socks, to keep the wool from getting shiny.

Across the street, Steven could see the hoodies huddled, hands in pockets, shoulders hunched and hoods shading their faces from the bright sunlight that had found its way back to Exmoor. They shuffled quietly and stared at the house but didn't approach. Steven thought they probably wouldn't ever again.

Things had changed.

Lewis had told him how they'd all come up the hill. The men running, Lettie keeping up with them in racing panic in her bathrobe and half-tied trainers – and his nan rolling and panting behind, the shopping trolley bouncing over the heather, keeping her upright when she should have fallen a dozen times, gripping Lewis's sturdy bicep until he bruised.

Lewis's dad had been the first to reach Steven and Arnold Avery, but Lewis's account of what happened next was uncharacteristically sketchy. He would only say the men had dragged Avery off Steven, and then his eyes would slide away and he'd get all unsure about quite what happened next, although Steven had already heard snatched whispers of Lewis's dad being questioned and released by the police without being charged, and of Lewis's dad never having to buy another drink in the Red Lion.

Then Lewis's memory would reassert itself about how Nan had seen Steven lying there with a pale green cardigan wrenched tight around his neck, and blood running from his eyes like something out of *Jeepers Creeper*s, and how she'd first sat down and then fallen over in the purple flowers, and how the men – once they'd known Steven would be OK – had all rushed to help her. And it was in *this* context that Lewis allowed his father to be the hero of the hour, belying Steven's waking vision of Lewis's dad standing by in a blood-spattered daze, while others helped.

Steven didn't care. Lewis deserved the good half of that sandwich.

As his nan's flaccid arms jiggled over the socks, Steven wondered where the all-terrain wheels were now. It would be nice to have them back. The police had carried them off the moor in bags – along with the smashed and bloodied trolley, his spade, the pale green cardigan, and Arnold Avery.

Unconsciously, Steven touched his throat, which was still swollen and achy and allowed him to eat ice cream and jelly by the ton. Helped by Lewis, of course.

Feeling his throat under his fingers made him shiver, even though the gas fire was on in what was proving to be a warm summer. Touching himself like that made him feel like the killer. The tender skin under his fingers, the strange dips and gristle of his own windpipe, the throb of his vein. The odd, floppy vulnerability of it all. Enough squeeze, enough press, enough cold intent, and it could all collapse and crush so easily.

Steven had thought a lot like the killer in the past two weeks. He'd thought a lot about Blacklands and a lot about Uncle Billy.

And a lot about that patch of white heather.

Avery had been sitting there, waiting for them in the white heather.

He'd forced Steven up the mound and made him kneel in the white heather.

'*Get down!*'

Steven shivered again.

'Cold?' Nan looked at him sharply.

Steven snuggled further under the duvet she'd carried down from Uncle Billy's bed for him, and shook his head.

Nan stood the iron on its end on the metal grille and lifted the brown paper bag.

'There,' she said.

Steven sat up and took the socks from her. They were still his old socks but they were as good as new. Better than new.

She watched as he pulled them on and wiggled his Manchester City sky-blue toes.

He looked up at her and suddenly had to bite his lip hard to keep it from getting away from him.

She saw the tears in his still-pink eyes and put a hand on his head, absolving him of the need to speak his thanks.

'Nan?'

'Mm?'

'I think . . .'

He grunted and started again, his voice still cracked and whispery.

'I think I know where Uncle Billy is.'

Her hand on his head twitched minutely, and Steven flinched under it in sudden fearful memory, but he didn't pull away. He forced himself carefully back to calmness and let her hand stay there, not hurting him, warm and cosy on his head.

He could feel her thinking, as if through the very flesh that connected them.

Nan didn't say anything for the longest time and, when she did, she smoothed his hair gently as she spoke.

'You get better,' she said. 'That's the important thing.'

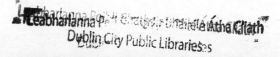

Author's Note

Blacklands was never intended to be a crime novel. I thought it was going to be a very small story about a boy and his grandmother.

The spark for it came when I saw the mother of a long-murdered child on TV and started to wonder about the impact of crimes such as Avery's, how they affect people for years, lifetimes – maybe even generations.

I thought: 'If I were the grandson of a woman whose son had been murdered, how would that affect *me*? What would *my* life be like?' Immediately I got an overwhelming sense of the sad fragmentation of a family, which went beyond all my preconceptions of forgiveness and noble suffering. Already thinking as a twelve-year-old boy, my only question then was: 'How can I change this?'

As Steven, writing to Avery for help seemed entirely logical. As Avery, manipulating this seeker of truth for my own gratification was a cruel pleasure. From there, the feeling that this could all spiral out of control drove *Blacklands* into unexpectedly dark territory.

This is a work of the imagination. My characters are not based on any real person, living or dead, and any similarity to actual persons is entirely coincidental. However, Avery's escape over the Longmoor wall is inspired by an actual prison break which took place in 2003.

Acknowledgements

Blacklands was written with the much-appreciated help of a Writer's Bursary from Academi. Thanks to Christina Pomery for her help with prison research and to Jack Cryer for being the hand of Steven. I am grateful to my agent, Jane Gregory, and the teams at Transworld and Simon & Schuster Inc. for taking a chance on a first-timer. Also to Eve and Michael Williams-Jones for their generosity in instituting the Carl Foreman Award, without which I would never have been able to give up the day job and become a writer of any description. Last but not least, thank you to all my wonderful friends and family, who always had faith in me – even when I was sure they were wrong.